A Time

Book 9
Marti Talbott's Highlander Series

By
Marti Talbott
© 2010

CHAPTER I

SHE WAS TOLD NEVER to go off alone, but Mackinzie Campbell had a mind of her own and Laird Campbell had given up trying to control her years ago. The color of her hair was more red than brown, her eyes were green, she had a smattering of freckles across her nose, and her favorite place in the world to be was standing in the tall grass on the crest of a hill overlooking the crashing waves of the sea below.

To the north, an island where some of the Campbells lived, often tempted her to cross the water but she doubted she would be any happier there. In the opposite direction, the land rose up into high cliffs that curved around the bay, and never was there a lack of seagulls gracefully gliding in the wind.

The dark clouds on the horizon and the ferociousness of the waves hitting the rocks was a sure sign another storm was approaching and if she waited too long to go back, she was sure to get soaked to the bone. Still, the rhythm of the sea often held her spellbound as it hit the rocks, rushed up the sandy beach and then subsided.

The sun was still shining on the hill and the pleasant meadow behind it, which was rimmed with tall Scots Pine trees and a thickness of undergrowth. A path at the bottom of the hill led from the ocean to a waterfall that offered plenty of fish easily caught.

Mackinzie loved the feel of the wind in her unbound, waist length hair. She wore the light blue and yellow plaid of her clan and a blue shirt, with the customary measure of plaid over her heart and shoulder.

Orphaned at an early age with no siblings, she often wondered what it would be like to have a real family. She never seemed to abide with any one set of parents for very long. After all, they did have valid reasons for sending her away, like a cottage too small, her unwillingness to obey, or a mother who could abide her silence no longer.

By the time she reached seven she realized rejection most often occurred when she spoke out of turn. Since she was never quite certain when her turn was, she spoke less and less to avoid the problem. On the other hand, when she was not fond of the family who kept her, talking out of turn was very beneficial.

There were other reasons for her silence, but those she kept to herself. At thirteen, Laird Campbell had had enough of her unruly behavior and decided to give Mackinzie a cottage of her own. That suited her just fine.

She might have feared for her safety living alone, but her devil may care attitude and the gift of suitable weapons from an unknown benefactor, made her a better fighter than most men. Everyone was well aware she would not hesitate to kill if she needed to. Likewise, she was a good hunter and when she wanted something more than meat, she offered to wash clothing. The unmarried men and women who were occasionally unwell greatly appreciated her efforts, but otherwise kept their distance.

It was true, Mackinzie had no friends, having insulted every member of the clan at one time, or another, and no Campbell was likely to marry her. If any man had asked for her, which she doubted, Laird Campbell most likely warned against it. Always before she did not care, but as she got older, loneliness began to plague her. Her life, therefore, was one unhappy day after another for which she sought relief, as she did on this day, at the top of the hill overlooking the sea.

She was about to leave when she spotted a magnificent black stallion running along the edge of the sea with its tail lifted and its head held high. He seemed to enjoy the feel of splashing through the water's edge and he was almost out of sight when he stopped, turned and looked up at her.

Never had she seen such a wondrous sight and she was even more pleased when the stallion started up the hill toward her. His eyes were as black as the rest of him, but she saw no danger and when he stopped within reach, she smiled and patted the side of his head. She expected him to bolt and run away, but when she moved closer and stroked his neck, the stallion stood perfectly still and let her. He seemed larger than most horses and to mount him she would need a rock to stand on, so she contented herself with just petting him. A few minutes seemed to be enough for them both and soon he turned, went down the hill, crossed the meadow behind it, and walked into the forest.

Somehow, her spirits were lifted that day. It was a good omen that put an uncommon smile on her face, and for a reason she did not understand, she felt her life was about to have meaning.

As soon as it started to sprinkle, Mackinzie hurried down the hill and headed back to her village.

NEASAN MACGREAGOR HALTED his horse at the end of the long, wide MacGreagor glen and listened. A guard, hidden somewhere in the forest, whistled and soon the whistle was repeated until it reached the ears of all those living in the large village, where the paths meandered between dozens of cottages at the other end of the glen. Behind the cottages sat a three-story keep where their laird lived and conducted the clan's daily business. In front of the Keep, two halves of a short, semicircle stonewall skirted the large courtyard and the wide gap between them began the path down the center of the glen. The ends of the walls were beginning to crumble, but everyone was certain they would be repaired someday.

Decided upon generations before, each whistle had a different meaning, the longest of which meant danger. This whistle, however, only prepared them for a visitor. A visitor? Had he changed so much in seven years the men no longer recognized one who was born and raised in their village? It must be so, for as he started his horse down the path in the middle of the glen, no one came to greet him as he expected. Perhaps they were too shocked.

Strapped on a two-wheel cart built especially for the hauling, his horse pulled an enormous, curved bone that had already astounded many a Highlander. Few had seen the ocean, let alone the bone of a sea monster.

Any other man might have been happy when Laird Justin MacGreagor sent him away, for Neasan MacGreagor had seen far more of the people and the land of Scotland than any of them had. It was true, in his youth, Neasan craved adventure, but being allowed to leave was not the same thing as being forced to. Neasan was forced to go and unjustly too, for even if he was guilty, Laird MacGreagor had no proof.

The other two men sent with him were not accused of any crimes and did not suspect the true reason for their sudden departure. Neasan did. He suspected they were sent away for no reason other than being greatly disliked by their laird. The truth be told, Neasan didn't like them much either, but he needed them and kept silent on the matter. Laise and Osgar thoroughly enjoyed the journey even when food was scarce and the nights were cold. Like them or not, their ultimate fate was also an injustice, one which Neasan could not forgive or forget.

NEASAN WAS A VERY LARGE man, as most MacGreagor men were, with blond hair, blue eyes and a nose that had been broken more than once. His beard and mustache covered most of his lower face, save for where a long, unsightly scar on one cheek marked his greatest battle. It was a battle fought alongside Laise and Osgar near the end of their first year away and it did not go well, but the MacGreagors would never hear the real account.

The seeds of Neasan's wrath were planted long ago, although he could not precisely say what first caused his discontent. Yet on the day his face was scared and his good looks vanished, his bitterness quickly increased. Until that day, Neasan thought of himself as a handsome man, at least as handsome as any other was, and his ability to attract women with a smile proved him right. Now, women quickly looked away. That too was Laird Justin MacGreagor's fault.

The one woman Neasan truly wanted was Justin's daughter, Paisley, but Justin let few men near her. Paisley had sparkling blue eyes, hair the color of snow and many men dreamed of having her. For months, he watched her from afar, but not once did she notice him or favor him with her smile. Her coy and rude behavior toward him was an unthinkable insult.

Even if Justin had allowed Neasan to court her, MacGreagor women had a say in choosing their husbands and it was unlikely Paisley would have chosen him. Therefore, it served Justin and his daughter right when Laird Macalister abducted her and Neasan was only too willing to help.

Unfortunately, after she was recovered, she married a laird from another clan. That too made Neasan furious. He did not love her, that much he knew, he only wanted to claim her as his prize. All was not lost, however, for husbands died all the time and hers would be easy to kill.

Soon after he was accused of aiding Paisley's abductor, Neasan was abruptly sent away. His punishment was much worse than death or banishment—he and the other two were sent to find something that should have been impossible to find - the bone of a sea monster.

Spending his nights alone after the other two died and wandering the shores of Scotland looking for the impossible only served to further increase his rage. Then one day his luck changed. His horse nearly tripped over the tip of a bone sticking out of the sand and upon closer look and extensive digging, the fragment turned out to be the gigantic rib bone of a beached whale.

At last, he brought the impossible home and people were beginning to recognize him. Neasan MacGreagor completed his ride to the village with pride and pretended smiles for them all. He was a hero of sorts, and when he stopped his horse, dismounted, and untied the cart, nearly all of the people were gathered to admire the bone. Best of all, they had a mountain of questions he was going to enjoy embellishing for the next few days at least.

Laird Justin MacGreagor did not come to greet him and Neasan took that to mean he was not welcome back, until he learned his laird was ill. That was unfortunate indeed. For months, Neasan savored the idea of calling a healthy Justin out and fighting to the death. Now he had to wait until the man either regained his health or died.

Yet two of Justin's sons were there, Sawney, who looked like a younger version of his father and Hew, who appeared more shy and quiet than Neasan remembered. Both were fully grown now and if it came to that, Neasan thought neither would be difficult to defeat in battle.

"What of my son?" asked a woman.

As the crowd quieted, Neasan lowered his sorrowful eyes. Appearing sympathetic was something he practiced the night before and he neglected to answer for just the right length of time. "Laise and Osgar fought bravely and died with honor."

The mother caught her breath and as her eyes began to tear, Neasan tenderly took her in his arms. It was not something he enjoyed, but it had to be done if the clan was to think him a changed man.

ONLY FOUR MEN WERE seated in chairs around a table in the small cottage, but the rest of the room was filled to the brim with the curious, all wanting to hear the first of Neasan's exciting accounts.

"Aye, we fought them," said Neasan, "'twas a fine battle easily won. We were as dancers, spinning here and jabbing there until all five lay dying on the green. Before that first battle, I did not know how well we could fight. I tell you true, were the MacGreagors conquerors, we could rule half of Scotland."

"Will the king mind if we take half of Scotland?" one of the men jokingly asked.

Neasan grinned and lowered his voice a little. "I vow not to tell him, what say you?" Determined to be well liked, he was pleased when the men roared with laughter. It appeared to be working.

In the back of the crowd, Sawney was not laughing. He remembered his sister's abduction well and had a two-inch scar on his neck to remind him. One moment he was standing next to Paisley and the next, a man held a dagger to his throat while another man carried her away. Her abductors had help and it wasn't long before it became clear Neasan was the traitor.

It was Sawney's Aunt Carley who saved Neasan from being either executed or banished. Once they were convinced Neasan was guilty, Justin, Carley, and Sawney talked long into the night in Justin's bedchamber trying to think of the best way to rid the clan of a man they could never trust again. It was not for Neasan's sake Carley pled on his behalf, but for his mother's, who was Carley's closest friend.

Now, an enormous whalebone stood in the middle of the glen, the other two men were dead and Neasan sat in his mother's cottage gloating over his accomplishment without noticing her absence. She did not believe the rumors of his treachery, faithfully watched each day for her beloved son's return and his name was the last she spoke before she died two months before. Indeed, Neasan was laughing instead of mourning and Sawney seemed to be the only one disturbed by it.

Sawney had heard enough. The MacGreagors were not conquerors and it did no good to excite the minds of warriors. He turned around, eased between two men standing behind him, went out the door, and walked away.

CHAPTER II

ALL THEIR LIVES THEY lived a peaceful existence in the MacGreagor glen; falling in love, marrying, giving birth to the next generation and dancing to the flute player's music. Most assumed they would be buried beside the long, wide glen where tall headstones marked the graves of those who had gone before.

The glen was surrounded by massive forests that offered good hunting, and a river behind the village supplied them with plenty of fresh water. They washed clothing and bathed in the convenient loch, had ample grazing for their livestock and good soil for growing herbs, grains, and vegetables. More importantly, Justin managed to keep them out of wars with the other clans.

His father gave him the name of Alaisdair, but the clan called him Sawney. He was not yet twenty-one, had Justin's same height of 6' 5", a well-developed build, dark hair and bright blue eyes. Yet to those who remembered her, his features were more like those of his English mother. He wore a green kilt, the same as all MacGreagor men, with light blue threads enter-woven to separate the green into squares. His leather shoes laced up to his knees and he wore a sun-bleached white shirt with a measure of plaid over his heart and shoulder.

Sawney enjoyed life more than most. He often went with the hunters or took a turn standing guard in the forest. The best of times were had when he came across men from other clans. By the time he reached eighteen, he had a reputation of being friendly, fair, and fun to exchange gossip with. Not once did he neglect to share his wine and food with strangers.

As he got older, the need of a wife occupied his mind more often than he cared to admit. He expected he would become the clan's next laird, and if that happened, he needed a good woman to stand by his side. The problem was, he had not fallen in love since he was fifteen.

"You are too particular," said Hew. A little less than a year younger than Sawney, Hew looked enough like him to be his twin. The brothers often took up the hunt together, something they both greatly enjoyed. However, the day after Neasan's return the hunting was sparse and after half a day, they decided to sit in the forest and rest for a while. "You find fault with their smiles, the way they walk and even their laughter."

"A lifetime is a long time to enjoy a lass's laughter when it sounds remarkably like the bark of a red fox."

At first Hew chuckled, and then he got serious. "Of whom do you speak? I am in want of a wife as well, you know. Or do you hope I will marry her and not find out until after?"

"Would I do such a thing to the only brother I have left?" The mention of lost loved ones made both of them pause. Each generation, it seemed, suffered some sort of disease that killed many as it spread throughout Scotland, and this generation was no exception. It began with a feeling of ill health, then a fever, a sore throat, a cough and a rasping sound in their lungs.

For a full month, they did nothing but care for the ill and bury the dead. Still, some of the weakest lived, others didn't even get sick, and everyone tried to guess why. Thyme, the elders finally decided—those that didn't get sick were partial to thyme. Others thought the idea ridiculous but began to consume more wild thyme just in case. Thankfully, the illness was behind them now and although they lost friends and relatives, the mourning period too had passed.

Seated on a fallen log, Hew stared at the ground. "We lost so many I know not which to miss most."

"I think of our brothers constantly. Our bedchambers are so quiet at night I can hardly sleep. We still have Father…and Paisley did not die."

"True, we should see about Paisley more often. 'Tis but a short ride to the Graham markets."

A slow smile crossed Sawney's face. "Is it Paisley you wish to see or might it be the comely lasses who go to market there?"

Hew picked up a stick and tossed it at his brother. "Are you as witless as all that? Do you not know if my dear sister happens to be there, I will enjoy seeing her as well."

"That is what I thought." Sawney leaned back against the trunk of a tree and sighed. "Finding a wife is not as easy as I once thought."

"And a wife, our next laird must surely have. Wives have a way of calming the clan when there is trouble."

"But not just any wife will do. She must be kind, resourceful and…"

"And in love with you?"

"Aye, and I in love with her, as Father keeps reminding me. He is right, of course." Sawney paused for a moment. "I wonder brother, what opinion have you of Dena?"

"Dena is comely, kind, resourceful on most occasions, and she has a pleasant smile. Unfortunately, I have not heard the sound of her laughter. Do you fancy her?"

"I admit she is a bonny lass and I do consider her occasionally, which is not to say I am in love with her. I begin to think I understand nothing when it comes to love. Have you considered her?"

"I have considered all but the widow Gormelia. As you said, marriage is forever and a lad cannot be too careful."

Sawney wrinkled his brow. "You do not favor Gormelia?"

"Brother, she is sixty if she is a day." Hew brushed a spider off his kilt and then changed the subject. "Father believes he will die soon, am I right?"

"The pain in his side grows stronger and for his sake, I hope it does not linger much longer. I will greatly miss him, but if death is the only way to stop his suffering..."

"I guessed as much. It is why he insists upon telling us the old stories after our evening meal."

"He wants to tell them and I never tire of hearing them. There is much to learn from those who have gone before, although I do not quite believe our great-grandmother married a Scot yet loved an English king."

Hew grinned. "It is that story Father loves telling most, just after he makes us pledge it is for the ears of our family only."

The brothers were quiet for a time, listening to the birds in the trees, for movement in the forest that might mean a fruitful hunt or a neighboring clansman with gossip to tell. At length, Hew broke the silence. "What will you do with Neasan now that he is back?"

"I am not certain. Father says to send him off again, but I doubt he would stay away this time. He did not come back to see his mother, that much is clear, so why then did he come back?"

"To boast of his accomplishments?" asked Hew.

"Or because no other clan would have him."

"He seems a changed lad, perhaps he values his own clan more now."

Sawney lowered his gaze. "I pray you are right."

TO NEASAN, NOT MUCH had changed except the ages of the people that remained. The ones he called friends before his departure were a bit wiser, but still as bored with life as he had always been. It was these four he sought to speak to first and for his plan to work, he needed to know whom he could trust. With the first friend, he stood guard, with the second and third he joined in the hunt and with the last, he helped prepare the skin of a deer for tanning.

All the while, he talked of the things he had seen and the great Scottish wealth easy for the taking. He chose his words wisely and in only a few days, other men began to seek him out. Whatever they desired to do, be it to fight, see the world or have valuable possessions, Neasan exaggerated the possibilities. The best of their desires was to become conquerors; the one he favored most himself. Yet these men were still too few and after careful consideration, he knew what he had to do.

DENA MACGREAGOR HAD Neasan's same blond hair and blue eyes, which made her pleasant enough to look at, Neasan thought. Moreover, she had exactly what he needed—she was closely related to several well-respected clansmen who could persuade others. Everyone believed Justin would die soon and that meant Neasan had no time to waste. "I wonder," he began as he walked to where she stood in the glen.

At first, Dena stared at the scar on his face until she realized her rudeness and looked away. "You wonder what?"

"I was wondering if a lad with a scar such as mine might hope to have a wife someday."

Dena's marriage possibilities had not been all that abundant and his question made her smile. "'Tis not a lass, but a lad who is too particular. Some desire a lass with dark hair and brown eyes, or red hair with green. They choose tall, short, thin, round..."

He chuckled. "You are right, but what do you prefer?"

Neasan was far more emboldened than MacGreagor men usually were and Dena liked that. Even so, she took a moment before she answered. "I prefer a lad who is kind, gentle and keeps only unto me."

"Then my scar does not make you think ill of me?"

"It might have, had I not known you before. The scar may make you look fierce, but I recall a very pleasant face."

Neasan quickly hid the fact that he did not remember her and smiled. "Then I am encouraged. Will you walk with me?"

Dena found his request very tempting even though accepting meant she was sure to be the subject of the clan's propensity to gossip. She too had fanciful notions and considered what accepting his advances might mean for her. More than anything, she wanted to be the clan's mistress and she didn't care who she had to marry to accomplish it.

Everyone said Sawney was likely to be their next laird. Although she thought he might fancy her a little, he had never made his intentions known. On the other hand, there were rumors Neasan wanted to be the next laird, rumors she neither fully believed nor disbelieved. There was something very exciting about a man who knew what he wanted and wasn't afraid to say it. Now it appeared he wanted her and she found it very flattering. At last, she nodded and when he began walking, she walked beside him.

A FEW DAYS LATER, LAIRD Justin MacGreagor's long, and for the most part, happy life came to an end sometime in the night. If he greatly suffered before he died, he told no one and when he was found, it looked as though he went peacefully in his sleep. His body was washed and then laid out on the long table in the great hall.

In the great hall, Justin's prize weapons hung on one wall, a faded tapestry hung on the other and the large, stuffed, colorful pillows his mother, Glenna, made lay along the walls. He liked his home clean and warm, and the women liked pleasing him. Yet to keep his body cool, they did not light the fire in the large hearth.

For two days, those who chose to viewed his body and mourned the loss of him. Then they laid him in a box and once the lid was nailed shut, a green MacGreagor plaid was draped over it. With the Priest saying prayers and the clan following, Laird Justin MacGreagor was carried to the peaceful graveyard on the edge of the glen and buried next to his wife, Deora.

The next day, the ache in Sawney's heart over his father's death was overwhelming. The aging three-story building he called home was so ghostly quiet he could not bear it, so he went outside to walk for a time and then sat down on a log facing the glen with his back to the graveyard.

He watched the men and women go about their chores as usual, watched several clouds drift across a blue sky and listened to the birds chirping in the trees. All seemed oddly peaceful as though nothing was wrong in their world. Nevertheless, he knew the calm would turn to chaos if the clan had no laird to guide them.

Sawney grew up knowing the clan might choose him as their next laird, just as they had his father and his father before him. He hoped they would, but he had not realized what a painful time it would be. Now, he had a few very important choices to make concerning whom he trusted to hold high positions.

He ignored the whistle announcing yet another visitor come to pay their respects and watched instead the man and woman walking hand in hand toward the corrals. Hew mentioned it, but Justin's death made Sawney pay little attention at the time. Now he saw it for himself. Dena, the woman he considered marrying, walked in the glen and her smile was for the man who held her hand - Neasan.

Sawney closed his eyes and tried to remember if they were cousins. It would not be unusual for a brother and sister, or even cousins to walk together holding hands, but Neasan had no sisters, of that he was certain. Sawney charged himself to ask about that later and turned his thoughts back to the matters at hand.

If chosen laird, he needed to consider strong men to protect him, advise him, and take command on his behalf when he needed them to. His cousin, Keter, would be a good choice for his second in command. He liked him well enough, he was a strong warrior and usually wise when it came to the ways of the world. Keter's brother, Blare, would do equally as well.

"Can you forgive me?"

Sawney recognized her voice immediately and looked up to smile as his sister. "You have come after all?"

"My husband refused to bring me."

He quickly stood up, took Paisley in his arms, and hugged her. Then he helped her sit on the log beside him. Paisley was still a vision of beauty with light blue eyes and white hair hidden under a dark blue scarf. When they were younger, he saw nothing remarkable in her looks, but once he began seeking a wife, he could not help comparing them to his sister. Perhaps that was the reason he found it impossible to choose a wife.

"The river is high this time of year and I feared crossing, but as you can see, I managed it without getting too awfully wet."

"You came alone?"

"Chisholm had banished me."

Sawney's jaw dropped. "What?"

Paisley puffed her cheeks. "My husband is petitioning the pope to have me set aside."

"He sets aside the most becoming lass in all of Scotland? Why?"

"I am accused of adultery."

Sawney put his arm around his sister and let her lay her head on his shoulder. "Who would believe that?"

"Chisholm does. My hair is a curse, you see. At first he only glared when a lad looked at me too long, then he began to draw his sword and twice he became enraged and nearly killed a lad."

"Simply because he looked at you?"

"Aye. After that, he commanded his guards to be with me where ever I went, which I found as annoying as they did. Then yesterday, he turned on his guards. He convinced himself I was bedding one, or all, and killed two of them."

"He has gone daft."

"That he has." She pulled off the scarf that matched the dark blue of her plaid and let her braided white hair show. "'Tis my hair they stare at, not me, but I could not convince him. I am truly cursed."

Sawney hugged her a little tighter and laid his head against the top of hers. "There may be a remedy."

Paisley pulled back to see his eyes. "What remedy?"

"Just last week Father told of a lass who boiled the fall leaves and turned her yellow hair to red. Aunt Carley will know how to do it."

"Why have I never heard that story?"

"I had not heard it either until a few days ago. I suppose Father only just remembered it himself. 'TIs the story of Charlet."

"You must tell it to me someday."

"Yesterday I could think of nothing but the stories he told. How shall I remember them all? Hopefully when all is settled, I can tell them and see if you and Hew remember them more clearly."

Paisley smiled. "As I recall, you are not fond of being corrected."

"As I recall, you are quite fond of doing the correcting." It was so good to have her back even under such awful circumstances. She filled a void in his heart the way only a sister could and he vowed to do all he could to take away her suffering.

Sawney's attention was suddenly drawn to his brother. Hew's pace was not urgent as he walked toward them, but his expression and the purposeful way he walked told a different story. Sawney often accused his brother of being part gray wolf the way he managed to sneak up on people. All their lives they shared a bedchamber and if anyone knew how to read Hew's moods, Sawney did.

CHAPTER III

BOTH BROTHERS WAITED while Hew held out his hand to his sister, helped her stand, and then took her in his arms. "I heard."

Paisley closed her eyes. "I did not think the gossip would spread so quickly."

"A rider came the back way." Hew intentionally kept her in his arms for fear she would collapse once she heard the news. "There is more. The rider said to say Chisholm went completely mad after you left."

She leaned back and stared into his eyes. At length she looked down. "Has he killed himself?"

Hew hung his head.

Paisley's reaction was so unexpected, the brothers exchanged worried glances. She did not catch her breath and no hint of a tear rolled down her cheeks. Paisley let Hew hug her once more before she moved away, stepped over the log and walked to her Father's grave. "I am happy I bore him no children."

Paisley had not realized anyone else could hear her until she noticed the gravediggers. She watched them finish putting the carved stone in the hole at the head of Justin's grave, replace the loose dirt and pack it down with their shoes until the stone was secure. Each respectfully nodded to her and then walked away, but it wouldn't be long until the whole clan knew every detail of what had happened.

"You did not love your husband?" Hew couldn't help but ask as both brothers stepped over the log and went to stand on each side of her.

"Aye, at first I loved him with my whole heart, but brother, a lad can kill a wife's love, particularly if she is falsely accused constantly. He found error with everything I said and everything I did. I will perhaps mourn and even miss him once I have had time to reflect, but for now I am glad to be shed of him."

It was difficult to grasp falling out of love with someone, but if Paisley said it, Sawney had no reason to doubt it was possible. The best thing to do was change the subject. "Come with me, wee sister."

"Wee? I am older than you." Paisley looked up at one brother and then the other. "I am *wee* compared to the two of you."

She was smiling and it unnerved both her brothers, but as they had since they were children, Sawney and Hew locked arms to make a chair, swooped her up, turned her around and then carried her back over the log. Abruptly, they dumped her out, which always made her giggle.

It was glorious to be back with her brothers and although she did not giggle, she did smile. As Paisley walked with them into the glen, men watched her, including Neasan whom she barely remembered, but that was normal and she paid them no mind.

"I am so happy you have come," said Hew. "We have been far too mournful and you bring back the sunshine."

Paisley stopped walking, which made both of her brothers stop as well. "There are rumors among the clans." She had their full attention and wanted to tell her brothers where no one could hear her so she quickly glanced back. "They are about you, Sawney. They say you will be challenged now that Father has passed."

"Do they say by whom?"

"Nay. Do be careful, I could not bear losing Father *and* you." Finally, tears filled Paisley's eyes. "Father came to see me just last month and I pretended all was well. I could tell he suspected, but I did not want him to see how dreadful my life had become."

Hew hid his own sorrow. "'Tis all behind you now, wee sister. You will start a new life with us. Aunt Carley lives in *that* cottage and she will be pleased to have you stay with her."

Paisley was surprised, pulled a cloth out of her belt, and quickly wiped the tears off her cheeks. "*That* cottage?"

"Aye, Father moved her there two months ago. It was better, he said, to have her closer to Keter and Blare where they could see about her often."

"Is everything still in *that* cottage?"

Sawney smiled, "Aye, all is well with the MacGreagor wealth and we three are the only ones who know about it."

"We three and Aunt Carley," Hew corrected.

NEASAN, A GIANT OF a man in his own right, watched the brother's take Paisley to her Aunt Carley's cottage. She was back, at least for now, and he was very pleased.

Dena was not pleased. She could not help but notice him watching Paisley and found it disdainful. "I have always hated her," she said in a somewhat whiny voice. "Why has she come without her husband do you suppose?"

After days of wooing her, Neasan was as tired of holding her hand as he was of her. He let go of her hand, yet forced himself to be pleasant. "She means nothing to us. She will be gone soon enough."

"Not soon enough for me."

He was becoming steadily irritated and it would not do if he were to keep her convinced. "I have heard you prefer her brother?"

"Perhaps I did before..."

"Before what?"

Dena shyly turned away. "Before you came back."

Both her jealousy and her words convinced him he had completely captured the affection of this stupid, stupid girl. There was one more thing he wanted to tempt her and her family with. "Tell me, if you were mistress, what would you change first?"

The possibility pleased Dena more than she was willing to let on. It was exactly what she wanted, but she held her answer so as not to look too eager. "I suppose if I lived in the Keep, I would change everything. The furnishings are old, the tapestries are faded and..."

He cared not to endure the boring details and interrupted her. "I am glad to hear it." Neasan took her hand, started them walking again, and ignored the silly grin on her face. His next move was for her to spread the word and for that, he needed to let Dena get back to her family. He stopped, took her in his arms and lightly kissed her on the lips. Then he whispered in her ear. "I must leave you now." Abruptly, he walked away.

Dena was so thrilled, that she hurried off in the opposite direction. Her dreams were coming true and she could not believe her good fortune. Neasan wanted her and she wanted to be a mistress. They were a perfect match.

She told her father first. Markus, one of the few remaining elders, beamed with pride. Having a daughter in the Keep opened all sorts of possibilities for his entire family. Perhaps his other daughters would be approached by men of more quality. Furthermore, his sons might hold positions of honor under Neasan, such as advisors, or even second and third in command. Markus told his wife and his other daughters, who went to tell all the relatives and soon the glorious news began to spread all across their peaceful glen.

SAWNEY AND HEW LEFT Paisley in the care of her aunt and then busied themselves gathering the red and gold leaves for Paisley's hair dye. Carley, Justin's only living sister, already had a pot of water boiling over the fire in the hearth when they returned to the small cottage. She wore the same white shirt and green pleated plaid the rest of the clan's women wore, only Carley's thin frame did not show her figure off as well as it once did. Her hair had turned gray, she has bags under her eyes and crow's feet marked the corners.

Her cottage was much like all the others with sod walls and a thatched room. It was small with only two rooms, one for eating and one for sleeping, yet it held a bed in each room for the times someone wished to stay the night. A small table and four chairs were placed in the middle of the first room and a shelf along one wall held the water bucket, wooden bowls, goblets, and spoons. Her beloved second husband's weapons hung proudly on one wall and an old, tattered, yet colorful tapestry handed down through four generations hung on the opposite. It was of a red deer and all who saw it marveled at the meticulous craftsmanship.

Carley quickly added the red and yellow leaves, plus a few green ones, to the pot of hot water and stirred the mixture. Adding green leaves made the dye more brown than red and in no time at all, the water began to darken.

Once the brothers wandered off to let the women tend the chore, Paisley changed out of the dark blue of her husband's clan into the green colors of her father's. She was home, glad of it and as soon as the mixture cooled, she stepped outside and let Carley carefully poor it on her white hair. It appeared to be working. The last step was to let it dry in the sunshine so she and Carley carried chairs outside. Already, Paisley was beginning to feel like an altogether different woman.

HEW WALKED WITH HIS brother to the corral and wanted desperately to ask if he would become Sawney's second in command. On the other hand, he would know soon enough and putting pressure on his brother at a time like this seemed unfair. Instead, he watched a sleek horse trot around the inside of the corral fence. It had a beautiful golden coat, a white mane, and a long tail that touched the ground.

"What will you do with Father's horse?" Hew finally asked.

"He is old, does not come when anyone calls but Father and he deserves to be put to pasture."

"I agree, he has been a faithful friend. Do you suppose he senses Father has passed?"

"Who is to say what a horse does and does not sense? Perhaps Paisley will want him. Training him to come when she calls would take her mind off her troubles."

"That is a grand idea," said Hew. "You don't suppose he will try to eat her hair now that she smells like leaves, do you?"

For the first time in days, Sawney chuckled. "I had not thought of that." He turned around to lean against the fence and his smile quickly faded. The people were gathering in the courtyard and it could only be for one reason—to choose their next laird. He had not expected it so soon, but getting it all said and done would suit him just fine.

NEASAN STAYED IN THE back of the crowd in the courtyard so as not to be obvious. Yet the one person he wanted to see was not there and he thought it odd. Perhaps Paisley was still with her aunt or better yet, inside the Keep. No matter, the Keep would be his home soon enough and then he could go in and find her. Her husband's suicide was his good fortune. He intended to kill Laird Chisholm Graham soon anyway, and the man just saved him the trouble.

Neasan's plan was coming together very nicely, he thought. For years, he suspected the MacGreagor laird held vast wealth, and the proof was in the golden chalice offered for Paisley's safe return when she was abducted. No one had ever seen it before, but Justin made certain all of them saw it the day after Paisley was taken. Where there was one thing made of gold, there were bound to be others.

The only question was—where did Justin keep his wealth? It had to be in his third-floor bedchamber, the one Justin allowed only a few people to see. One way or another, Neasan would have that bedchamber and all the wealth to himself - even if he had to fight Sawney to get it. Moreover, if all went as planned, he would have Justin's title, his wealth, and his precious daughter. The thought made Neasan smile.

Only one thing stood in his way - Sawney MacGreagor. The people liked Sawney well enough, but he offered no adventure, no excitement, and not nearly enough merriment. Neasan was willing to let them have all that and more. Hopefully, it would be enough.

Standing in front of him, Dena turned to smile at Neasan, a smile he gladly returned. He anticipated great pleasure once he got her in his bed, but she was not the one he would marry. A willing woman could never be the mistress of *his* clan. Of course, she thought she was to be the next mistress and to encourage her; he put his hand on her shoulder. Her large family would keep her future in mind as they cast their shouts in his favor, and touching her as if it were pleasing to him, added further encouragement.

CHAPTER IV

SEATED ON A CHAIR OUTSIDE Carley's cottage, Paisley finished brushing her brown hair dry. While Carley went to the courtyard to watch the choosing, Paisley was content to just sit in the sun and await the predictable outcome. She had yet to shed a tear for her husband. Perhaps the tears would come later, but for now she was a MacGreagor again, savored her newly found freedom and anticipated a better future. One very good thing had come from Chisholm's death - she was now a widow instead of being marked as an adulteress.

Paisley avoided looking at them when people walked past, and none seemed to unduly notice her. She too was surprised the clan wanted to choose a new laird so soon, but if that's what they wanted, so be it. It would be an exciting day for Sawney and there would be a very large celebration after. Perhaps it would be fun to attend the festivities and see how long it took the clan to recognize her.

THE CROWD WAS AS LARGE as it was ever going to get when Sawney and Hew walked from the corral to the courtyard. The people were a sea of green all anxious to cast their votes and several of the men came to stand with Sawney, all of them very large and all them the surviving sons or married to the daughters of Justin's four sisters.

As was the MacGreagor custom, the eldest of the elders climbed up to stand on the short wall and then held up his hand to quiet the crowd. Markus, Dena's father, wore his age of 56 years well despite his graying hair. "We all mourn the loss of Laird Justin, but 'tis time to get on with it. We choose this day the new laird." He paused for just a moment before he asked, "Whom do you choose?"

The first shout was for Sawney, but it was not long before shouts for Neasan drown Sawney's supporters out. "Neasan, Neasan, Neasan," they chanted until Markus held up his hand again. The old man could not hide his joy and grinned at Dena. "The people have chosen Neasan!"

Before the crowd could cheer, Daniel spoke out, "Neasan is a traitor, and you all know it!"

"He has changed!" a Neasan supporter yelled.

Sawney took a step closer to the elder. "My Father said the people are to choose, but can you truly follow a traitor? How long before he betrays all of you as well?"

Neasan pushed his way through the crowd and then turned to face Sawney. "Prove I am a traitor." He watched Sawney look at his brother and then lower his eyes. "I thought not. Heretofore, I shall be your laird and you shall be my followers. Get your belongings out of my keep!"

Blare was furious and stepped forward to stand next to Sawney. "Dare you command Justin's son? I will not follow you and I fear for those who do!"

"Then you shall be banished, you and all those who hold with the old ways," said Neasan.

"What old ways? Those that protect our lasses and children and keep us out of war? Do these offend you?" asked Keter.

Neasan smirked. "I see no glory in staying out of war. How does a lad prove himself if he never fights? As to the other," Neasan continued, "our lasses are willful. They put upon the lads unthinkable demands knowing there is no punishment. Let them feel the wrath of their husbands and mind their place."

"I choose banishment!" Keter shouted. "Cursed be the lad who lays a hand on my wife and daughters!"

"Banishment it is then," Neasan yelled back. "Go now, take your family, and be gone with all of you!"

A long silence fell on the crowd as Neasan and Sawney glared at one another. Men on both sides kept their hands at the ready to take up swords, but it was up to Sawney to give the word and he had not yet said the word.

Both her sons now faced banishment and Carley looked the most horrified. For generations, the men in Justin's family held command of the clan with pride, but it appeared all was suddenly lost. She had lived too long, she thought, yet if ever she was to speak up, now was the time. "And our belongings? Are we to leave without..."

She was the one woman Neasan respected and for her sake, he turned away from Sawney and lowered his voice. It was Carley who spoke up for him that night so long ago and he knew it. "Let it not be said the MacGreagors cast *you* out with nothing."

The people parted to let her through. Carley ignored everyone and walked forward until she stood directly in front of the new laird. "Let it not be said that *you* are MacGreagors and *we* are not. 'Tis my ancestors who gave over the name."

Neasan lowered his gaze and thought about that. "Perhaps you are right. The MacGreagor name will be vile to us now and we should choose a new one." His eyes suddenly brightened over the idea of passing his first edict. "Heretofore, I the son of David, decree our new name to be Davidson. Be gone with you, all you MacGreagors and do it before the sun sets this day. I care not to look upon your faces ever again!"

PAISLEY HEARD THE SHOUTS of the crowd and knew Sawney had lost. Yet it was not until Carley came rushing back that she began to truly believe it.

Nearly out of breath, Carley took her hand, pulled Paisley inside, and closed the door. She recited what happened while she went to the back wall of the cottage and began to wiggle the first of two stones free. Two generations before, it was a new cottage with a hollow hiding place built into the wall and it was there Justin hid his wealth.

"Sawney, Hew, Daniel, and my sons have been banished. You will go with them. Make haste, Paisley, untie your belt. You must wear the golden sword under your plaid."

It took a moment for Paisley to make sense of her aunt's words. She would go with her brothers, of that she had no doubt, but was it wise to take the sword with them? Most of Scotland believed the rumors about a golden sword were just part of an old legend, but there truly was a sword with a blade made of gold, and Carley wanted her to take on the enormous responsibility of keeping it safe. "Nay Aunt, 'tis fine for standing, but the sword will show when I mount a horse. Is there no other way?"

Carley reached into the hiding place and withdrew a long sheath with the sword inside. "Then wear it without. No one knows we have it and Neasan will think it normal for you to be well armed."

Paisley took the sheath Carley handed her and started to wrap the strings around her waist. The heavy sword was obviously meant for a man, but she was tall enough to keep it from looking too out of place. "What of the rest of it?"

Carley put the stones back. "Let it stay with me." Next, she grabbed an empty cloth sack and looked around for supplies to send with them.

"You are not coming with us?" She was about to cry and had to deeply breathe a couple of times to control her emotions.

"I am old, dear one. I would slow you or worse, die on the way."

"But where will we go?"

SAWNEY WANTED TO FIGHT—TO lash out at anyone who opposed him, but he remembered his father's admonishment to first keep himself alive. Besides, he knew not which he could trust and without many a good man on his side, he feared fighting would be a fatal error. It was difficult to turn away, but he forced himself to do just that and headed for the large three-story keep.

As the faithful in the crowd gathered around him, Neasan languishing in his new found fame and did not seem to notice both Sawney and Hew go inside the only home they had ever known. He had not considered banishing the brothers, but just now, it seemed a brilliant stroke of fortune to have done so. This way, he did not have to worry they would find a way of preventing him from claiming Justin's wealth or making Paisley his bride.

He looked down at the woman he had his arm around and smiled. Dena would be a delight this night and he deserved a private celebration, unless he drank too much. If he did, her virtues would surely keep until the next night.

SAWNEY AND HEW MIGHT have relished a moment to savor being inside their home for the last time, but instead they hurried up the first flight of stairs to their bedchambers, stuffed belongings in sacks and grabbed weapons. As soon as they were finished, they quickly went back down the stairs and escape through the back door.

As he walked out, Sawney heard Neasan and his men enter the great hall and begin to shout in celebration. It made him sick and he vowed not to forget that feeling all the days of his life. The clan, his father's beloved clan, was in for murderous times and there was nothing he could do about it.

NOT ALL WERE HAPPY to see Justin's family go and some were tempted to go with them, but for one reason or another, they decided against it. Nevertheless, they risked Neasan's retribution by preparing mounts and loading pack horses with enough food and water to see the MacGreagors through for a couple of days. It was the least they could do for Justin's sons.

There wasn't much time. The afternoon sun seemed to be moving across the sky more quickly than usual and Sawney wasn't even certain who was going and who was staying. The best thing to do, he decided, was for him and Hew to mount their horses and wait in the middle of the glen for the others... if there were others.

WITH HER FAMILY STANDING inside her cottage, Carley held up her hand to silence her pleading sons. "I will stay, and that is an end to it. Neasan listens to me and perhaps I can help those who remain behind."

"Then we will stay as well," said Keter, her eldest son. He wrapped his arms around his mother and kissed the top of her head.

"You cannot, you have been banished and Neasan will kill you. You can best serve me if you take my grandchildren to a place of safety and hold dear the old ways."

Carley hugged Keter's wife, Gavina, and their daughters, Dolina and Elspeth. The girls were not yet ready for marriage, but they were not little anymore either. She picked a mirror with a carved wooden handle up off her shelf and gave it Gavina. "This belonged to our great-great grandmother, see that it stays in the family." Carley waited for Gavina's nod and turned to her second son

Blare took his turn and held her for a long moment. "We will come back for you, Mother."

She pulled away and smiled. "If you can. First, you must see that everyone survives and Justin's son is protected. By the time you come back, many will have tasted Neasan's treachery long enough." She kissed Blare's wife, Jennet, and each of their two nearly grown sons, Daw and Cormac on the cheek and then went back to her shelf.

Carley took the lid off her jar, reached inside and retrieved a small cloth sack. She pulled the strings apart, opened it and let Keter see the jewels. "Justin gave them to me some weeks hence and you can use them as barter." She added the small sack to a larger one containing the few oats she had on hand, and watched him tie it around his waist.

Then she turned to her younger son again. "Remember the old stories and tell the children often so they know from where they came."

"We will, Mother," said Blare.

Daniel's wife passed in childbirth, but he still had three children, Senga, a daughter old enough to marry, Logan, a son age five and three-year-old Flora. He was having trouble controlling his anger, as he always did, but when Carley came to him, he let it pass.

"You are my sister Brenna's son whom I love very much. You are the eldest and you must give your advice to Sawney with great care. You should have your grandfather Neil's sword, but I suppose Neasan has it now. Perhaps someday..."

Daniel returned her embrace and smiled to comfort her. "I assure you, we will be back to reclaim it."

She paused to take a deep breath and hoped she was not forgetting anything. Her heart was breaking, but she didn't let them see. Instead, she hugged Paisley and then turned her attention back to Keter. "Begin a rumor...say," she paused to think of something,

"Say you saw a gray wolf with eyes the color of the sky. Then I will know you are safe."

THE SUN WAS MIDWAY to setting when Paisley went out the door of Carley's cottage with her cousins and their families. With pride, she walked to her brothers in the glen and was surprised to find her Father's horse waiting for her. As soon as Keter helped her up and handed her the reins, she adjusted the golden sword to make certain it did not look out of place. Everything was happening so fast, too fast for any of them to comprehend what it truly meant.

Both Sawney and Hew had to take a second look at the woman with light brown hair just to be certain she was their sister. At length, both smiled their approval, which pleased her very much.

The packhorses had straps over their backs with full baskets and cloth sacks tied on each side. Paisley took that to mean there were several who cared about their survival and it warmed her otherwise cold heart. Then Daniel put little Flora, in Paisley's lap and that helped even more. She had someone to care for now and it gave her renewed strength.

Sawney remained on his horse next to Hew and waited for the others to collect and mount their horses. They were the ones he expected would go with him, but then he saw something he did not expect. Carrying their belongings, Lenox, Moffet, and Diocail made their way through the watching crowd and started toward them.

Sawney could not have been more pleased. These three were unmarried, had no family left, he trusted each of them and he needed more men to protect the women and children.

AS SOON AS HE COULD leave the celebration in the great hall, Neasan rushed up the first flight of stairs to find Paisley. She was not there, but he was not concerned. In the window of a second floor bedchamber, the very bedchamber Paisley occupied before her marriage, Neasan watched the MacGreagor's gather in the glen. It was then he realized he was not truly familiar with any but Justin's sons, and had no idea which woman was married to which man. It did not matter, the woman with white hair was not among them, and furthermore, Carley was not going either. The people honored Carley, listened to her and she could be of great benefit to him in the future.

He continued to watch just to make sure Paisley didn't change her mind. How easy it all was. Had he guessed, he might have taken the clan from Justin years ago.

THEY STAYED IN A ROW across the glen and waited for the last three men to get on their horses. Then they waited a little longer for Sawney to give the signal. They numbered nine men, all well trained warriors, three women who held their eyes down for fear they would burst into tears, and seven children ranging from age three to not quite eighteen.

Silently standing in front of the village watching were Neasan's new Davidson followers.

"How can this be happening?" asked Blare, seated on his horse next to Sawney.

"I do not understand it either." Everything Sawney believed in seemed to be slipping away in one short afternoon. "The lads do not come to fight with us and the lasses do not cry. How have they so easily turned against us?"

Keter leaned forward and patted the neck of his agitated horse to calm him down. "I wonder if Justin knew."

"Surely he would have warned us," said Hew. "How do they forget their pledge to Father so easily?"

"Father is dead," said Sawney. "They have no pledge to him now."

On the other side of Hew, Daniel sighed. "Unless Neasan is even more witless than we think, they'll not be without a new pledge for long."

"And if they do not give their pledge?" Hew asked.

"Then he will most likely kill them. If not, he will banish them as he has us, and they will try to find us," Daniel answered.

"If they can," said Sawney. For a few minutes longer, he looked at the faces of all the people he knew and loved. Did they expect him to say something, he wondered. Was he to forgive them before he rode completely out of their lives? There was no hint, no goodbye waves, no tears, and he believed, no regrets.

"Which way, brother?" Hew asked.

Disgusted, Sawney took his eyes off the people. "I have always wanted to see more of northern Scotland."

"So you have, we go north then."

Sawney glanced down the row to his right and then to his left. The men were all armed with swords, daggers, bows made of carved wood, and strings made of hemp. They carried a full count of arrows in sheaths hung over their shoulders and kept their bows at the ready, an easier weapon to use since the heavy swords often took two hands to wield.

The women were being very brave, the older sons had control of the packhorses and the children were quiet. He nodded to Paisley, raised his hand and waved them on.

With Keter and Blare in front and Lenox, Moffet and Diocail in the back to protect them, the small clan of MacGreagors turned around and started down the path that would take them out of their beloved glen

Blare looked back once more searching for his mother, finally spotted her, nodded, and closed his eyes for a moment. No harder thing had he ever had to do than to leave Carley to the devices of an evil man. Yet she was right. His first responsibility was to his wife and children.

A short distance after they left the glen, they found where the paths crossed and turned up the one that would take them north, to the best place to cross the river.

ON A HORSE WELL HIDDEN in the trees, Bearcha took his time before he started to follow. Why Neasan chose him to do so was not a mystery; Bearcha was the only man left in the courtyard when Neasan came back out of the great hall. His command was simply to report back and it took no time at all to discover that the MacGreagors had taken the northern path. Even so, he followed for a time.

A hunter by choice, Bearcha had a full head of shoulder length brown hair he tied in the back. He kept his brown mustache and beard trimmed shorter than most warriors, which made him appear less fierce. He also had a wife and one infant son who was born after the fever passed. While he seriously considered going with Sawney, he was not about to risk losing his wife or their only remaining child.

NEASAN LEFT THE SECOND floor window and hurried down the stairs where several of the men were already celebrating. "Lads, come with me," he shouted. He walked to the end of the great hall and opened the door, *his* door he was happy to realize.

CARLEY WATCHED UNTIL she could no longer see her sons and was glad to leave the silent crowd. They were truly gone and as soon as she walked down the path, stepped inside her cottage, and closed the door, the tears she held back began to run down her cheeks. All alone, she sat down at her table and soon, her tears turned to sobs.

NEASAN CLIMBED UP SO he could stand on top of the short wall in the courtyard and shouted for his followers to gather. He felt like a king looking down on his kingdom and couldn't help but grin. He took a moment to look for Paisley, but again she was not there and he was not overly concerned. No doubt, the sorrow she felt over her husband's death caused her absence and it was understandable.

"The lasses and children will leave us now and the lads will give me their pledges." Neasan watched as the women, including Dena, took the children away, albeit in a slightly unnerving silence. Nevertheless, when they did as he said, he felt even more empowered. They were beginning to comply, as well they should.

The men stood alone in the courtyard, some smiling and others not. "He who will not give his pledge to obey my commands shall be banished, but his family shall remain." He listened to the shocked murmurs with great satisfaction. There it was finally, his ultimate threat against those who were not completely on his side. Now they would be forced and a MacGreagor would never break his pledge. Suddenly, he wrinkled his brow. He'd forgotten to consider those who had no family.

Neasan only half listened as one-by-one the men gave their pledges, and tried to think what to do should any of those without families decline. There was the possibility Sawney would come back to fight if he had more men, and banishments would certainly send him what he needed.

Some of the men wore grins as wide as his, especially those in Dena's family, and some seemed to hold back, but in the end, Neasan worried for nothing. Each man gave his pledge and the hardest part was over.

Now it was time to choose his second and third in command. He'd thought about it often and decided it made little difference. He could appoint any man so long as he was not from Dena's family. Choosing one of her brothers or even her cousins could be a grave error once it became clear he did not intent to marry her.

"William will be my second in command and Catan my third. Keep to your normal duties until I say otherwise." He noticed a disappointed look on the face of one of Dena's brothers and wanted to laugh aloud. The brother was obviously just as witless as his sister was.

Neasan turned his grin toward the other men and shouted loud enough for all to hear, "Let the feast begin!" He hopped down from the wall and headed back inside his new home. Just as he opened the door to the empty great hall and stepped in, Neasan remembered standing before Justin as a boy to receive his punishment from some unimportant infraction of the rules or other. For a moment, he thought Justin was standing there with his legs apart and his arms folded frowning. The foreboding passed as soon as his men filed in and began filling their goblets with wine.

It was time to take a better look around. With his men watching, Neasan crossed the room, opened the back door, and got a good look at the kitchen. Then he came back and started up the stairs. His men wanted to follow, but if Justin kept the two upper levels private, so would he. He put a hand out to stop them, walked up the first flight of stairs and opened the door on his right. It appeared to be the bedchamber Justin's two younger children shared before they passed. Neasan quickly closed the door.

The opposite bedchamber was where Paisley grew up and although he had already been in that room, this time he would enjoy it more. Once he walked past the room Sawney and Hew left in a mess, he opened her door and savored the memory of seeing her standing in her window on a hot summer night. He could almost feel her there still. Perhaps he would take her in her very own bed, but then he had not yet seen Justin's chamber and bedding his precious daughter in Justin's bed would be even sweeter.

Amid the laughter and the shouts of his men, he retraced his steps and started up the second flight of stairs. At the top, he paused. He was about to discover all that wealth and he wanted to cherish the moment. Slowly, he pulled the handle down and opened the door.

The room held an ordinary bed, a table, four chairs, and two trunks. Neasan's eyes sparkled as he walked to the first trunk and opened it, but what he found inside disappointed him. Blue plaids from long ago were nearly in shreds, the drawing of a child was faded and the only other items were two daggers, possibly belonging to previous lairds. Neasan closed the lid and opened the other trunk. Inside, the belongings were even more meager. It held a worthless goblet, extra candles, and spare leather belts.

Neasan put the lid down and rubbed the back of his neck. It was here...somewhere...it had to be. He looked up and examined the ceiling for a hidden door or shelf, but nothing stood out. Still, he was not overly concerned. The wealth was there, where else could it be? Perhaps there were loose boards in the floor. That must be it.

At any rate, this was his bedchamber now and he had all the time in the world to find Justin's gold. Just then, he looked at the bed Justin died in and thought he saw something move. A new feeling of foreboding washed over him and suddenly he could not get out of that bedchamber fast enough.

CHAPTER V

MACKINZIE CAMPBELL'S long, red hair was braided, she wore a sword, a dagger, and a lightweight bow with three arrows in a sheath strapped over her shoulder. This day she was not happy, even though she was standing in her favorite place on the crest of the hill overlooking the ocean. She had not seen the stallion for days and she felt as if her only friend had deserted her. She looked for him on the beach, in the forest and near the waterfall, but he was nowhere to be found.

Twice since that first day he had come back, casually walked up to her, and even let her ride once when she found a rock high enough to stand on so she could mount him. He seemed such a gentle horse, yet she could feel his strength and had no doubt he could outrun every other horse in Scotland.

At first, she thought him wild, but he seemed not to fear people so it was possible he belonged to someone and had just wandered off. Now, most likely, his owner found him and he was unable to come for a visit. It deeply saddened her and with a heavy heart, Mackinzie went down the hill, turned north, and walked along the sandy beach toward home.

IN THE COURTYARD THAT now belonged to the Davidsons, Grant motioned for his brother, Bryce, to take a walk with him in the glen where no one could hear. They were married to sisters, both of which were Justin's nieces. "We should have gone with them," said Grant when they were far enough away from prying eyes and listening ears. Already, many were uncertain whom to trust even if they had a need to share their thoughts, but these two brothers-in-law were normally likeminded and confided in each other often.

The taller of the two, Bryce nodded. "Smile, we must pretend happiness even if we do not feel it."

"I shall do my best, but 'twill not be easy," he said through a forced grin. "Davidsons? Sons of David we are not!"

"Lower your voice, Grant."

It was not any easier for Bryce to pretend, but he tossed his head of bountiful, curly blond hair back and laughed. "The man is daft."

"Of that, I am certain. He is dangerous too."

"Agreed."

Best friends since childhood, they were as different as night and day. Bryce was far more bold while Grant was most often the wiser of the two. Even the color of Grant's dark hair stood in stark contrast to the blond Bryce, although they both had blue eyes. Both hunters, each day they challenged each other in one way or another and still neither stood out as the clear winner.

The volume of the clan's celebration was beginning to increase and both stopped to look back toward the Keep. Bryce nudged his friend and said, "My wife swears she will not serve Neasan, nor will she prepare food for his feast. I may have to strike her."

This time, Grant truly laughed. "Do allow me to watch."

Bryce wrinkled his brow. "You wish to watch me strike my wife?"

"Nay, I wish to see what she does to you in return. Neasan may think it is simple, but a wife has many devices of revenge."

Bryce playfully slapped his brother-in-law on the back. "That she does, that she does."

ON HORSEBACK AND FOR the better part of two hours, the MacGreagors formed a single line of white shirts, green kilts and plaids. The women fought back tears while the men held their anger, worried about the future and fretted over the women and children. They kept to the narrow, winding path through the forest, going ever northward, first over two rolling hills, across a pleasant meadow and then past a good sized puddle where the last rain had not yet seeped into the ground.

Birds chirped in the trees but the sorrowful MacGreagors did not notice, nor did they notice the sweet smell of the Scot Pine trees. But then, they lived with that smell all their lives and were used to it.

Abruptly, Keter put his hand up to stop them and everyone tried to see what might be the matter. A beautiful black stallion stood on the path blocking their way to the river bank.

Sawney had his father's sword tied around his waist and touched it often, but it didn't seem to help. His sorrow was sometimes clouded by moments of rage and he feared such sudden changes in his emotions meant he was going mad. He needed a distraction and this horse did just that.

When Sawney made his way to the front of the line and slid down off his mount to get a closer look at the black horse, the MacGreagors held their breath. "'Tis unwise to approach a wild horse, Sawney," Keter cautioned.

"Grandmother Glenna told of a horse like this once. He led the clan to our new land in the glen. Do you not remember the story?"

"Aye, but that was not a wild horse. This horse has never seen a bridle; he has no marks on his head."

Sawney walked closer. The horse seemed to be looking him in the eye and Sawney truly saw nothing to fear. Instead, he reached out and rubbed the horse's nose. From the tip of his ears to his hooves, the horse had not one spot of any other color on him. Even his eyes were black and when Sawney moved closer still, patted the horse's neck and grabbed a handful of mane, the stallion held still and let him swing up on his back.

Blare shrugged, "An extra horse will be a blessing. Turn him around so we can cross the river before dark."

Even with Sawney's urging, the horse would not move. Instead, the stallion pawed the ground. "He warns us not to cross," said Sawney.

Keter rolled his eyes. "A horse only knows how to eat and sleep, nothing more."

While they were stopped, Lenox took the opportunity to make his way from the back of the line, past the women and children, and halted his horse facing Sawney. "We are being followed, at least we were. I believe he has left us now and gone back."

"Did you see who it was?"

"Aye, it was Bearcha. He let me see him."

Sawney continued stroking the side of the black stallion's neck. "Bearcha let you see him?"

"Aye he did and he is very good at hiding when he does not wish to be seen."

"Neasan sent him to see which way we went, but why? What does it matter?"

Lenox shrugged. "Whatever his reason, we best not let him find us."

"I agree. You have done well, Lenox."

Lenox nodded, turned his horse around and went back to guard the clan from the rear.

Sawney exchanged glances with Keter who was thinking the same thing. The path on the other side of the river would take them through more than one narrow passage where archers could easily cut them down one by one.

KETER LOOKED TO HIS right and then to his left. There was a path beside the river that would take them east and perhaps that was a better choice. He walked his horse a few feet down the path and then halted to study the river. Convinced it was not too deep, he went back and motioned for the clan to follow him. To his relief, the black stallion carrying Sawney fell in behind Hew.

The last man dismounted, untied a bucket he refused to leave behind, and threw just enough water on their tracks to make them unrecognizable.

It was slow going, the horses found the rocks in the riverbed difficult to master and as soon as he thought they had gone far enough, Keter led them back onto the path. Hopefully, they would be far away by the time the Davidsons discovered they had not crossed the river. Yet time was not on their side, darkness still came early that time of year and the children were getting tired.

Where the path going east and west crossed one going north and south, Keter took neither and instead led them into the forest. He kept going deeper and deeper into the woods until he found a small clearing where they could rest for the night.

Emotionally numb, few said anything as they unloaded their things and let the horses wander away to graze. Sawney watched to see which way the stallion went and fully expected never to see it again. Justin's horse followed the Stallion and since it did not yet come to any of them when called, he feared they would lose his Father's horse too. None of them dared leave the clan and there was little he could about it now.

Darkness was almost upon them when they ate a meal, although most of them were not hungry. Using their long cowhide cloaks, they made beds, settled the younger children, and gathered to decide what to do.

Jennet could not help but stare at Paisley's hair. "How have you done that?"

"Does it please you?" Paisley held her breath hoping for a positive reply.

"It is so very different; I hardly know what to say. Perhaps when we have become more accustom to it." The eldest of the women, although not by much, Jennet could always be counted on for an honest opinion. For as long as Jennet could remember, Blare had been the man for her and together they had four children.

Blare and Jennet's sons, Daw and Cormay, were in their teens, capable of handling the packhorses and could fight if need be. The couple lost two daughters in the fever, one older than the boys and one younger. It wasn't hard to see that grief had taken its toll on Jennet, and now they had no home. Deciding if she liked Paisley's hair helped keep her mind occupied.

"I find it very pleasing," said Hew. "As I recall, it was that color when we were growing up."

Paisley was a little disappointed in Jennet's reply, but perhaps she was right, it would take a little getting used to. She took a moment to look at all their faces. Was this truly all that was left of Justin's beloved MacGreagors? Not truly, five cousins were left behind, married to men who did not bring them and what was a woman to do in that case? Paisley was sincerely grateful not to have a husband to decide her future. Perhaps remaining unmarried would be a good thing.

"I choose Sawney to be our laird. Do you agree?" Keter asked, breaking the silence. He waited for the others to say yea or nay, but there were no nays. Tears finally streamed down the cheeks of the women and it was good for them to release their emotions. Keter and Blare comforted their wives and older daughters while Hew put his arm around Paisley.

"We should have fought him," said Daniel. He was proud of his warrior skills and still having trouble holding back his anger.

Before Sawney could speak, Keter put a hand on Daniel's shoulder. "We might have died and you must not leave your children without a mother *and* a father. We are charged with protecting Justin's sons and it is a great honor."

Daniel knew Keter was right and lowered his eyes.

At just fifteen, Keter's daughter Elspeth looked more worried than sad. "I thought half the clan would come with us."

Keter lovingly touched the side of her face. "They are frightened. The lads feared their families will not live."

"Will we live, Father?" Elspeth asked.

Keter was quick to let go of his wife and hug his eldest daughter. "I will not allow any of us to die. We are MacGreagors and we have survived worse."

Elspeth nodded and then turned her attention to Sawney. "Do you think Grandfather Justin watches over us?"

Sawney smiled. "I pray he does, I am in need of his wise counsel."

Still a little angry, Daniel slightly raised his voice. "Their families might not survive Neasan. Justin should have done away with him years ago."

"He thought to, but Mother stopped him," said Keter.

"She erred," Daniel shot back.

Blare put a finger to his lips and cautioned Daniel to speak softer. "Just now Mother is our greatest advantage. The clan will listen to her and perhaps turn on Neasan. Then we can go home."

Still awake, eleven-year-old Dolina sat up in her bed. "But why must we be quiet always?"

Keter exchanged glances with his brother and then decided to tell his youngest daughter the truth. "We believe Neasan will try to kill us so we cannot go back and fight him."

Her eyes widened. "Oh."

Blare smiled to comfort his niece. "We will not let him kill us, wee one. Someday we will go back and Neasan will not have a peaceful night until we do. He will worry we are in the trees, just across the river or perhaps even in his bedchamber late at night. He will go daft and I say we stay away until he does. Do you agree?"

Dolina considered it, nodded and then settled back in her bed next to little Flora. She was sister to Elspeth with five younger siblings to help her mother care for normally, but the fever took them. It was too much sadness and just now, she thought an adventure was a fine idea. They could not go home, so she might as well enjoy herself even if it meant sleeping on the hard ground.

Sawney listened but he hadn't said much. He noticed Hew watching him occasionally, but he was relieved that Keter and Blare easily answered all the questions. After it seemed the others had little more to say, he assigned the order in which the men would guard them through the night, named Keter his second in command and Blare his third just as he planned to do before the clan chose Neasan.

Hew lowered his eyes and Sawney knew he was hurt. "Brother, there are not many of us just now, but I need a good lad who will see to the training of the warriors. Are you willing?"

It was a perfect position for him, one Hew had not thought of, and he was pleased. "Aye."

Little about their future had been decided, but by the time the adults spread their bedding in a circle around the children and Lenox took the first watch, the exhausted MacGreagors quickly fell asleep.

FOR NEASAN, THE EVENING had just begun. He remained pleasant, joked with the men, flirted with Dena and drank his share of Justin's wine. As soon as he could manage it, he slipped out the door and went to find Paisley. He had to know where she was and guessed she was with her aunt Carley.

Yet when he walked up the path to Carley's door, he hesitated to knock. It occurred to him he was not as sober as he should be when he approached Paisley. He could command her, and would if he had to, but just now, he didn't want her to know his intentions. On the other hand, she would be mournful and might find it endearing to think he cared enough to seek her out. Indeed, it was a very good idea.

Emboldened, he knocked on Carley's door. When she answered, she held a candle in her hand so she could see who it was better. Carley looked older than she had only a few hours before and her eyes were red from crying. "I have come to see about you."

Carley nodded and then stepped back so he could enter. As far as she knew, Neasan had not asked anyone about his mother, but perhaps he meant to now.

"Where is Paisley?"

His question took her aback. "Paisley?"

"Aye, she did not go with her brothers, so I expected to find her here with you. Does she sleep elsewhere?"

"I must wonder why you wish to know? Has she caused harm to someone?"

Neasan had endured his fill of being pleasant and narrowed his eyes. "Tell me where she is!" He saw the fear in Carley's eyes and instantly regretted his harsh tone. This was not at all what he planned. In a calmer voice he said, "I merely wish to satisfy myself that she is well taken care of. I am aware of her husband's death and..."

Carley set the candle down on the table and grabbed the back of a chair with both hands. She felt fine, but pretended to be unsteady hoping to buy time so she could decide what to tell him. The MacGreagors were barely away and she was certain there was more on Neasan's mind than he was willing to admit.

He reached out to steady Carley, pulled a second chair away from the table, and helped her sit. His concern was genuine. It occurred to him she might die and he needed her to keep the others calm. "I did not mean to upset you." He watched her put her hand over her heart as she took two deep breaths. "Perhaps I should come back in the morning."

Carley kept her pitiful expression and nodded. "'Twould be best." With her back to the door, she listened as he opened it and then closed it behind him. Relieved, she folded her arms on the table, laid her head down, and closed her eyes.

Neasan did not go far before he paused to think. Carley had not been faint at heart that afternoon. If anything, she spoke more boldly than any of the others. She was hiding something, she had to be, and he suspected it was Paisley.

He should not have been so forthcoming with his desire to see Paisley. It was, after all, his first night as laird and Carley might have suspected he intended to make Paisley celebrate with him, or worse, thought to force her. If anyone knew about his long time desire for Paisley, Carley did. That was probably it. All he needed to do was wait and find her tomorrow.

Neasan took a few more steps and stopped again. Was it possible the brothers took Paisley with them? He did not think so. He saw no evidence of it and why hide the fact? Sawney could not know Neasan wanted her, unless...Carley warned him.

It was beginning to make sense. Paisley must have hidden in the forest as soon as she got word the MacGreagors were banished. Paisley and Sawney had always been close and Sawney would never leave without his precious sister. She might have refused to go and could be in any one of a dozen cottages, but Neasan doubted it. He was right; he knew he was. Paisley was gone and his blood was only just beginning to boil.

BEARCHA RODE BACK INTO the glen, dismounted just before he reached the courtyard and handed the reins of his horse to a boy. He had just started into the courtyard when he noticed Grant coming toward him. He and Grant had always been good friends, they trusted each other, and he was eager to hear what Grant had to say.

"Neasan made us give our pledge under threat of banishment...without our families."

At length, Bearcha nodded and watched Grant quickly walk away.

Neasan entered the courtyard a moment later and was glad Bearcha was back. He listened to his report and then went back inside the Keep. Six men, good with a bow and arrow, would be enough to kill the MacGreagors and bring Paisley back. He did not care what happened to the other women and children; they meant nothing to a man of his newly acquired importance.

Once back in the great hall, Neasan downed a goblet of wine and held up his hand to silence them. "I will have six lads to do my bidding this night, who is willing?" Two eager men instantly stepped forward but the others seemed hesitant. "Did you not just give me your pledges?" His words and his glare made each of them nod. It was not the kind of loyalty he hoped for, but that would come with time.

First, he whispered something in Dena's ear and watched her go outside to wait for him. Next, he chose six, appointed a leader, and sent the others away. It was then and only then, that he let his fury show. "They have taken Paisley with them and I want her back."

"Why," William, his new second in command, asked before he realized his mistake.

Neasan put his hand on his sword, gritted his teeth and glared into the William's eyes. "Dare you question me?"

William quickly took a step back. "Nay, forgive me."

Neasan relaxed a little, lowered his hand, and paused to take a forgotten breath. "They have gone north. Do what you must, but bring her back. Do as I command and your reward will be great."

William was worried. The message was clear; he was to kill Sawney if need be. Success would be rewarded, but what if they could not find the MacGreagors?

OUTSIDE, BEARCHA LEANED against the wall of the Keep, put the bottom of one foot against it, and folded his arms. He could not decide if he should remind Neasan he had not yet given his pledge, or wait to see if Neasan noticed. Bearcha could always claim he was gone and did not know about the pledges so he decided to wait.

He watched Dena and several men come out of the Keep and in a few minutes more, six more warriors left and headed for their horses. He waited and waited, as did Dena, but it appeared Neasan had forgotten them both.

AS SOON AS THE MEN left, Neasan began to pace from one end of the long great hall to the other. With Paisley gone, his plans were not working out as well as he thought. At least he still had the wealth...or did he? Vaguely, he remembered telling Sawney to get his belongings out of the Keep. Did Sawney take Justin's wealth with him?

Too dark to search Justin's bedchamber once more and not partial to going back up there again in the dark, he continued to pace. He should have told William to search their belongings. Why did he always think of these things too late?

Neasan yanked open the door, ran across the courtyard and into the glen just in time to see his men disappear into the darkness. When he looked around, Bearcha was still in the courtyard so he hurried back.

"Bearcha, catch up to them. Tell the lads to search their belongings."

"Who's belongings?"

Was he to face stupid questions every time he uttered a command? Neasan was tempted to mount his horse and do the chore himself, but why should he have to? He was laird and laird's do not do things themselves. "Do as I say or I will have your head! The men went north and if you hurry, you will soon catch up to them. Tell William to look for Jewels in Sawney's belongings."

Bearcha nodded and headed for his horse. He thought it ironic that Neasan told him to go north, when it was Bearcha who followed them and told Neasan which way Sawney went. Furthermore, was he expected to stay with the men or come back and report? Neasan didn't say and Bearcha didn't ask.

Still sitting on the short wall in the courtyard, Dena heard every word. She watched Bearcha run to get his horse and then watched as Neasan walk right past her, went into the Keep and close the door.

THE NEXT MORNING, THE small MacGreagor clan quietly ate, gathered their things, rounded up their horses, and got ready for a full day of riding. The black stallion did not come back, but fortunately, Justin's horse did so Paisley still had a mount of her own.

Which way to go was the question, and if they did not know already, soon the Davidsons would discover they had not crossed the river. Sawney looked at each of his men and raised his voice just enough so they could hear. "Perhaps we should go to the Swinton."

"Aye," said Keter, "'Tis a large enough clan to hide in."

"Listen," whispered Blare. At the sound of voices, he dismounted, handed the reins of his horse to his son, and quickly crept through the trees until he could see where the voices were coming from.

He knelt down behind the bushes and was surprised to see four Kennedy hunters so close to where the MacGreagors camped for the night. They seemed not to have a care in the world, talked loudly, and were enjoying a morning meal of oat cakes cooked over an open fire. Blare stood up, stepped out of the bushes, and showed himself.

Alarmed, all four men quickly got up and started to draw their swords. Their leader recognized Blare just in time and put out a hand to stop them. "MacGreagor, you are on our land," said he.

Blare raised an eyebrow. "I have always assumed this to be MacDuff land. Have you gone to war with them without my knowing?"

Caught in his lie, the man grinned. "Perhaps it is MacDuff land at that, but they never come this far. What are you doing here?"

"Have you not heard? Justin died and Neasan is laird now. He has banished the MacGreagors."

"Justin died?" The man wearing a red shirt and kilt lowered his eyes. For as long as he could remember, he liked Justin and his skill at preventing clan wars was highly held by all in that part of Scotland, even though most suspected Justin used trickery to do it.

"Aye, three days past," Blare answered.

"I am grieved to hear it. Did you say you have been banished?"

"All MacGreagors have been."

"Who is this Neasan? I have never heard of him."

"He is a traitor Justin sent away years ago. He returned, somehow turned the clan against us, and now calls them Davidsons."

It took a moment for the men to take it all in. "These Davidsons, will they attack us?" asked the second man.

"Neasan claims there is no glory without war. Aye, he will try to take your land. Trust him not."

Aghast, the first man slowly ran his fingers through his hair. "Are there none left we can trust?"

"Perhaps, but we were given no time to find out which they are. Neasan has many faithful followers, and until you are certain, I would trust none of them."

"Your warning is well taken. Where will you go, how will you get on?"

Blare took a deep breath and slowly let it out. "We know not where to go, we will become wanderers, I suppose, until we are strong enough to come back and fight."

The third man finally spoke up, "Do they hunt you?"

Blare lowered his eyes. "Neasan dared not kill us in front of the clan, but he dare not let us live either. Aye, he hunts us or soon will. 'Tis what I would do."

The man nodded. "How can we help?" He looked Blare up and down and thoughtfully stroked his beard. "Wanderers will cause people to gossip and you know how quickly that spreads. If his lads do not find you, this Neasan will hope for word of wanders wearing green." He glanced down at his own kilt. "I am partial to red myself."

Blare began to smile. "Aye, but in green you can more easily spy on the Davidsons."

"A fine idea, very fine indeed. How many of you are there?"

"We are nine lads, but we will trade whatever you are willing." Blare waited for their nods, slipped back into the trees, and in a short while returned with Sawney, Keter, and Hew.

Before long, the four Kennedys had on green kilts and the four MacGreagors were dressed in red. The Kennedy's also gave them the red plaids they used for bedding, although they were faded and not very clean. Nevertheless, they would do for some of the women to wear once they were washed.

"You have warned us and we will not forget, MacGreagors." The four Kennedys watched the MacGreagors disappear back into the forest.

BLARE LED THE OTHERS back, burst into the small clearing, and started to mount his horse before he realized his different attire startled the women and children. He quickly slid back down, pulled his wife into his arms, and kissed her passionately. "Does a Kennedy kiss like that?"

Jennet pulled back and put one hands on her hips. "Are you suggesting I find out?"

Blare rolled his eyes, kissed her once more, and then lifted her up on her horse. "I've a good feeling about our future, wife. Happiness is ours for the taking."

Blare's words seemed to lift everyone's spirits even though they were still worried the Davidsons would find them. Everyone understood when Keter did not return to the path and instead led them through the thick and often forbidding forest. Their clothing caught on bushes and scratched their legs, but not badly enough to cause any serious damage.

NEASAN AWOKE LATE IN the morning and it took a moment for him to realize he was in Justin's bed on the third floor of the Keep. How he got there, he could not be sure and at first, it unnerved him enough to make him quickly stand up. Then he remembered it was, after all, his bed now. Just as quickly, he reached up and held his pounding head with both hands. This was his first full day as laird and it did not appear to be starting out well. Too much wine the night before gave him a headache and his men had not come to tell him Paisley was found.

Furthermore, when he went downstairs none of his men were there and the women had not brought his morning meal. Was he always to be plagued with disobedience? He walked to the front door of the Keep, opened it, and stepped outside. The sun was too bright, the courtyard was as empty as his great hall and it served to further enrage him. "Where are you?" he bellowed, quickly grabbing his aching head again.

Leaning against the wall of the Keep just as he had the evening before, Bearcha puffed his cheeks. "They are not yet awake."

Neasan turned his glare on Bearcha. "You are awake enough."

"I have not slept. You sent me to tell the lads to search Sawney's belongings and I have only just returned."

"You told them?"

"As you commanded."

Neasan finally lowered his voice. "Have they found the MacGreagors?"

"Not yet. They were forced to stop for the night."

"They will find them soon. With lasses and children, Sawney cannot travel fast and my lads are not likewise encumbered." Neasan took a couple of steps across the courtyard, stopped, and turned to face Bearcha again. "Why is there no morning meal prepared for me?"

"Tell me who you commanded and I will see what has caused the delay."

He wrinkled his brow and shifted his eyes from side to side. "I do not recall."

"Perhaps in the future, you might make those arrangements before you..." Bearcha hesitated.

"Before I what?"

"Before you attend the feast." He waited to see just how upset Neasan was going to get before he went on. With no sleep, he did not want to have to fight him and was relieved when the man seemed calm. "Laird Davidson, you are in need of wise counsel."

At the mention of his new title, Neasan brightened right up. "I choose you!"

"Me, but I am not worthy."

"I say you *are* worthy."

"And if I decline?"

"Why would you decline? 'Tis a position of honor."

"I am a hunter and you would keep me from it."

Neasan thought about that. In one regard, he did not appreciate being turned down, but on the other hand, he had yet to meet anyone as honest and forthright as Bearcha. The man did not fear him and there was something very appealing in that. "I say you will advise me, like it or not."

Bearcha slightly nodded, walked away to see about a morning meal for his laird and left Neasan standing alone in the courtyard.

Neasan watched him go, went back inside the great hall, sat down at the head of the long table, and waited. Being laird appeared to be a bit more complicated than he imagined, but he had no doubt he could manage. It did not help that he slept half the day away and he vowed not to let that happen again.

To fight his pounding head, he poured himself a goblet of wine, drank half and then used the side of his arm to clear the used goblets off his end of the table, sending them crashing to the floor.

Soon, Bearcha returned with a bowl of hot oats, milk, and butter, placed it before him and then took a seat a few chairs down from the head of the table.

Neasan quickly consumed the meal, allowing milk and oats to dribble down his beard and onto his shirt without his notice. When he was finished, he wiped his mouth on his sleeve, belched twice, and moved the bowl away. "How many are we?"

Bearcha frowned. "I have never counted. Shall I do it now?"

"Aye and give the count before the day's end."

"Will you call them to the courtyard so I can count them? 'Tis what Justin..."

The fury in Neasan's eyes was unmistakable. "Never say that name in my presence again, do you hear me?"

Bearcha slowly nodded and wondered just what he'd gotten into.

Outside in the courtyard, a man gave the whistle signaling arrivals. Expecting his men to bring Paisley back, Neasan quickly got to his feet and rushed to the door, but before he could open it, two Swinton warriors burst in.

"You dare come in here?" demanded Neasan.

Not knowing what to say, both of them ignored the question. "We have come to pay our respects to Laird MacGreagor," said one.

"He is dead."

"Aye, we know, that is why we came. Perhaps you might tell us where to find the new laird."

"*I* am the new laird and we have changed our name to Davidson."

The second man's eyebrows shot up and then he glanced around the room. "We mean to see Sawney. He is..."

"Sawney is dead," said Neasan.

The Swinton warriors exchanged astonished looks. "We had not heard that. We are saddened..."

"Be gone with you," Neasan shouted, turning his back and returning to the table. "I have much to do and you annoy me."

It didn't take long for the Swintons to leave the room, mount their horses, and ride back down the glen. Neasan watched them go, slammed the door, and turned his glare on Bearcha. "Have you something more to say?"

Slowly, Bearcha stood up, moved the chair away and turned to face his laird. "Nay, I will count the people after I have slept."

"After?"

"Aye, after." He did not bow and did not ask permission to leave. Bearcha simply walked out the door.

CHAPTER VI

FOR HALF A DAY, THE MacGreagors rode up one hill, down another and stayed off the beaten paths. The fear of being hunted weighed heavy on all their minds. They stopped twice to rest the horses and see to their comfort, and then did not stop again until Keter found another clearing and a stream where they could refresh their water flasks.

Sawney looked for him, but the black stallion did not catch up. At least he had his best friend, Paisley, with him and that brightened his mood.

Careful to keep her voice low, Paisley took hold of Sawney's hand. "I wish we could walk the stiffness out."

"'Tis not safe enough yet."

"I know, but promise you will take me when it is. The people, your people now, wish a little privacy and I wish to enjoy the love of a good brother...even one who wears the colors of a Kennedy."

Sawney smiled. "I tell you true, sister, if ever I find a lass like you, I will marry her with all due haste."

"Not too quickly, I pray. A hasty decision is not always best, I have learned."

"I am your laird now, I will choose your new husband and you must obey me."

"Not true, I am an elder and the MacGreagors do not command elders."

"An elder by only..." Sawney looked around and his eyes widened. "I am surrounded by elders? Nearly all of you are older than me."

She grinned. "I am pleased you noticed."

"Do you mean I am laird over little?"

"Well, there are always the wee ones who know no better."

"I am relieved." He kissed his sister on the forehead and then nodded to Keter. "The sooner we get on with it the sooner we can take a day of rest."

The women tried not to groan and the children were being as good as tired children could be when they were lifted back up on the horses.

Keter was wise and Sawney was pleased with the way he led the clan farther from the danger. Sawney often looked back to see to the well-being of the women and children, as any good laird should. Sometimes the littlest child was with Paisley and other times asleep on Jennet's or Gavina's shoulder. The weight of a sleeping child was a lot to ask of a woman riding a horse hour after hour, but it could not be helped. The men needed their hands free to protect them.

THE FOUR KENNEDY WARRIORS, wearing green MacGreagor colors, hurried to return home and tell their laird all they had heard. Known to most as thieves, the Kennedys once boldly took livestock from other clans, but it cost them greatly in a war with the Swintons many years before. Having learned their lesson, they took to stealing smaller things such as weapons, milk stools, shoes, and even kilts when they could get them. Stealing kilts made it possible to spy on another clan without being noticed and facilitated their favorite pass time, which was stealing without getting caught and bragging about it.

They and their neighbors suffered losses when the fever came just as the MacGreagors did, and all of them decreased in size that summer. Therefore, the Kennedys had no real need to steal. Just the same, a new reason to do just that brought them great joy.

When Laird Kennedy heard the MacGreagors would come back to fight for their land someday, he smiled. "And we will help them. For now, we will put our skills to best use against these Davidsons." He paused to spit on the ground, a show of complete disgust. Then he turned to his second in command. "See that our lads steal all the weapons they can and set extra lads to spy on them. We must know when they think to attack. And send word to the Swinton, the Haldane, the Graham and the MacDuff. None are safe this day."

The Kennedys made ready to sneak in and out of the Davidson hold to steal what they could, the spies were sent to watch their every move and each time the name "Davidson" was uttered, they spat on the ground.

Before the day was done, Kennedy riders spread the word to the other clans, who also sent men to spy on the Davidsons. Yet it was the Haldane who worried most. Their land bordered that of the Davidsons, they were the smallest clan and knew they would be the easiest to conquer. To prepare, they took all but their bare necessities into the woods and hid them.

Then a new rumor began, one that would tear at the hearts of all the clans. Swinton warriors said they heard Sawney was dead. If it was true, it meant the MacGreagors would not be coming back to fight and the other clans had to deal with Neasan themselves.

FOR AS LONG AS THEY could that night, the six men Neasan sent to bring Paisley back followed the MacGreagor tracks until darkness made it too difficult. At first light, they took up the search once more and when they reached the river and crossed, they could not find enough fresh tracks on the other side to indicate several riders.

William led his men back across to the path beside the river, got down and examined it. Still there were not enough tracks and for a moment he wondered if they'd walked their horses in and let the water carry them downriver. That would have been dangerous, but not unheard of if people were desperate enough.

William thought it was a fool's errand Neasan sent them on anyway. He saw no woman with white hair and he'd watched every move the MacGreagors made before they left. Even so, the only decision left was to take the path along the riverbank going east or west.

He thought to split his men up, but three against the MacGreagors had no chance, so it was best they stayed together. He shrugged and turned his horse east up the path along the river.

It was not long before he found new tracks that appeared to come out of the river, and he was certain he had found the MacGreagors. He encouraged his men to go faster, but when they reached the place where the paths crossed, they found three MacDuff warriors in the way that quickly threw down their swords and surrendered.

The MacDuffs were well known for avoiding a fight at all costs and the other clans normally just let them be. It was better than capturing lazy people and then having to provide for them. Whether they were truly lazy or not, no one was quite certain and few cared to find out. Rumors were enough to make most people think they were.

"Do you know Sawney MacGreagor?" William asked. Two nodded and one shook his head. "Have you seen them today?" To that question, all three nodded, but when William asked which way they went, each pointed a different direction.

William took an exasperated breath, hopped down off his horse, and studied the tracks on each of the paths. The path leading north and south had very few, while the one going east had many. He got back on his horse, waited for the MacDuff to get out of his way, and then waved his men forward.

It was long after time for their noon meal by the time they caught up with those leaving the tracks. Instead of MacGreagors, the people were from a clan who had gone to barter for goods with the Grahams.

Disgusted, William turned his men around. They were tired and the horses needed rest, so he found a small clearing just off the path where they could rest.

MACKINZIE HAD AN ODD sort of happiness in her heart. It was as though something marvelous was about to occur—something just around the bend, across the meadow or on the hilltop overlooking the ocean she loved so much. When she went to fetch the basket of wash from elder Tavan, she actually smiled.

"Are you unwell," he asked. Crippled since the age of nineteen when a horse threw him, Tavan used an ornately carved tree branch for a cane and often asked for Mackinzie's washing services. She once called him an 'old scunner,' but he paid her no mind. He could not name one single person she hadn't called that at one time or another.

Still standing in the doorway of his cottage, Mackinzie wrinkled her brow. "Do I look unwell?"

"Not at all, it is just that you smile so seldom, I thought..."

She leaned down and picked up his basket of clothing. "Tavan, do you believe people can feel good things coming?"

"Well now, let me see. Aye, I do believe..." Before he could get all his words out, Mackinzie turned and walked away. It was quite possibly the longest conversation anyone in the clan had had with her in months. Tavan put his cane on the table and sat down in his chair. His cottage was larger than most and once belonged to the

Campbell laird and his wife. That was before the King of Scots came and built a castle by the sea.

Now the overly large and lavish castle cast its morning shadow right across Tavan's cottage and most were happy not to live in it, even if it afforded more space. Two wives and seven children ago, he thought to ask Laird Campbell for a different abode, but the subject just never seemed to come up. Now his children were grown and at the old age of 56, his hands hurt too much to make fancy woodcarvings the way he once did. On most days, he simply sat by the river and watched the water flow to the sea.

It was out of concern he'd taken a special interest in Mackinzie. He could do his own wash, but his children provided for him well and he could easily give her anything she needed. Yet Mackinzie was far too proud to accept charity.

Tavan suspected she liked him too, although she never said so. When she was not yet eleven, she came to ask about the death of her parents, a question she might well have asked anyone. Just the same, she asked him and he was honored she trusted him to tell her the truth.

Mackinzie always had a look about her, a look of mischief that made people wonder what she was up to, but Tavan was wise enough to see beyond that. Inside was a hurting little girl no one knew how to help. That day, she seemed satisfied with the answers he gave concerning her parents, and was just as quickly gone again. Nevertheless, if anyone could have a special connection with Mackinzie, it was Tavan.

He took a deep breath and slowly let it out. "That one needs a husband and at least twenty children to love!"

ONCE THEY WERE BACK to the place where the north and south paths crossed those leading east and west, William halted his men and scratched his head. It was the very place Keter took the MacGreagors into the forest, but William was looking for tracks, not broken branches or trampled foliage.

William knew that crossing the river could be accomplished in several places, although not as safely or conveniently as the first, and going north seemed the most likely direction the MacGreagors would go. On the other hand, South to the MacDuff or east toward other clans was just as likely. In the end, William only had one choice—go back and find the place where the MacGreagors left the path.

THEY WERE ALL EXHAUSTED, yet Keter urged the small band of wanderers on, hoping to put more distance between them and the Davidsons. They had enough daylight left to travel another two hours but the children were fussing, the women shed more tears and even the horses began to balk at the prospect of having to wade up yet another creek.

Sawney finally said, "'Tis enough," and Keter stopped in the next parcel of flat land he found.

They ate the last of their fresh bread and cheese, put the small children to bed, and gathered to talk over what they would do next. It felt good to stand up, yet even the eyes of the adults drooped, and their minds were cluttered with random thoughts.

All the women had stiff muscles plus headaches from crying, and were content just to move around a little and let the men talk. Of the seven children, four were nearly grown and they were more interested in standing nearby listening.

Sawney finally said, "Tomorrow two lads will hunt along the way."

"Perhaps there is a village where we might barter for food," said Blare.

Keter somehow looked older than the day before. Perhaps they all did. "We do not know how far we are from the nearest clan."

"Aye, but dare we build a fire to cook the meat? Let us not forget, Davidsons know everything we know about tracking someone through the forest. Smoke would easily give away our location," said Blare.

"I cannot help but wonder. How many of the ones we left behind would truly try to kill us?" Sawney asked. "I have seen no ill will and they loved Father, I know they did."

Keter shook his head. "Sawney, a laird is sometimes the last to know. I have heard their rumblings from time to time, although sadly I did not take it to heart."

Daniel rubbed one of his tired eyes. His anger had subsided from the night before and his tone was much softer. "They shouted for Neasan to lead them and if they have pledged themselves to him, they will be honor bound to fight us. What else can they do?"

"I do not believe Bearcha would do it and there must be others," said Lenox. "I too have heard their rumblings each time word came of fighting in other clans, but for a MacGreagor to fight a MacGreagor just to please a laird is something I would never believe."

Moffet agreed. "All of us are related by blood in one way or another. Scots do not kill their blood."

It was the first time Sawney realized Lenox, Moffet and Diocail, were first cousins. They even looked somewhat alike with thick red hair, scruffy beards more brown than red and the same wide shoulders. "Yet we too are their blood. How do we go back and fight them? Would they surrender?"

Diocail shook his head, "Nay, they will not surrender. They will fight if they must to honor their pledge, but only if we attack them first."

Sawney closed his eyes and rubbed his forehead. "We are too tired to speak of this now." He walked to his sack of belongings, opened it, and began to spread his extra plaid on the ground. Before long, the others did the same and soon most were asleep. Moffet took the first watch, Hew the one after and Blare's son, Cormay, took the next.

The night air was cold and with no fire, Cormay pulled his heavy cloak tighter around his neck. At least the moon shed some light on the small meadow and he would be able to spot danger. Just then, he heard the far off howl of a wolf and decided to wake his brother, Daw. Two could keep watch better than one and a pack of wolves were known to carry off small children when they were hungry enough. Just to be sure, Cormay picked up little Flora, bedding and all, and laid her between Blare and Daniel.

Daniel heard the wolves too and pulled Flora closer to him. Then he rose up to see where his five-year-old son, Logan, was. Nestled next to his older sister, Senga, Logan was sound asleep.

IN A VERY SHORT TIME, it seemed nearly everything had changed in the Davidson village. That morning, Carley went to the loch to bath with the other women, which had been a MacGreagor custom for as long as she could remember. Few women were there and none of the warriors were gathered in the glen for their training, which was probably a good thing considering the amount of wine they consumed the night before. A warrior without his wits about him could get hurt.

Carley went about her life as usual, gathering herbs, taking the vegetables she needed from the store house and praying Neasan would not return to inquire about Paisley. So far, the morning was peaceful.

Her peace did not last long. News soon came that Neasan sent six men to find Sawney and bring Paisley back. Then in the afternoon, word spread that Sawney was dead.

Carley didn't believe it and doubted anyone else did either. Still she felt a great sadness and lay down in her bed hoping death would finally take her. She was about to drift off to sleep when there came a soft knock on her door.

At not yet twenty-four, Grant spent his days hunting and fishing with Bryce to feed their young families. When the hunting was good, as it was on this day, Grant took extra meat to those in need, and lately added Carley to his list of elders now that her sons were gone.

As soon as she answered the door, he went inside and closed it behind him. With the dim light of evening filtering through her pulled back window covering, he set a skinned rabbit on her table and then turned to face her. "Four Kennedys saw Blare on MacDuff land. They are certain Sawney is not dead."

Her relief was so great, she closed her eyes and nearly collapsed in his arms. A moment later, she asked the inevitable question. "But are you certain they were not killed after the Kennedy's saw them? Neasan sent six…"

"If they were dead, Neasan's lads would have come back by now and we would have heard it from their own lips."

Carley left his embrace and sat on the edge of her bed. "That is true."

"Rest Carley, believe they are alive and find comfort in it." Grant tenderly put a reassuring hand on Carley's shoulder. She was not just an elder, she was his wife's aunt, and everyone loved Carley.

HIS FIRST DAY AS LAIRD did not go as well as he expected and Neasan quickly grew weary. From the moment he finished his morning meal, which was after noon, men began to come in wanting to know if they should do this or that. A farmer complained that the cows were bawling, the women did not come to do the morning milking, and he was put upon to do it himself. Another came to ask if the clan needed him to butcher a cow for meat, and yet a third wanted to know which pasture to move the cows to since the sheep cropped the grass too low for his herds to eat.

All this chaos Neasan blamed on Justin. Justin coddled the men, made decisions they could easily make themselves and now, he had to endure the constant annoyance. How was he supposed to know Justin set the schedule for the women to do the milking and Justin decided who needed what and when? Seething by the third hour of it, he could not have hated Justin more than he did on this day.

DENA WAS CONFUSED. Neasan left her waiting outside for so long the night before, she gave up and went home. She took a long walk in the glen that morning, two in the afternoon and still she was ignored. What did it mean?

Customarily, the unmarried women gathered in the courtyard of an evening, talked, pretended not to notice and waited to see if the unmarried men would ask to walk with them. Yet this evening the women were not there, nor were the men.

Dena found a tree stump to sit on not far from the courtyard and waited. Maybe they were just being quiet. After all, everyone knew Neasan had a headache. She wondered if he was unwell and that worried her even more. All her desires could come crashing down if Neasan died.

It was almost dark by the time William and his men broke through the trees, rode into the glen and then into the courtyard. William barely had time to dismount before a furious Neasan bolted out the door and marched to him.

"Where is Paisley?" he bellowed at the top of his lungs. His uproar drew the attention of other men who quickly gathered to see what was happening.

"We could not find them," said William.

"You could not find them?" His teeth were gritted, his fists were clenched and his eyes looked like they were going to bulge out of his head.

William kept an eye on the hand Neasan used to draw his sword and got ready to quickly back away. "They did not cross the river, of that I am certain. We found tracks on the path leading east, but when we caught up, 'twas not MacGreagors."

"They went into the forest!"

"Aye, but where and in which direction. Tell me and we will go back."

Neasan was so enraged, he could hardly think. He wanted and even needed to kill someone. Slowly and deliberately, he turned to look at the men in the courtyard watching him. "Get your horses, lads, tonight we attack!" Not one man among them moved and if he could have, he would have killed them all. He gathered all this breath and shouted, "Did you not hear me?"

In the forest on both sides of the glen, men from all five neighboring clans hurried off to warn their people.

DENA DID NOT MOVE EITHER. "Paisley?" she whispered. She remembered the way Neasan watched Paisley, but he said she meant nothing. Now he was demanding to have her back?

SO FAR, GRANT MANAGED not to be included in Neasan's circle of trusted men and such was the case when the men mounted their horses to attack another clan. His brother-in-law, Bryce, was not so fortunate.

For hours, it seemed, Grant waited inside the cottage he shared with his wife and small son, walked the floor and waited for word. At length, he blew out the candle, opened his door a crack, and peeked out.

The moon offered just enough light and at last, Bryce walked up the path, slipped inside, quietly closed the door, and quickly sat down at the table. "None dead."

Grant's mouth dropped. "None?"

"Not one and Neasan is beside himself. Someone warned the Haldane we were coming. When we got there, Neasan lit a torch and tossed it on the roof of the Haldane keep, but no one ran out. Neasan roared his fury, drew his sword, and commanded us to burn the village to the ground." Bryce had to pause long enough to deeply breathe and gather his thoughts.

"I could not do it. We pledged years ago to protect the Haldane, not kill them. I watched for people to come out of the cottages, but there were none and in the end, Neasan did not even care if the forest caught fire. Do you see? Neasan commanded us to burn the Haldane in their beds and I could not, nor could two others. We shall surely be put to death."

"Where are the other two?"

"They wait for me in the forest."

"You must go to Sawney and tell him what has happened," said Grant.

"I fear leaving my wife, she is with child."

"Neasan will call you out if you stay. I will see to her and Neasan will calm with time."

"Should we come back when he calms?" asked Bryce.

"Nay, do not come back. Go to the Kennedys, learn which way Sawney went, and go after him."

Reluctantly, Bryce stood back up. "You will see to our families?"

"Aye, tell Sawney we need him to come back." Grant locked forearms with his best friend and a moment later, Bryce was gone. In the distance, Grant could hear an angry Neasan spewing his rage on his men and then it got oddly quiet. Certain Bryce was caught, Grant closed his eyes.

BEARCHA'S GLARE WAS as fierce as Neasan's, who stood face to face with him in the courtyard. "You have conquered their land. Must you have their blood as well?"

Neasan still wanted to kill someone, but with all the strong wine he drank on the way back from the Haldane attack, his rage was beginning to wear off. At length, he blinked and looked down. "True, we have conquered their land." Then he remembered and turned to look at the other men. "Three disobeyed me, find them!" Instantly, those who were still in the courtyard ran in different directions.

William did not move. He was one of the first men Neasan confided his desires to and William thought a life of conquering sounded exciting. Yet how exciting was it to attack quite possibly the smallest clan in all of Scotland? Long hours searching for Sawney and then taking part in the attack made William bone tired, and he did not intend to spend the night looking for the traitors. "They'll not find them in the dark."

"They will, or they will die instead."

"How many can you kill before the people turn against you?" William had had enough.

Bearcha watched Neasan go into the Keep and then watched William walk down a path. He was surprised William stood up to his laird. He assumed William and Neasan were of the same mind, but now he wasn't so sure.

CHAPTER VII

MORNING CAME EARLY in the Davidson glen. On the third floor of the Keep, Neasan opened the lids of Justin's two trunks and used both hands to pull everything out. Aging blue plaids, a drawing on parchment, daggers in their sheaths, goblets, belts, and spare candles went flying across the room. Then he searched every inch, inside and out, for hidden pockets or false bottoms. When he found nothing, he closed the lids, picked them up one at a time, and hurled them against the wall. The aging wood splintered and broke apart.

He had not one jewel to his name and what kind of laird was he without wealth? His next victim was the bed he slept little in the night before. The feather stuffed mattress sat upon a grid of ropes tied to a square frame. Perhaps the legs were hollow, or the gold was hidden inside the mattress. With his dagger, Neasan ripped through the tightly woven cloth, tore open the mattress, and clawed through the feathers until he was satisfied nothing was inside. Frustrated, he turned the cloth inside out and threw it on the floor sending hundreds of feathers high into the air.

Next, he carefully examined the legs of the bed, but each was a solid piece of wood with no indication that anything was inside. At last, there was nothing left to do but tear up the boards in the floor.

Out of sight of the Keep, people gathered to share news of the raid on the Haldane the night before. Three men were now branded as traitors and three families were without them, but at least the men had not been captured. Not yet, anyway.

No one in the Davidson clan was more upset than Dena. Neasan seemed to have completely forgotten her and she was not the only one who suspected she'd been used. Feeling bad for her, some had a look of pity on their faces as she walked past and some even refused to look at her.

It was hardly a secret Neasan sent men to bring Paisley back, he yelled loud enough for the whole world to hear, and it made her look the way she felt—cast off. Because her morning walk proved so unpleasant, Dena spent the rest of the morning sitting on her bed waiting to see if he would send for her.

Neasan didn't ask her to serve his meals, but then, that might be a good sign. A future mistress would never be asked to serve the laird before her wedding. Yet if he wanted Dena, why did he send men to bring Paisley back? Little by little, her sorrow was turning to spite.

ANTICIPATING WHAT NEASAN would demand once he got through destroying the inside of the third floor, William gathered the same five men, and had the horses and supplies prepared. They had finished and were waiting in the courtyard just before Neasan burst out the door. Their laird had bags under his eyes, his hair was mussed, and his beard seemed to have grown a full jagged inch since the day before. They noticed, but none of the men dared laugh, at the feathers in Neasan's hair.

If Neasan was pleased to see his men mounted and ready to go, he didn't show it. "Find them and bring them back!"

William also heard the rumor that Sawney was dead and he feared asking, but it was better than coming back empty handed again. "Find who...?"

"The traitors. Bring them to me and then you can chase after Sawney."

"Sawney is not dead?"

"Where did you hear that?" demanded Neasan.

"It is said the Swintons first reported it."

Standing not far away as he always seemed to be, Bearcha could tell by the shocked expression on Neasan's face that the man just now realized his own words had come back to haunt him. Of course, the Kennedys had seen Sawney quite alive, but Bearcha saw no reason to share that information with Neasan.

Laird Davidson once more glared at William. "If Sawney be dead, then Hew will have Paisley, but first find the traitors. Any lad who refuses my commands must die."

There was nothing William could do but nod and mount his horse. Neasan gave no indication as to where they were to search for either the traitors or the MacGreagors, and the burden of making wrong decisions lay heavily on William's shoulders.

He led his men down the middle of the glen, followed the path to the crossroads, and turned west. It was as good a direction as any to look for the traitors. Hidden in the forest, the Swinton, Haldane, Kennedy, and Graham spies quietly watched. The MacDuff were there too, albeit hidden far deeper in the woods.

BRYCE AND THE OTHER two men who refused to take part in the Haldane attack were warn out. Bryce managed to slip back into the forest just before Neasan ordered his men to find them. The three spent the remainder of the night trying to avoid being caught by men who knew the paths and the forest as well as they did. Darkness was clearly on their side, but none of them slept a wink.

As soon as the sun began to rise and they were certain Neasan's men had given up searching for them, they managed to slip across the path before William and his five warriors left the glen. Instead of west, they headed southeast toward the Kennedy village.

Two hours later, they stood before Laird Kennedy in his courtyard, stripped of all their weapons with their hands tied behind their backs. "We are at your mercy," Bryce said. "Help us find Sawney and bring him back."

"How do you know Laird Davidson..." Laird Kennedy paused to spit on the ground, "did not kill all the Haldane?"

"We saw for ourselves. Someone warned them, they must have, for the Haldane were not there when we arrived. I heard no child cry, no lass scream and no lad shout a warning. I tell you true, they are yet alive and hidden somewhere. And there is more."

"Go on."

"Laird Davidson left straight away. For all we know, the forest is on fire. I fear..." When all the Kennedy men spit on the ground, Bryce was beginning to see a pattern.

Kennedy started shouting orders and before another word was said to Bryce, ten Kennedy warriors were sent to find the Haldane and see that the fires were out. It took a little while for Laird Kennedy to calm down. While Scotland was a place of ample rain, there were always dead trees and bushes this time of year and a forest fire could wipe out all of them, including the Davidsons.

"The lad is witless," Kennedy finally muttered.

"Aye, more so than you think," Bryce agreed.

"Sawney said to trust no one so why would I tell you where he has gone?"

Bryce hung his head. The rope around his wrists burned a little, but he ignored it. "I have no words to convince you, but I beg of you, help us find him. He is our only hope."

A TIME OF MADNESS

FOR SAWNEY THERE WAS a bit of good news. The black stallion was back and seemed to want them to follow. The stallion pawed the ground, and then waited until the men got everyone situated on the horses. Keter looked to Sawney for advice but Sawney only shrugged. As long as they were not going back the way they came, why not follow this odd horse. Besides, a horse could find water and a rider-less horse was even better at it.

At length, the stallion led them up the side of a hill and from the top they could see a magnificent glen, nearly as grand as the one they left behind. At the edge of the valley sat a village not unlike their own, except this one had a tall wooden fence around it to keep attackers and wild animals out.

Inside the fence, the people appeared to be going about their normal day. "They look peaceful enough," said Daniel. He dismounted, took little Flora out of Paisley's arms, stood her on the ground and held on until she got her balance.

Keter got off his horse too, as did the other men, and each helped the women and children down. Soon they stood together looking at the tranquil scene before them.

Blare pointed at a large square of tilled land to the right of the village. "They farm and the land is good. Perhaps they let us barter for food."

Paisley was worried. "'Twill do no good, we have nothing to barter with."

"Aye, but we do." Keter untied the string around his waist, opened the sack, dug inside, and withdrew the small sack Carley gave him before they left. He handed it to Sawney and then watched to see the delight in his laird's eyes.

Sawney poured the jewels into the palm of his hand and watched them sparkle in the sunlight. "She took them out of the goblets?"

"Mother said Justin did," Keter answered.

Sawney lifted his eyes upward, "Thank you, Father."

Lenox was astounded. "Are there more golden goblets?"

Sawney smiled. "Aye, there are."

Now Diocail was worried, "Will Neasan find them?"

Sawney put the jewels back in the small sack keeping only one large ruby out. "I assure you, Neasan will never find them."

Paisley smiled at the three unmarried men who unselfishly came with them and was tempted to pull her sword. If any deserved to see its golden blade shimmer in the sunlight, they did. However, now was not the time.

Hew noticed it first, nudged Sawney until he looked, and only then did both recognize the familiar handle sticking out of the sheath Paisley wore. Sawney smiled, quickly looked away, and turned his attention to the village below. "If we can see them, they can see us."

"True," said Blare. "Perhaps if we walk instead of ride, they will think us peaceful as well."

"How will we explain why we wear different colors?" Gavina wanted to know.

"Better still, who do we say we are?" asked Jennet.

WALKING INSTEAD OF riding made them all feel better. With Keter once more leading the way, they went down the hill, turned up the path, and leisurely strolled toward the village. Sawney noticed the black stallion did not come with them and assumed that was the last they'd see of him.

Paisley even managed to pick a few wild flowers along the way, the children ran forward and then ran back, and as they got closer, two puppies scrunched under the wooden fence and raced out to greet them. The children were delighted, even the older ones, but especially little Flora.

As soon as the tall wooden gates opened, four guards came out with swords drawn and Sawney quickly called a halt. He made certain the women and children were behind the men, but he did not draw his sword. A moment later, an unarmed man walked through the gates. He looked too young to be a laird and seemed overly interested in the women, but as he drew near, his guards kept him well protected.

"We have come to barter for food and clothing if you have them to spare," Sawney said.

"Who are you?"

"We are Fergusons. A flood took our village, our land grows little anyway, and we seek new land."

"We have heard of no village flooding."

"Perhaps the news has not yet reached you."

"Perhaps." He seemed not to notice how much bigger the MacGreagor men were than his men and instead gawked first at Paisley and then at Jennet. "I am Laird Macfarlane."

"Have you food to spare?" asked Sawney.

Laird Macfarlane looked fifteen-year-old Senga up and down, but when he looked a little too long at Gavina's hips Keter found it difficult to control his annoyance. "She is my wife."

"And the others?" he asked, not bothering to stop staring.

Keter stepped in front of Gavina just before he answered. "All married."

"Pity." At last, Macfarlane turned his attention to the task at hand. "What have you to barter?"

Sawney slowly opened the palm of his hand, showed Laird Macfarlane the ruby, and watched the admiration in his eyes. "'Tis yours in exchange for ample food for us all."

Laird Macfarlane quickly changed his expression from delighted to demanding. "'Tis not enough."

"'Tis all we have."

Macfarlane stared at the largest ruby he had ever seen and pondered the trade for a moment. "I shall have it first."

"Nay, you shall have it last. Bring out the fare and if we find it agreeable, then you shall have the ruby. I give you my pledge."

At last, Macfarlane nodded to one of his men, who rushed back inside the gate. At first, he returned with only two yellow plaids, one sack of oats, a smaller one of vegetables and a third of apples. Sawney rolled his eyes. The man was sent back for more three times before the MacGreagors were satisfied and Sawney gave Macfarlane the ruby. Soon they were on their horses and riding down a path that took them around the village and into the forest beyond.

They followed the path for just a short time before Keter took them back into the woods. It would not be the first time a clan bartered and then attacked to get their goods back. Once more, the bushes scratched their legs, they had to push tree branches out of the way or duck under them, and once more, the going was far slower than it would be on the paths. Still, two hours later they were safely away.

WILLIAM WAS NOT ALL that unhappy to be captured. After hours of following tracks without finding Sawney or the traitors, he and his men were suddenly surrounded by no less than thirty Swinton Warriors. Even as big and as strong as they were, six against thirty was certain death so they did not put up a fight. Then, when he mentioned the name Davidson, each and every Swinton spat on the ground and it was plain to see, they knew all they needed to know about Neasan.

At least William did not have to face his laird with yet another failure and about that, he was very glad. Once they were stripped of their weapons, the Davidsons were taken to an empty cottage and held captive. Not long after, two men brought them an evening meal. "'Tis from Sawney," said one. "He wishes us to keep you well-fed."

William's mouth dropped. Not only was Sawney alive, William had found him after all. Unfortunately, there was nothing he could do about it. He wondered just how long it would be before Neasan heard where Sawney was and that his men were captured. What would he do then? Neasan, he decided would declare an all-out war.

Nevertheless, William was a little embarrassed. Captured by another clan? That was something that never once happened to the MacGreagors and if it had, Justin would simply ride into the Swinton village and ask for them back. He would barter, trick, or do whatever else he must to save his men, but he would not go to war unless it was his last alternative.

William took the bowl handed him, crossed his feet at the ankles, sat on the dirt floor and began to eat. The feeling that the clan chose the wrong man to lead them was growing stronger by the hour and now there was something else to worry about. If Sawney managed to defeat Neasan, William's future would be in doubt. It was too late to worry about that now, he supposed. He was Neasan's second in command, a pledge was a pledge and he'd given his to Neasan.

HUNTING FOR HER OWN meat was a mundane chore that had to be done and when Mackinzie could not find a deer, chickens running wild or a rabbit to kill, she decided to go to the waterfall to fish for salmon. It was not far from the hill she loved and instead of going the long way around on the beach, she took a shortcut through the trees, where she could cross the creek without getting wet by hopping from rock to rock.

The feeling of something splendid coming her way was gone, this day she felt wistful and decided it was because she'd given up seeing the black stallion ever again. With that on her mind, she was not being overly aware of where she was, or where she was going when she found herself not five feet from a Scottish Wildcat.

Mackinzie had encountered wildcats before, but this one was by far the biggest and looked to be the most dangerous. From its nose to the tip of its tail, it was as long as her leg, had ruffled brown and black stripes and a jaw that looked unusually wide when it hissed.

Everyone knew these cats didn't hesitate to kill especially to protect their young. They were sly cats, fearless and powerful, known to kill birds as large as eagles and easily walk away with one of the Campbell lambs clamped tight in its jaws.

Now, Mackinzie stood between the cat and the fish it most likely wanted to catch with its very long and very sharp claws. She was terrified. Cautiously, she began to back away while at the same time drawing her dagger. Again, the monstrous cat hissed and for a moment, she wondered if she should attack first.

The cat suddenly hunched down as though it was preparing to leap and when it did, Mackinzie turned and ran. She nearly missed two rocks as she scrambled across the creek, but she managed and continued to run through the trees all the way back to her village.

She feared no man, but a wildcat was an altogether different matter and when she looked back, she was relieved to know it wasn't chasing her. Out of breath, she slowed as she started down the path between the cottages.

Mackinzie told the first man she saw about the wildcat. He was surprised she spoke to him at all, but his worry soon matched hers and he hurried away, shouting a warning for mothers to keep their little ones inside and for extra guards to watch over their extensive herds of sheep.

She took one more look down the path just to be sure the cat was not behind her and went home. Her cottage was very small with barely enough room for a bed, a table and one chair. It was located not far from the castle, most likely chosen so Laird Campbell could keep an eye on her. Likewise, the path was straight and she had a clear view of the castle's large double doors, which meant she could keep a close eye on him as well.

It was a pleasant village all in all with the usual cottages made of rock and mortar. Thatched roofs were different colors, depending on the age of the materials used to build them. Most of the men helped herd sheep north of the village, often moving them from hillside to hillside with the aid of border collies. Save for a trip down the coast to sell their wool once a year, the Campbells were not a seafaring clan. Yet spring was approaching and nearly everyone in the clan was busy with something that had to do with getting the wool to market.

Their total inattention to her suited Mackinzie just fine. As she entered her cottage and closed the door, she decided she wasn't that hungry anyway and settled for a meal of raw white carrots, turnips and berries. A short time later, she heard the men on the path say they had killed the wildcat and she was greatly relieved. Now she would not be scared to go back to her beloved hill.

When she finished her meal, Mackinzie looked around her sparsely furnished cottage. This day she had something amazing to tell and was sadly and acutely aware of having no one to tell.

She shrugged, got up, and pulled her small weaving loom away from the wall. Each evening she passed the time by working her loom while the sunlight still allowed her to see. She liked the soft lamb's wool and some mornings when she went out to greet the day, a new ball of spun yarn, just the right color, lay on a rock near her door. Always, she looked around, but she still had not discovered who left such wonderful gifts for her.

Kilts and plaids were made of eighteen rows of light blue followed by three rows of yellow, a pattern she found boring and tedious. Instead, she liked to experiment with different colors and make designs. Why not? The clan had more than enough weavers to supply their needs. It was just a way to ease her loneliness and she had no intention of letting anyone else see them.

ONCE DENA GOT WORD that Neasan sent the men out to find Paisley again, she was not just annoyed, she was as furious as he had been the night before. Becoming mistress of the clan was something she'd dreamed about all her life and she would not let Neasan deny her now. Besides, she found him exciting as well as alluring. She could not wait to be in his arms and thought he felt the same way. After all, he did kiss her and that was as good as being betrothed.

Dena spent hours sitting on her bed trying to think of some other reason he wanted Paisley back. Alas, there was no other reason. Neasan intended to marry Paisley and that was that.

The thought grated on her very soul—he was the man for her and Dena was right for him, even if he did not know it. Perhaps it was time she did something about his misguided intentions and there was only one sure way—Neasan could not marry Paisley if he was already married. A plan certain to work was beginning to form in her mind, but to make good on it, she had to be alone with Neasan, and that didn't appear likely anytime soon.

Nevertheless, if there was a way, Dena was determined to find it.

AT THE TOP OF THE NEXT hill, the black stallion rejoined them and once more took the lead. The MacGreagors continued to follow him, not because they believed the horse knew what it was doing, but simply because they could see no reason not to. Had the stallion turned south or north, they might have reconsidered, but the horse led them through the forest until it came to a well-worn path.

Keter hesitated for a moment, decided they were far enough away, and when Sawney nodded, continued to follow. All were glad to be out of the bushes, and from the path, they could see more of the countryside. They marveled at the vast lands and rolling hills of Scotland, behind which they could see far off mountain peaks.

Only once did they leave the path to hide from men coming toward them. The men tried to catch the black stallion, but it managed to stay just out of reach until the men got tired, gave up, and went on their way.

Though the MacGreagors remained watchful, they saw nothing of the Davidsons and began to breathe easier. When it rained, they covered their heads with heavy cloaks and kept going. When evening came and it stopped raining, they found dry land under the ample trees in the forest to sit on. Then they ate their fill and were happy to drink strong ale to soothe their aching muscles.

A hearty meal and the freedom to walk the stiffness out helped their mood. Just before time to put the children to bed, Sawney told one of the old MacGreagor stories. "Our Great-great-grandfather was in want of a wife. He lived in a faraway place where..."

STILL NEASAN DID NOT send for Dena and it was time. She undid her braid and brushed her long hair until she was satisfied it looked as good as she could make it. She parted it a little to one side, looked in the small, broken mirror on the wall, and was pleased with the way it framed her face. Late evening was finally upon them, the clansmen were taking part in their third night of celebration and the time seemed right to put her plan into action. She picked up the extra clothing she intended to wear after she bathed, opened the door, and walked down the path toward the courtyard.

Dena was delighted to find Neasan outside with the men and he did not appear to be as agitated as he had been most of the day. At least it meant Dena did not have to think of a way to tempt him out of the Keep, although she would have come up with something if necessary.

He spotted her too, which was exactly what she hoped. Dena stopped, smiled at him, lowered her eyes, and then turned, and headed down the path to the loch. Normally, the men bathed in the late afternoon and if she was very fortunate, those who still held with the old ways were finished by now. Cautiously, she paused as she approached the loch, peeked through the branches of the last tree, and assured herself they would be alone. So far, everything was perfect.

She set her pile of clothing down on a rock, slipped out of her shoes and began to untie her belt. Then she waited for what seemed like quite a while until she heard footsteps behind her. Without looking back to see, she released her belt and let her plaid fall to the ground. The footsteps stopped and she knew he wanted to watch. Her long shirt still covered all but her legs and just to tantalize him, she leisurely opened her shirt and let it slowly slide off her back.

Abruptly, she ran into the water and started swimming away. When she glanced back, she saw him undressing and knew his strength would enable him to catch up with her quickly, but she had considered that when she made her plan.

She swam around the bend until she was out of sight, hurried out of the water, and grabbed a blanket she left there earlier. Next, she slipped on an old pair of shoes and ran into the forest. By the time Neasan arrived, Dena was well away.

The forest was darker than she thought it would be and before long, she ran right into the low-hanging branch of a tree. She hit it hard, cut her cheek just below the eye, and nearly knocked herself out. It hurt something awful, but she never made a sound for fear Neasan was close.

She lifted the branch over her head and then stopped to see if she could hear him. When she heard nothing, she took a moment to wrap the plaid around her naked body better and proceeded to walk right into a tall, thorny bush that scratched both her legs.

Dena planned to beat Neasan back, but now she wasn't sure she could. Oh well, being found hiding in the forest would work just as well, and she wasn't so far from the loch that she couldn't go back.

CHAPTER VIII

IN THE DAVIDSON COURTYARD, Bearcha noticed when Dena smiled at Neasan. He also noticed Neasan leaving to follow her and he feared the worst. Yet Neasan was laird and could do whatever he wanted. On the other hand, what kind of man would let another attack a woman? Causally, he glanced around to see if any of the other men noticed and was certain they had. Yet none of them was willing to do anything about it. Dena could not know what she was doing, could she? Bearcha had never paid enough attention to Dena to know.

He was still mentally debating when Neasan came back. His cloths were dry, but his hair was clearly wet and again people noticed. Bearcha thought he should go see about Dena, but decided to wait a little longer. It would not do for him to see her before she was fully dressed.

He waited and waited and waited. Dena did not come back and Neasan began to drink more heavily than before. He had an odd look on his face and Bearcha could not quite make out what it meant.

It was almost completely dark and he was about to walk that way when Bearcha noticed Dena's father and brother head down the path. That was best, Bearcha thought. Let them discover what had happened.

A few moments later, he heard Dena's father call for her. It was clear she was not still at the lake and Bearcha joined several other men who headed that way. Dena's father was beside himself with worry. Her clean clothing were still on the rock, the ones she took off lay where she left them on the shore and Dena was nowhere to be found.

NEASAN DIDN'T CARE what happened to Dena. What he cared about was her attempt to trick him and how easily she managed it. The truth be told, he hoped she drowned. Just now, all he wanted was a good night's sleep. Neasan dumped his wine on the ground, tossed his goblet away, and walked inside the empty great hall. It was obvious no one had come to clean up and he made a mental note to see about that tomorrow before the rotting food on the table began to smell.

He was halfway up the second flight of stairs when he remembered he'd destroyed the mattress in the top bedchamber. He stopped, turned around, and went back to the second floor landing. Dragging another mattress up would not be too difficult, he thought, but when he opened the door to Sawney and Hew's old bedchamber, he decided just to sleep in there instead. He vaguely heard men still calling that despicable Dena's name.

ON THE FOURTH DAY WITH the sun shining bright and with no sign that they were being followed, the MacGreagors happened upon a stretch of beautiful grasslands between two hills complete with a nearby stream. It was a good time to do it and Sawney decided they would stay and rest for a while. They bathed and washed their clothing, let the children play and let the horses graze. Moreover, they had time to cook, take naps and discuss what to do next.

Sawney bent down, grabbed a handful of dirt, and let it slip through his fingers. "Aye, we could stay and build our home here, but is it far enough away? Neasan's lads could easily find us in two days' time."

"If they know which way to go," Daniel reminded him.

Keter sat on the ground, stuffing Dolina's green clothing in her sack. She now wore the yellow plaid of the Macfarlane just as her sister did. "I have been thinking about that. They are sure to think we did not go north as Bearcha reported, and the MacDuff have never known a secret they did not tell. Therefore, we did not go south either," said Keter.

"If they ask the Macfarlane, they are sure to know which way we went," Daniel pointed out.

Sawney pulled a long blade of grass out of the ground and examined it. The horses were happily grazing, the little children were napping, and the women were content to brush each other's hair with the wood-handled bush Carley sent with them. "They might think we went north. Grandmother Glenna was from the far north and they might think we seek sanctuary in her clan."

"I've a better idea," said Diocail. "The next time we see lads on the path, two of us will say we saw an odd clan turn south somewhere between here and the MacFarlane."

Sawney reached over and playfully slapped Diocail on the back, "How have you come to have your wits about you?"

"He is right," said Blare. "To the next, we might say the clan argued among themselves and parted ways, some going south and some heading back the way they came. That should confound the Davidsons, they'll not know which way to look."

Keter seemed exceptionally pleased, "Aye, and we can say we are from a different clan each time."

"It is settled then," Sawney agreed. "We will keep going."

A TIME OF MADNESS

IT WAS QUIET WHEN NEASAN woke up, climbed out of Hew's bed and stretched. Unaware he'd slept half the day away again, he went to the window that faced the river behind the village, and decided a little fishing would do him good while he waited for William and his men to bring Paisley back. He saw none of the people, but perhaps they were still sleeping. Curls of smoke rose from hearths in the cottages just as they always did, dogs slept along the paths and a cow had somehow managed to wander from the pasture to the river.

Again, he found no morning meal waiting for him downstairs and he let out a frustrated huff. However, this time Bearcha was seated at the table waiting for him instead of leaning against the wall outside like he normally was.

"There is no lass serving me again this day?"

"They fear you now, so you'll not likely get any of them to enter without a lad to protect them."

The volume of Neasan's voice started to rise a little. "Why, what has changed? They did not fear serving me yesterday."

"They have seen Dena's face?"

Neasan walked to the table, grabbed an overturned goblet, and started to pour himself some wine, only to find the pitcher empty. Furious, he threw the clay pitcher against the wall and watched it shatter into a thousand pieces. Rotting food was beginning to smell, the colorful pillows along the walls were stained and there were three deep cuts in the long table Neasan often coveted before he became laird.

"'Twas your last pitcher," Bearcha muttered.

Neasan took a deep breath and tried to calm himself. "What has happened to Dena's face?"

"She claims you struck her."

"Would that I had. She tempted me to go with her, swam away and was gone before I could catch up."

"That is not how she tells it."

Neasan couldn't believe what he was hearing. He tried to run both hands through his tangled hair, gave up halfway through, and slowly sat down at the head of the table. "Does she say I forced her?"

"Aye." Bearcha slowly stood up and moved the chair away. He had seen Neasan's rage often enough to stay out of reach. "The people await you in the courtyard."

"Tell them to go home."

Bearcha took several steps toward the door before he stopped and turned around. "Only their laird can make them go."

Neasan needed time to think and watched Bearcha walk out the door without saying another word. If the clan believed Dena, they would demand he marry her and that was the last thing he intended to do. He rubbed the back of his neck and stared at the table. What could he do? He needed her family to become laird, but now those same men would turn against him if he did not marry her.

Again, he rubbed the back of his neck and closed his eyes. Then it occurred to him he might manage to find a way out of it after all.

THE GRASSLANDS OFFERED soft beds on the ground and a place to fill their flasks with fresh water. Yet it gave the MacGreagors no place to hide. Just as they were about to mount their horses and continue their journey, they noticed two horsemen riding down the side of a hill toward them.

The MacGreagor warriors immediately prepared themselves to defend the women and children, but these strangers were not looking for someone to fight. They were curious and once they halted their horses, glanced over all the people, and noticed their different color attire, they had plenty of questions to ask.

Sawney said they were Forbes and they were sent to find new land worthy of growing hemp. The strangers seemed to accept that since everyone used hemp to make a variety of goods including rope. About the different colors, Sawney laughed and said their weavers were simply not the best. That too the strangers easily accepted and one even showed the odd threads in his own kilt.

"Where might we find good land?" Keter asked. Just as he hoped, one of the strangers pointed south. Keter nodded, and began to help the women and children mount. "South it is then."

Satisfied, the strangers rode away and did not look back.

"Brother," Paisley said when Sawney lifted her up on her horse, "Why do you think the black horse stays with us?"

Sawney handed little Flora to her and waited for Paisley to get a firm hold on the reins and the child. "I believe he has fallen madly in love with my mare."

Paisley giggled. "Horses do not fall in love."

"You cannot know that. Perhaps they are the same as people."

Paisley smiled. "Or perhaps you have lost your wits." A sharp pain in her side made her wince. "Sawney?"

"What?"

She hated bothering him especially since they were all suffering, but she had to before her injury got worse. She held tight to Flora and leaned down to whisper in his ear. "The sword it too heavy. The strings are cutting me when we ride."

He looked shocked. "Hew, come." He pulled Flora back out of her arms and handed her to his brother. "Forgive me for not realizing. Of course it is too heavy." He lifted Paisley down, quickly untied the leather strings, and noticed blood on her side just above her belt. "You tie it too high, sister."

"I tie it around my belt, but the weight pulls that side down and the strings ride up."

A wound that would not heal could cause death and it was something they all feared. Sawney handed the golden sword to Hew and while Paisley held her shirt closed in the front, Sawney lifted it enough at the waist to see her injury. It was not cut too badly, but enough to cause him concern and to cause Paisley a great deal of discomfort.

Sawney took Flora out of Hew's arms. "Stow your sword on one of the pack horse and wear hers. While Hew did as he said, Sawney handed Flora to Senga. Paisley is hurt. At fifteen, Senga was happy to help. She loved children and hoped to have one of her own someday.

"I will stay back to protect her," said Hew when he returned.

Sawney smiled, "You are a good brother." He waited for Paisley to get her shirt on properly, then lifted her up again, careful not to touch her cut. "We cannot lose you."

His love for her was endearing and made her smile. "I'll not die; you need me to keep you from marrying a lass who is too willing."

The last to mount his horse, Sawney raised his hand, motioned them forward and they too left the pleasant valley.

NEASAN FINALLY OPENED the door of the Keep and walked out. Just as he expected, the entire clan was there waiting for him, including Carley. What he didn't expect to see was the Priest. Dena stood by her father with her eyes held down and true enough, she had a horrible bruise around her eye and a cut on her cheekbone. Briefly, he wondered how hard she had to hit herself to accomplish that. In a way, he admired her trickery, except she was playing it on him.

Dena's father shoved her behind him and turned to face Neasan. "You have shamed my daughter and you will marry her this day."

"She lies."

"She does not lie."

Neasan gritted his teeth. "Tell him, Dena. Tell him I did not put a hand on you."

Dena was careful to stay hidden behind her father's back. "You did, do not deny it."

"No man shames my daughter and then does not marry her. If you refuse to do right, I will call you out, and if I do not kill you, her brothers will."

Neasan was caught and it was not wholly unexpected. "Very well then, I will marry her." He paused just long enough to let the crowd start to murmur. "However," said he loud enough for all to hear, "You will not call Dena mistress. She will not live under my roof, nor come to me with any request. Heretofore, she will not so much as speak to me."

Neasan paused again just to let his words sink in. "She is not to attend a feast, not to walk in the glen when I am there and no lad shall speak her name to me." He gritted his teeth again and glared at Dena's father. "She will be guarded at all times to prevent any lad from bedding her." He turned to look at one of the men, who quickly nodded.

Neasan continued, "When it is certain she is not with child, I shall set her aside for her trickery. Then, I will send her away—never to return."

Not be mistress? Dena was horrified and tried to think of a way out of her quandary. Before she had a chance, her father pulled her out from behind him and stood her in front of the priest. Neasan came to stand beside her and the entire time the priest conducted the ceremony, she never heard a word. How could she have made such a mess of things? More importantly, how was she to keep the clan, and especially her father, from knowing she lied? Then it occurred to her she might entice the man sent to guard her, and if not, she could plead her case to the priest. After all, not all women conceived on their wedding night.

Her father wasn't listening either. He dared not think what would happen to Dena out in the world alone if Neasan sent her away. Clearly, he would have to take his family and go with her, but he was an elder, this was the only home he had ever known and he knew the world beyond the glen could be harsh and cruel.

Nor was Neasan paying attention. His mind was on Paisley and how she might feel about what he was doing. Marrying Dena, if he were guilty, would be the honorable thing to do. Being forced into a marriage would not bode well with the daughter of the former Laird, a laird who would never let himself get caught in such a trap.

No indeed, Justin was saintly, never said a harsh word to a woman and remained faithful to that skinny, English wife of his. Justin was not even human, as far as Neasan was concerned, and living such a virtuous life ruined it for every other man. There were always women who were willing and Neasan knew exactly who they were, but he doubted Justin did. This was all Justin's fault. A woman's word should never be believed above that of a man.

Paisley was probably just like him—just as proud, arrogant and stubborn. As soon as William brought Paisley back, he would make her live in the Keep. Let the people think what they want and soon they will think her as common and as wanton as Dena. It would serve Paisley right!

At last, Dena and Neasan said their "I do's" and went their separate ways, him into the Keep and her back to the cottage she shared with her parents and her siblings. Only this time, there was a guard posted outside her door.

IT WAS TWO LONG DAYS before the news they had been waiting for came and Grant was careful to take aunt Carley for a walk in the glen where no one could hear. "They are safe. Bryce made it to the Kennedys and they have gone to find Sawney."

Carley took the arm he offered for her to hang on to and heaved a sigh of relief. "I am happy to hear it and I am certain their wives are the same. Once they find..."

"We do not know if they can find Sawney. The Kennedy's traded kilts with them and who knows what colors they are wearing now. 'Twill be hard to know which way they went."

"Is there no gossip of a small clan on the move?"

"Aye, three clans have been seen. Scots move from place to place more often than we knew."

"None are Sawney? How can you be certain?"

"Our lads are very large and we would hear if..."

Carley smiled. "I had not thought of that."

They strolled across the glen until they neared the graveyard. It was the first time she had seen the stone placed at the head of Justin's grave and she approved.

"'Tis very fine work," said Grant.

"Indeed it is," Carley agreed. "I wonder that William and the lads have not come back."

"I wonder too, but I have heard nothing of them, no one seems to know where they went. It is uncommon not to hear."

Carley smiled. "Now that Neasan is married, perhaps he is not so eager to have Paisley back."

"Never have I seen such a wedding and true to his word, Neasan has not sought Dena out. It is unnatural for a lad to have a wife and not take her to him."

"In this case, Neasan may well be right. Dena deceived us all and God be with her if she is not with child."

"I had not thought Dena that shrewd."

"She had her eyes on Sawney first and made it known last year. Then she easily took to Neasan. Aye, she is shrewd enough to trick Neasan into marriage." Carley let him turn them away from the graveyard and walk toward the corral. "What of the Haldane?" she asked after a time.

"The Swintons have them."

"The Swintons? They are not the best of friends with the Haldane, not since a Haldane accused a Swinton of stealing his horse."

Grant smiled. "True, and they have yet to find that horse, but this is a different matter. When there is danger, the clans put aside their differences and stand together."

Carley leaned down, picked a flower and smelled its fragrance. "I have heard their muttering. Neasan thinks to attack another clan soon. Do you know which one?"

"Nay, he has not yet decided."

"We must do something."

"Such as?"

Carley thought about it for a moment. "I do not know...distract Neasan somehow. Perhaps if he has more to worry about in the glen, he might not be so happy to lead another attack."

THE MACGREAGORS ENCOUNTERED men heading their same direction too, although at a much faster pace. As they agreed, all hid except two or three MacGreagors, which allowed them to spread the rumors they planned. Conversely, the men they met had plenty to say about a banished clan and recounted all the same gossip Carley heard. Several different rumors about their banishment appeared to be spreading across Scotland, and the MacGreagors were fascinated to learn how easily the truth got confused.

Then came the worst possible news. A very small clan had been completely wiped out by men of great strength. Who else could do such a thing but Neasan, and the clan that was no more, had to be the Haldane.

The MacGreagors continued their journey trying to hide their sorrow from one another. The Haldane had always been small with few of their own warriors to protect them. At last count, they numbered only twenty-seven adults and they were good neighbors to the MacGreagors. The two clans occasionally intermarried which meant some were related.

The names and faces of the Haldane were on every mind and when Jennet burst into tears Sawney stopped the horses. Blare was quick to dismount and take his wife in his arms to comfort her. Soon, all the women were crying and all the men felt just as bad.

It was time for their noon meal anyway and Keter suggested the elder children carve a mark into a soft stone for each of the Haldane. It seemed to make them all feel just a bit better and they watched as the two eldest boys stood the stone upright along the path.

Paisley's side was hurting and it was Lenox who noticed it the most. Now that little Flora rode with one of the other women, he often saw Paisley hold her side. After the stone was carved and placed near the path, Lenox took Sawney aside and told him.

Paisley didn't want them to bother, but her brothers insisted, so the women held a plaid up in front of her. Sawney made Paisley undo her belt and with only her long shirt on, he carefully parted it, poured wine on his cloth, and held it against her wound. It was the only medicine they had and he knew it hurt, so when he thought he had held it there long enough, he gathered her in his arms and let her cry.

When they mounted their horses this time, it was Lenox who helped Paisley up, and instead of holding onto her waist, he put an arm under her legs and lifted all of her up. Lenox grew up with her and they had always been friends, save for the times she threatened to kill him. Pleasing her was occasionally difficult when they were young, but he didn't mind. She was fun to be with and interesting to talk to. Perhaps he cared for her a little more than the other men because of it and now he meant to see to her care.

Paisley was happy for his attention, although she saw nothing more in it than an old friendship. She was also happy Lenox was taking a burden off Sawney, who always seemed to be fussing over her. She did not deny her pain, but there was nothing anyone could do to relieve it, so she carried on as though nothing was wrong. All of them had aches and pains they were not complaining about and she did not want to be the fainthearted one among such strong people.

IF ANYTHING COULD DISTRACT Neasan from planning a new attack, it was the fact that William and the men had not come back, with or without Paisley. The more he thought about it, the more he paced and loudly yelled his complains about the multitude of things that irritated him. His bellowed list of threats was long and growing longer.

More and more, the Davidson's were getting tired of his ranting and more than once rolled their eyes over his latest outburst. It seemed nothing could please him, even his meals, which he continued to wolf down as though someone was set to take it away before he could finish.

It appeared to be the perfect time to act, so Carley boldly walked to the Keep, opened the door, and went in. Neasan was the only one in the great hall and she was not surprised. The Keep, her brother's home and her father's before him, was filled with the foul remainders of drunkenness from the previous nights.

She had lived through it all, buried them all one by one, and was thankful she was the only family member left to see their pleasant world crumbling.

As the old people often do, Carley remembered far too much of her youth and how her innocence was shattered when she married the wrong man—a man who was not buried in the graveyard with the family members. Instead, he was put in the ground next to other nefarious members so his soul would not taint those of the beloved. It was there she hoped to see Neasan put someday. For now, however, there was something she could do to help secure the return of the clan to the MacGreagors, and she was willing to risk her life to do it.

Carley smiled, sat down next to Neasan at the table, and tried to ignore the filth around her. "You need a wife."

Seated at the head of the table where Justin and his father before him always sat, Neasan eyed her suspiciously, "I have a wife."

She did not take her eyes from his. "Have you gone daft?"

At that, Neasan smiled. "Not completely. If you speak of Dena, I do not need her. I have all the pleasure a lad could want."

"Pleasure is a good thing, but what will you have to impress other lairds when they come to pay tribute? Surely they will, once you become a great conqueror." She took a moment to slowly look around. The large, colorful pillows her mother kept along the walls were cut open with the stuffed feathers hanging out. Coals in the hearth were shoved aside to make room for new wood and left where they lay. Rotting food remained on the table and the floor was littered with dropped goblets and stains from spilled drinks. When she looked back, Neasan was looking around too. "What will they think of you?"

Again, Neasan eyed her suspiciously. "You wish me well, do you? Am I to believe that?"

"Believe what you will, I care not what you do. 'Tis only something to talk about."

"Something to talk about?" He got up, walked to a table, grabbed a flask of wine, and returned to fill his goblet. "What are you up to, Carley? Why have you come to see me?"

She waited for him to sit back down. "When you were but ten, you killed a red fox and found pleasure in it. I guessed you to become a great hunter, but you desired more. When you hurt a woman without kind regard, I talked Justin into sparing you because you were too young. I confess it was not hard to do, Justin did not wish you to be his first execution. Now you are free to hurt, force and even kill every lass in the clan if you so desire. Therefore, I have come to ask you to spare me."

Both his eyebrows shot up. "Spare you? I wish you no harm, Carley. How have you come to think that?"

Carley started to get up. "'Tis but gossip then. I feared being slain in my bed and now I will sleep more peacefully."

He quickly grabbed hold of her arm. "What gossip? What do they say of me?"

She looked down at the hold he had on her arm and did not speak until he let go. "I am old and I do not recall who said it, but then I am usually the last to hear."

"Hear what?"

"That you intend to do away with all the elders."

Neasan tried to remember if he actually said that. He must have, but as hard as he tried, he did not remember even thinking it. Worse, he had no idea whom he might have said it in front of. "But not you, Carley, I would never hurt you."

"There be but a few elders left. How do we plague you?"

Still flustered, he tried to think why he might have said it so he could explain. "Perhaps because the people listen to the elders."

"You fear the people will rebel? Then I will tell the elders not to recommend it. They will listen to me." Carley walked toward the door, stopped, and did not bother looking back. "You've a traitor in your midst who warned us, as well as the Haldane. Perhaps you should forget the elders in favor of seeking him out." With that, she walked out the door.

In a courtyard that was once filled with happy people, few were there standing amid still more clutter on the ground. Yet those that were there seemed happy to see her and when she smiled, they returned with smiles of their own. Carley hoped to discover which were still true MacGreagors by their smiles, but Neasan's men also smiled. At least there was some measure of respect left for the elders even on Neasan's side.

As soon as she left the courtyard and turned down the path, Carley nodded to Grant so he would know the deed was done. She had not yet managed to get to her cottage before Neasan started yelling.

The day before and behind Neasan's back, Grant and Bearcha formed an alliance, and it was Grant who then nodded to Bearcha. If Neasan decided who his traitor was, the two of them were set to help the man hide. It was Bearcha who guessed that Neasan, when he was sober, would believe Carley and he was right. Now all they could do was wait to see what happened.

A TRAITOR WAS JUST one of Neasan's problems. His warriors always seemed to be losing things. One lost a pair of shoes when he went to the loch to bathe and had to come back up the path barefoot to plead for a new pair. The items lost ranged from belts, weapons, spoons, bowls, baskets of washing the moment a women turned her back, and even some of the tools could not be accounted for.

On the morning of Neasan's eighth day of rule, he went to the window of his third-story bedchamber, looked out, and discovered his beloved whalebone was missing from the glen, cart and all.

It was as though he had run completely out of rage and instead, he calmly sat on the bed he carried up himself from a downstairs bedchamber. Neasan tried to think where he had gone wrong. Being laird should not be this difficult. He should have killed someone that first day, but whom, Sawney?

That was it, as long as Sawney still lived, the clan thought they had another choice. They did not fear Neasan as they should, and therefore his commands were not obeyed without question.

Where was William?

This constant disobedience, the infernal questions and the odd happenings were all carefully designed to make him go daft. Neasan could see that now. He too had expected half the clan to go with Sawney, and when they didn't, he assumed they were truly on his side. Apparently, he assumed wrong and for all he knew, Sawney was lurking just out of sight, waiting to find him alone.

There had to be a way to get control of the people. How had Justin done it? Love was not Neasan's favorite word. In fact, he was never quite certain what that was, but everyone loved Justin. Therefore, love had to be the answer, but how on earth do you make people love you?

A moment later, Neasan thought he had the answer—but first, he needed to bathe, trim his beard, and make himself presentable.

MACKINZIE CAMPBELL missed the horse more today than most days, but once again, it did not come back. Certain Laird Campbell was looking for her after she exchanged harsh words with one of the other women, she hurried out of the village and came to her peaceful, uncomplicated sanctuary at the top of the hill.

It was not as though she tore the plaid on purpose, Mackinzie was simply washing it when it caught on a rock in the riverbed. Such things were not her fault and it was not as though another plaid could not be easily had, for the weavers always had extras on hand.

Mackinzie supposed she should not have called the woman a 'scunner.' It was the worst name one person could call another, but the word just shot out of her mouth before she realized what she was saying. Nor did she apologize. She saw no reason to apologize for telling the truth, the woman *was* a scunner. She supposed she should try to control her temper better, but whatever for. They didn't like her anyway and Laird Campbell never punished her harshly.

She did wonder what he had in mind for her this time, but his drinking habits were such, that if she stayed away long enough he would forget her altogether.

It was then she heard voices in the woods behind her, ran down the side of the hill, crossed the path, and hid in the trees.

CHAPTER IX

ALL DAY THE MACGREAGORS noticed seagulls, smelled the pleasant aroma of the sea, and knew they were getting close. They remained on their horses, walked them out of the forest, across a small meadow, and then up to the top of the last hill.

The vastness of the Atlantic Ocean took their breaths away. Waves crashed against red rocks on the shoreline sending sprays of water into the air. The sea receded, gathered strength, and then crashed again in a mesmerizing, yet peaceful sort of rhythm.

Soon they dismounted, stood in the tall grass together, and simply watched the movement of the water. More seagulls soared through the air, landing occasionally on the water and then taking flight again. To the north, there appeared to be an island or two and in the opposite direction, the land rose up into high cliffs that curved around the bay.

No one minded that the horses wandered back down the hill to the meadow, or that their muscles hurt and they were bone tired. All they wanted to do was watch the magnificent scene constantly repeating itself before them.

MACKINZIE THOUGHT THEM an odd-looking band of people, some wearing red, some yellow, and some green. That was before she spotted the black stallion, *her* beloved black stallion and the very large man riding him. He rode without a halter and reins just as she always did, although that was not so very odd, many men did. She watched him dismount, stroke the side of the horse's neck and set him free. The man helped the women and children down and then turned to look out over the ocean.

He was the largest man she had ever seen when he stood atop her hill and although he had a pleasant enough face, she was certain he could be fierce when he wanted to be. The other men seemed unusually large too and it wasn't long before she guessed these were the ferocious giants from the north she once heard about.

Yet the women with them did not seem afraid and when one of the men put his arm around a woman Mackinzie guessed was his wife, she could see no fear in the woman's face. At least these people appeared to love the ocean as much as she and Mackinzie could not find fault with that.

"'TIS MAGNIFICENT," GAVINA said as Keter put his arm around her waist. "I never suspected."

"Nor I," Keter pulled his wife a little closer and lovingly kissed the side of her head. "Perhaps we have found our new home."

Sawney glanced back at the meadow. "I agree. 'Tis good land and..." He noticed the stallion wander toward the trees on the northern side of the hill and stop. The black seemed to be looking at something and Sawney was curious.

"Go away," Mackinzie whispered. When the horse didn't move and kept looking her in the eye, her heart melted and she lovingly stroked his nose. "Aye, I am happy to see you too, but I do not wish to be discovered." Still the horse did not move and she was becoming frustrated. Yet what could she do? Perhaps if she hugged him he would be satisfied.

Mackinzie ran her hand along the side of the horse's neck until she stood next to him and when he lowered his head, she looped both arms around his neck and hugged him. "There, that should do. Now..." It was too late. As soon as she stepped back and looked up, she discovered the man standing near the back of the horse staring at her.

"It he your horse?" Sawney asked, patting the side of the black to let the stallion know he was there.

She quickly took another step away from him. The man was even taller than she thought, his eyes were a shade of blue she had never seen before and he half frightened and half fascinated her. All she could think of to do was nod.

"What is his name?"

Why hadn't she turned and run? Her heart was racing, her mind was cluttered and he kept staring at her. "'Tis a horse too becoming to name." Why did she say it was her horse? She had gone daft finally and this was the proof.

"I agree."

"You do?"

The woman standing before him had the look of someone who was up to something and it fascinated him so much, he almost forgot what he was about to say. "Aye...we happened upon him at...well, 'tis a very long story."

She heard a man behind him whistle. The stranger quickly turned to look, then he turned back to face her again.

"Riders," said he.

"Where?"

"Along the water's edge, I suspect."

"'Tis Amos and Joel. Pray do not tell them you have seen me."

Sawney wrinkled his brow, watched her slip deeper into the forest and go out of sight. He supposed she had her reasons and he would honor her request, but she did not take the stallion with her.

He would have helped her mount, but now she was gone and the horse was beginning to drift back toward the meadow.

She was certainly pleasant to look at with her red hair, green eyes, and that patch of freckles across her nose. Very pleasing indeed. Sawney turned around and went back up the hill to have a look at this Amos and Joel.

In the woods, Mackinzie stopped, turned around, and looked between the trees until she was certain both the man and the horse were gone. Quietly, she made her way back to her original hiding place. She had hidden from Amos and Joel often in that very spot and not once did they notice her. Any moment now, they would ride up the path, down to the waterfall, fill their flasks, and then go back the way they came.

When they first spotted the two men wearing scarlet kilts coming around the edge of the high cliffs, the MacGreagor warriors made sure their swords were positioned correctly and prepared to protect the clan. In silence, they watched the strangers make their way along the shore. They didn't appear to be in any hurry and soon the MacGreagors realized these were men in the service of the King of Scots. The strangers sat upon scarlet plaids thrown over the horse's backs and wore matching kilts with scarlet capes to keep off the chill in the air.

The riders turned their direction, started up the hill, spotted the MacGreagors, and came to a quick halt. Then one of them shouted, "We are in need of the good water on your land, nothing more. We mean you no harm."

Sawney motioned for the strangers to come, then spread his legs and clasped his hands behind his back. "I wonder where the sweet water is?" he muttered.

Blare did the same and smiled. "I suspect they are about to show us."

"What clan are you?" the other stranger asked, guiding his horse up the north side of the hill until he was close enough to talk without shouting. Joel glanced at the women and saw one he found pleasing, but did not dare show it for fear she was wife to one of the men.

Sawney had been thinking about it and just that morning decided a new name might better help them hide. He was grateful he managed to warn the clan in time so they would not look shocked. "We are Kerr," He had never met a Kerr, but he'd heard of the clan often enough in the stories his father told of the war between his grandfather, Neil and Neil's brother Sween.

"Ah, we thought you might be the banished MacGreagor clan. I am Joel and he is Amos. We ride the beach daily keeping an eye out lest the English, the Normans, the Celts, or the Romans think to attack."

In unison, all the MacGreagors turned to look out across the ocean. None had ever seen a ship or even a large boat, let alone the dreaded Romans, and the thought they might see one someday excited them.

Amos found this little clan fascinating as well. It was not hard to see how tired they were, especially since the smallest one was sound asleep on a woman's shoulder. "From where have you come?"

Sawney wasn't sure which lie he told last, so he stalled for time by introducing each of them. He was relieved when Blare answered Amos' question.

"We come from the west. Our village caught fire and we have always wanted to see the ocean. Our choice was to rebuild there or find a new land."

"Are there many other clans nearby?" asked Keter before the king's men could ask any more awkward questions.

"Brother, you forget," Blare interrupted. "They are thirsty and our flasks are nearly dry. Perhaps they might show us where the water is first."

"Why?" Dolina asked, pointing toward the ocean. "There is water aplenty there." Speaking out as she did, at not yet twelve, embarrassed her and she quickly hung her head.

The strangers laughed and then felt bad when she glared at them. "Forgive us lassie, we should not have laughed," said Joel, "The water in the ocean will plague you, but first you become daft. 'Tis the salt in the water that kills, they say."

"We have heard that," said Keter. "We have little, but we are willing to share a meal with you."

Amos nodded his appreciation. "My wife will have our heads if we do not return as promised, but we will show you were the water is and come back tomorrow…and the next day…and the one after that. You'll find good hunting in these woods and fish in the streams. You will do well here, Kerr, and you are welcome to all the land you can hold. 'Twill be good to have neighbors."

Sawney, Keter and Lenox followed the King's men down the side of the hill to the path and then around a bend. Sawney could not help but look for the woman as he passed, but she was not there.

They expected a stream, but it was not just a stream, it was a three-tiered waterfall with a pond. The salmon were the largest fish any of them had ever seen and the fish were trying to jump up each tier of the waterfall. Some were even making it while others fell back only to try again.

Amos got off his horse and explained while he dumped old water out of his flask and filled it with new. "They go upstream to spawn and their yield comes back down to swim in the ocean." He watched with fascination as Lenox knelt down, suddenly reach in the stream, pull a salmon out, and toss it on the shore. His grin matched those of the other men and soon each of the MacGreagors caught enough salmon to take back to the clan for their evening meal.

"How far away is your village?" Sawney asked, standing back up and brushing the dirt off his knees.

"Just a piece up the way," Joel answered, pointing north.

Sawney was happy to hear it especially since the woman in the forest went that way. Joel and Amos seemed pleasant enough and he wondered why she did not want them to know he had seen her.

Just before Amos and Joel mounted their horses and were ready to leave, Keter had one more thing to say. "On our journey, we happened upon a gray wolf with eyes the color of the sky."

"Blue eyes? Never have I seen such a thing. A gray wolf normally has eyes the color of a fire," said Amos.

"That is what we always thought," Keter said.

"'Tis a pity you are not the banished MacGreagors. We heard tell they were all slain and hoped it was not true. Till the morrow, then." From the path going back to the beach, Joel glanced up the hill to see if the lass he found pleasing was watching. When fifteen-year-old Senga was, he smiled. At not yet twenty, he was more than ready to take a wife and thrilled to see they had new neighbors for him to choose from. Perhaps he might come back and help them build.

Sawney, Hew and Lenox picked up the fish, walked back down the path and then up the hill. He hated telling them what they had just heard, but it had to be done.

"They think we are dead?" Tears began to form in the rims of Paisley's eyes and when Sawney opened his arms, she gladly went into them.

"They'll not think it for long," said Keter. "I told them we had seen a wolf with blue eyes, which is what Mother said to say so she will know we are well."

"There, you see," said Sawney, "what news travels faster than that of a gray wolf with blue eyes?"

Paisley wiped the lone tear off her cheek, "And every lad in Scotland will hope to see it."

"That they will." Sawney hugged her again and then started down the hill to the meadow. "I say we build a fire and eat these wondrous fish."

In the trees, Mackinzie watched the tall man hug the woman and decided it was time to go home. He was obviously married and that was that, although she liked him and wished it were not so. She shrugged and headed home.

The older children helped by gathering sticks while Sawney and two of the other men went to the edge of the forest to find larger pieces of dry wood. The women cleaned and prepared the meat, the older children gathered dry leaves, put them in a pile, and added the sticks. Then one struck ironware against his flint stone and fanned the small flames with his hands until it began to burn.

Soon the smell of cooking salmon filled the air.

LAIRD NEASAN DAVIDSON had a lot on his mind. He managed to take a bath and trim his beard, but the more he thought about what Carley said, the more determined he was to learn who betrayed him. As soon as he got back, he called the twenty men he thought might have heard him say he was going to do away with the elders, and made them come inside the great hall.

Bearcha could not stand the smell of the place and began to gather the bowls of rotting food. He carried them out the door to the kitchen and went back for more. How a man could live in such stench was beyond him and as soon as Neasan began yelling, Bearcha decided doing this chore at a slower pace would keep him out of the line of fire. Often he stayed in the kitchen a little longer than was necessary, even though it smelled worse in there. It wasn't hard to hear every obnoxious word Neasan had to say, in fact, the whole clan could probably hear him.

First Neasan demanded to know who told Carley and when that produced no satisfactory results, he wanted to know what they had heard of William and his men. He received no reply to that question either and began to pound his fist on the table. "I command you to tell me!"

Bearcha decided he best go back and try to calm Neasan down before he destroyed the table. He took a deep breath, opened the door, and went in. "They do not hear where William is because the clans are not speaking to us. We have attacked the Haldane and they favor them more than they do us."

It was a reasonable answer and one Neasan contemplated for a moment. "Do you speak the truth?"

Bearcha took a deep breath and let it out before he moved an empty chair away from the table, turned it to face Neasan and sat down. "If there is news of William, I for one have not heard it."

"Nor I," said another man amid the nods of the others. It was true, they had not heard a word.

Neasan tried to see deception in their eyes, but these were fearless warriors who were taught to keep secrets from birth, even from their laird. Perhaps they were telling the truth this time. His thoughts quickly turned back to what Carley said and for an hour more, he threatened, ranted, and raved until his throat began to hurt. He needed more wine.

Bearcha found Neasan's silence more frightening than his ranting, watched him finally sit at the head of the table, and tried to guess what he would find to get upset about next.

Yet Neasan remained quiet for several minutes until he decided he had only one more question to ask, "Who took the bone out of the glen?" He carefully watched as the men exchanged glances.

"You did," Bearcha finally answered.

"What?" Neasan half rose out of his seat and stared at Bearcha.

"Do you not remember? You said you never wished to see it again, so we took it away."

"When?"

"Last night after...after you drank your fill. Shall we bring it back?"

Neasan slowly sunk back into his chair. This odd lack of memory after drinking the night away never happened before. Suspicious, he brought his goblet up to his nose and smelled it. It smelled the same as MacGreagor wine always had. Maybe he was getting old, and why not, being laird was a lot harder than he imagined. "Be gone, all of you."

Never had men left a great hall as quickly as these twenty and Bearcha was right behind them. Outside, he watched them scatter in different directions, breathed in the pleasant air, and finally allowed himself the smile he'd been holding back all day. Still, that was not the end of Neasan's demands and when he heard the door open behind him, Bearcha quickly hid his smile and turned around.

"Bring Dena to me."

That was the last thing Bearcha expected to hear and although he was shocked to hear it, he had no choice but to obey. Dena was the man's wife and a husband had a right to do as he pleased. Bearcha nodded and walked down the path.

When she answered the door, Dena seemed pleased her husband finally sent for her. Bearcha walked her to the Keep but he didn't take her in. He feared for her, did not want to hear what he suspected would happen, and went home instead to hold his own wife in his arms.

She too feared what might happen, but Dena made this mess and thought she probably deserved what was coming. She squared her shoulders, took a deep breath, and opened the door. To her surprise, Neasan was alone and didn't look at all angry, although he did not smile. The place was a mess, but she ignored it, stepped inside, and closed the door behind her.

"Come, Dena." Neasan noticed her hesitation and added, "I will not harm you." He waited until she came closer and then pulled a chair away from the table for her. "Tell me, why have you falsely accused me?"

She thought to lie, but he was her husband and she had always heard there should be truth between a husband and a wife. Yet she was not eager to confess either. "Why do you send lads to bring Paisley back?"

"Oh, I see. You misunderstand, Dena. I want Paisley here so her brothers will not attack us, nothing more."

His explanation was one she had not thought of. It sounded reasonable enough and now she was thoroughly ashamed of herself for trying to trick him. At length, she hung her head, but when he came to sit beside her, he put a finger under her chin and lifted it so she would look at him.

"How did you happen to hurt yourself?"

She couldn't help but smile just a little. "It was dark in the forest and I ran into the branch of a tree."

He had not expected her to so openly tell the truth and just now, he wished he had someone hidden nearby to hear her confession. Why did he always think of these things too late? He took his hand away from her chin and put her hand in his instead. "'Twas a wretched thing you did and now we are both trapped by it. Nevertheless, I have decided to forgive you."

"You have?"

"Well, not completely. Do you suppose if you lived here with me, you might manage to get the women to do a little cleaning and perhaps see that my meals are prepared? 'Tis what a mistress does."

At the mention of her being his mistress, Dena's eyes lit up, and her heart fluttered with anticipation. "Aye. Shall I go get my belongings?"

"Please." He watched her bounce up and race for the door, and as soon as she was gone, he shook his head. "Never have I seen such a stupid lass."

It wasn't long before she was back with her grinning mother and sisters in toe. Almost immediately, they began to clean the place and Neasan was pleased, although he soon went outside to avoid all their happy chatter.

That night when he went up to bed, he found Dena waiting for him in his third-floor bedchamber. "What are you doing here?"

"I thought...I..."

"You thought wrong. You tricked me into this marriage and for that; you will never be in my bed." He grabbed her by the back of the hair and shoved her toward the door. "And if you breathe a word of this to anyone, I *will* kill you." He opened the door and released her.

He was furious enough to throw her down the stairs, but that would not do...at least not yet. Instead he took hold of her arm, half dragged her down the first flight, opened the door to the room where Sawney's dead brothers once slept, and shoved her inside. Abruptly he closed the door, went down the stairs and out the door to find his pleasure elsewhere.

In tears, Dena sat down on one of the small beds and closed her eyes. She wept for what seemed like hours and then a thought occurred to her. He did not love her, that was clear, but perhaps if she was very good and did all he asked, he might someday. Until then, she had what she wanted—she was mistress of the clan.

EVEN THE GROUND SEEMED softer in the tall grass near the sea and sleep came easily to the MacGreagors. The sound of crashing waves comforted them, the fish filled their stomachs, and all of them agreed this was a very fine place to build a new home.

Their first morning on the new land meant a thousand decisions had to be made. What they needed most was a roof over their heads and four walls to protect them from the wind and rain. A large structure was always the first built and would become the Keep once there were cottages for the families.

Fortunately, the art of building had been handed down through the generations and they'd managed to bring a few tools. The tools, each of them realized, were thoughtful gifts from those left behind and they were very grateful.

One guard standing on the top of the hill could see for miles around in every direction and Daniel took the first watch. It allowed all the other men to turn their attention to gathering beer stones, a white chalky substance they could grind and mix with sand and water to make mortar. The tempting grass kept the horses from straying very far away and bright orange peacock butterflies flittering through the air dared the three and the five-year-old to capture them. All the while, the sounds of the ocean seemed like music to their ears.

Yet there was so much to do and with no mistress to make decisions, the women began to loudly discuss who would do what. Finally, Sawney started up the hill to try to sort it all out.

Just then, Daniel whistled and pointed up the beach. The women quieted, the men ran up the hill to protect them, and the little ones scurried to hide behind an adult.

On a dapple-gray, a woman dressed in a blue plaid rode along the beach. As she drew closer, it was easy to see she had a pleasant face, light hair, which she wore in two braids and she was likely in her forties. When she spotted them, she waved and turned her horse up the hill.

"She rides alone," Blare muttered. MacGreagor women were not allowed to ride alone and he hoped it meant dangers were few in this part of Scotland.

Sawney was disappointed it was not the woman he met the day before. He'd been thinking about her all morning and often glanced at the woods where he last saw her just in case she was watching them. If she was, she was very good at hiding.

Keter scratched the side of his face, "Perhaps she can say where we might barter for a cow and some sheep."

Gavina giggled. "Aye, but we have no churn for butter or a curds and whey press for cheese."

"We have no kiln to bake bread, on which to put the butter either, but we will make them, my love...in time. For now, we will do it the way the ancients did; we will put the milk in flasks, put the flasks over the backs of horses, and let their constant movement churn the milk." He winked, left her side and offered to help the stranger down off her horse.

The woman was unaccustomed to such help and regarded Keter with suspicion. Then she shrugged, put her hands on his shoulders and let him lift her down. "I am Brin of Clan Campbell. My Amos told me about the fire," she said in a voice a little too high pitched and a smidgen too loud. Brin handed her reins to Keter and then went to the woman she assumed was his wife. "How dreadful for you all."

She gave Paisley a quick hug and then looked over the people. "My, but you are a small clan. Amos said as much and he is never wrong." She spotted their meager belongings in a pile and sadly shook her head. You need nearly everything, I see. Which of you is Laird Kerr?"

Sawney nodded. "I am."

Brin talked so fast, the MacGreagors just stood there staring at her in amazement. "I suspected as much, and are these not the biggest men I have ever seen?" She quickly looked Sawney and Hew up and down, and then spotted Jennet. "You are with child, I see." Joel did not say of that. I've a box just the right size for a wee babe. I am old and I hope not to need it again myself."

Jennet suspected, but she had not mentioned her pregnancy to Blare and when she looked up at her husband, he had the question in his eyes. Jennet smiled and nodded. Forgetting the stranger, he took her in his arms, kissed her, and excitedly swung her around. Their sons, Daw and Cormay, were in their teens and all their younger children were lost to the fever.

This was a new life, a new beginning and the MacGreagors were just as happy as Blare. Brin smiled. She was pleased to be the first to break the news and waited until they stopped celebrating.

Yet Paisley had her mind on other things. "May we barter for a cow?"

"We will ask Laird Campbell," said Brin.

"Will your laird object?" asked Daniel.

"Most likely not, if he does not abide too much strong drink, that is." She noticed the look of concern on Daniel's face and quickly added, "Oh, he is not vicious when he has had a chalice or two, but he sleeps so soundly we cannot wake him up."

At last, the MacGreagors relaxed and smiled. All at once, it seemed, they had a thousand questions about her clan, other clans, the ocean, where to find this or that, and where to barter for oats and barley. Most of all, was there a place to bathe nearby where there were far fewer fish?

Brin answered the first two questions, glanced out over the ocean, abruptly stopped in mid-sentence, and pointed at the dark clouds on the horizon. "Gather your things quickly now. Amos said to bring you inside. He vows 'twill be a bad storm and Amos is never wrong."

Sawney hesitated. "Your clan will kindly give us sanctuary?"

"Laird Kerr, we live in the middle of nowhere because the King of Scots wants his western coast protected. Few come to see us and never has our clan wanted news of the world more. Now gather your things, the harsh wind will begin soon and 'tis not easy to abide."

She was right. As soon as they loaded the horses, mounted and started down the hill toward the beach, the wind was already starting to blow sprinkles of rain hard against their faces.

JUST AS AMOS SAID, the village was not far away at all. The path turned inland just before they came to a very large courtyard surrounded by cottages. Despite the harsh wind and the increasing rain, It seemed most of the Campbells had come out to greet them, although they weren't exactly cheering their arrival. In fact, they were all very quiet. Several women stood near the large double doors of a castle that consisted of two very long floors facing full south. A round, three-story guard tower on the end nearest the ocean was attached to the main building and when they looked up, two men stood in the open-air window watching them.

Riding beside Keter in the front, Brin giggled and nodded toward the waiting women, "They waste no time, you see. They are unmarried hoping to find husbands among the Kerr." She looked up, spotted her husband in the guard tower window, and waved. "There, do you see them? Laird Campbell is awake and stands beside Amos." She halted her horse and started to get down, but before she could, Keter dismounted and held out his arms to her.

Brin looked behind her, noticed the MacGreagor men doing the same for the other women and frowned. "Why is this done? Do you capture lasses and keep them from running off once they have set foot on the ground?"

Keter first wrinkled his brow and then smiled, "Nay, we do it to keep them from being trampled. Our lasses are free to leave whenever they wish, though we prefer they do not go alone. 'Tis too dangerous."

She finally accepted his help. "Indeed it is, what with gray wolfs, wildcats and wild boars in the woods. Did you truly see a gray wolf with blue eyes?"

"Aye we..."

Brin did not allow him to finish. One more glance at the threatening dark clouds alarmed her. "Inside, all of you, and quickly." She led the women and children in, but when she turned around, the Campbell men were staring at the MacGreagors instead of helping. She stuck her head out one of the huge double doors and yelled at them. "Have you no care to help them?"

It was as though their daze was at last broken and soon the answer to their hesitance was clear. The tallest of them was still more than a foot shorter than the MacGreagors, and their muscles were not nearly as well developed. Timidly, they helped lead the horses into the overly large stable and began to unload them.

It was then Sawney spotted her. Mackinzie stood alone near the side of the castle with her arms folded watching him. He stared at her for far too long before he realized what he was doing, nodded slightly and looked away. He helped unload the last packhorse and when he looked again, she was gone.

Just before the rain turned to a squall, the MacGreagor men walked past the giggling Campbell women, entered the castle and stopped to stare. The great hall was grander than anything they had ever seen. It was decorated in red and gold with a solid oak table in the middle of the room. The high back chairs had red cushions and on the walls hung an array of weapons the likes of which the men had never seen. Candles in iron holders on the walls brightened the room and there was even a very large chair at the far end, situated on a wooden platform.

"'Tis the king's castle," muttered Daniel. He bent down, picked up little Flora and then went to stand beside the women.

Behind them, Laird Campbell descended the last of the stone staircase. "Aye, when he is here, which has only been once in all these years." He was a rotund man with blond hair graying at the temples. His face was pleasant enough, but his unusually long mustache, longer even than his beard, drew their attention away from his kind eyes.

Brin ran to him, kissed his cheek and then she hugged Amos. "There, you see, I convinced them. I said I would and I did."

"Right you are, wife, right you are." This day Amos wore the blue with thin green striped kilt of his clan. "You are most welcome, Kerr. This is Laird Campbell and Brin is his daughter. We are..." As if on cue, lightening and then thunder boomed across the sky forcing him to hold his words until it subsided.

Little Flora screeched and tightly hugged Daniel's neck, which made Daniel smile and whisper in her ear to comfort her.

"As I was saying," Amos continued, "we could not abide leaving you out in this weather. You must agree to stay the nights with us until you have built proper comforts. Agreed?"

Sawney caught the hopeful look on the faces of the women and at length, nodded. "We will not be a burden, I pledge it."

Laird Campbell walked past the MacGreagors, to a table near the throne, picked up a pitcher and poured the entire contents into a large chalice. "Daughter, do you intend to let our guests go without?"

Brin winked at Gavina. "We keep only enough for one and hide the rest until later so he will sleep through the night."

"I heard that," Laird Campbell loudly said, "and I am not fooled. 'Tis my keep, when the king is not here, and I'll search until I find you out."

Brin giggled. "He always says that, but once he has had his fill, he forgets to go look." A moment later, a door at the other end of the great hall opened and three serving women came in carrying more chalices, a large pitcher of ale, and a platter of small round breads.

Sawney looked for her, but the woman with the magnificent green eyes was not among them and when he glanced down, Dolina had her hands on her hips glaring up at him. "What?"

"I wish to bathe!"

Of all the children, even the ones left behind, Sawney had to admit Dolina was his favorite. What she loved most in the world was to get his attention. "Now? Shall I toss you in the ocean, the waterfall on our new land or would you prefer to stand outside in the rain?"

"First I should like to eat." She looked at him for permission and when he nodded, she hurried to the table and helped herself to the bread. "I am hungry enough to eat a goat."

Laird Campbell chuckled. "Remind me to hide our goat." He walked back to where his daughter stood and then turned around. "We have prepared a grand welcome feast and the many bedchambers in this useless castle are done up for your rest." He quickly put up his hand to stop Sawney's protest. "I'll not argue the matter, not now when the lot of you look tattered and torn. Sit, Kerr, sit and be fat like me!"

CHAPTER X

THEY FOUND THE ALE too sweet for their liking although spices had been added to bitter the taste. Nevertheless, it was the first real meal they'd had in days and each of the MacGreagors greatly enjoyed it. It was wonderful to be inside listening to the rain instead of having to shield themselves from it the best they could with their cloaks.

Joel came late and found a place to sit next to Senga, which pleased her but not her father. She was old enough to marry, but Daniel was not ready to let her go. Still, whom a daughter loves is not always up to her father.

The Campbells had many questions and if they noticed Sawney did all the answering, they did not let on. So also did the MacGreagors have questions which the Campbells were more than willing to answer. Once Amos began to describe the ships they might see on the ocean, the MacGreagors had enough questions about sailing to ask long into the night.

THE RAIN HAD STOPPED by the time Paisley finished eating and decided to go for a walk. She was grateful no one noticed except Lenox. He looked concerned when she opened the door, but she smiled to ease his worry.

It was still cloudy but getting lighter and it was much warmer with only a gentle breeze moving the air. Paisley watched for puddles of mud, rounded the corner of the castle, and found a path. Several of the Campbells watched her, but none tried to prevent her, so she continued on and was surprised when it led to a river.

This time of year the water gently flowed to the sea instead of rushing and she soon found a rock to sit on. The cut in Paisley's side hurt, she didn't feel all that well and knew she should be resting. Still, it was the first time in days she had a peaceful moment to herself and that was worth it.

What she thought about was Chisholm. In the beginning, she loved him with her whole heart, now her husband was dead and she should be mourning the loss of him. Yet somehow, she still couldn't bring herself to cry. Therefore, when she spotted a Campbell woman carrying a basket of clothing down the path toward her, she was happy for the diversion.

Mackinzie almost didn't see the woman sitting at the edge of the river. When she did, she abruptly stopped and started to turn back.

"Do not go. Come sit with me."

Shocked to have a woman speak to her in a friendly way, let alone wanting her company, Mackinzie shifted her eyes. This was wife to the man who rode the black horse, she realized. Still, she was curious about these people and doubted she would hear about them from the other Campbells. Perhaps if she did not call her a scunner right off, they might be friends...for a little while. "I am Mackinzie," she said finally.

"I am Paisley. Will you sit with me?"

"For a moment."

Paisley smiled, waited for Mackinzie to find a rock to sit on and set her basket down. "How many are the Campbells?"

"I do not know." She wanted to, but Mackinzie was afraid to ask any questions.

"Brin said the Campbells do not care if we build a village close by and we are most grateful. Our home burned."

"I see."

Paisley tried to get more comfortable and Mackinzie noticed her slight wince. "Where are you hurt?"

"'Tis nothing."

"Hurting is never nothing. Tell me." Mackinzie stood up and took a step closer.

"The strings of my sword cut my side on the journey."

"Does it hurt more today than yesterday?"

"A little."

Alarmed, Mackinzie lightly touched Paisley's forehead with the back of her hand. It was hot. "I shall get your husband."

Paisley smiled. "I do not have one of those and I am very glad of it."

The Kerr man was not married after all, at least not to this woman, and Mackinzie was glad. "Who then?"

"Please do not ask any of them to come. Two are my brothers. They are tired to the bone and especially tired of caring for me. I am well enough, truly I am."

"I will get Tavan."

She was gone before Paisley had a chance to stop her. Perhaps it was best to let someone help her. The skin around her cut was red and hot, and denying it was foolish now that they were someplace safe. She waited for someone named Tavan to come but instead, Lenox was practically running when he found her.

"The lass said you are feverish." Without another word, he swooped her up in his arms and headed back toward the castle. Before he even got to the door, he started shouting. In his arms, Paisley's whole body was hot and Lenox was terrified. As soon as Sawney opened the door, Lenox carried her inside.

Mackinzie stood not far away watching. She possibly had a friend finally and it would be so very unfair to lose Paisley now. Upset, she turned and went back to the river to tend her washing.

LONG INTO THE NIGHT, Mackinzie sat on a tree stump beside her cottage and watched the big double doors of the castle. People came and went, but none of them was Paisley. Even the man she favored came out. He walked with another, who looked a lot like him and Mackinzie guessed they were brothers. They seemed in a hurry to check on the horses and just as quickly went back inside.

It wasn't until Tavan finally came out that Mackinzie got up and went to ask how the woman was.

Tavan seemed surprised by the question. "She will do just fine, Mackinzie, just fine indeed." He wanted to ask how she knew the woman was ill, but as usual, Mackinzie walked away before he could.

SAWNEY WAS ALONE FOR the first time in days in an unfamiliar bedchamber decorated far more lavishly than any he had ever seen. Paisley was asleep, at last, in the bedchamber next to his and he could hear her if she called out. Laird Campbell's brother, Tavan, brought a potent salve to put on her cut and Sawney could hardly bear watching the amount of pain his sister was in. Yet she would die without it and it had to be done. Brin offered to stay the night with her, which he regarded as most kind since the women in his clan were exhausted.

So much had happened in a very short time. His father was dead, he was banished, his sister was sick, and the daunting task of building a village lay before them. They required so much and the list of needs overwhelmed him. At least he could look forward to seeing the woman again, whatever her name was.

Just as he started to unlace his shoes, someone knocked on his door. "Enter."

Keter nodded, closed the door behind him, found a chair at the table and sat down. "How is Paisley?"

"She sleeps finally."

"You look as tired as I feel."

"I do not deny it."

"Cousin, you have done well these past few days."

"As have you." Sawney finally got his shoes off and set them on the floor by the bed. Then he seated himself in a chair across the table from Keter. "I am glad you have come. I fret over all the lies we tell. They are too many for the clan to remember, especially the wee ones."

"I have thought that as well but what can we do?"

"We should say the truth before we are found out and ask the Campbells not to say where we are."

Keter lowered his eyes and considered it. "Every clan has its traitors and every lad his price."

"Do we have a traitor?"

"I do not think so, but a laird must understand and keep watch. If we say the truth, the Davidsons may learn where to find us and if we stay the nights here, we put the Campbells in danger."

"You are right."

"And you are right as well. 'Tis too hard for the children to remember. Even I am not certain which lie we tell currently."

Sawney moved the candle aside so he could see Keter better. "We must go back and fight soon."

"Must we? The others did not come with us of their own choosing. Why not stay here? I could be very happy in this place of peace and adventure by the sea."

"I am tempted to stay as well."

"Sawney, how are we to win a war with so few?"

Sawney rubbed his brow. "I have thought of that. We could offer the jewels to lairds who are willing to fight with us."

Keter's tired eyes brightened. "For jewels, perhaps both the Swintons and the Kennedys would fight with us."

"If they are not already captured and killed."

"There is that. Perhaps the Campbells will help us."

"Perhaps so, once we tell them the truth."

Keter stoked his straggly beard. "I greatly miss Justin. He would know what to do."

"I miss him too. How did he become so wise?" Sawney lightly bit his lower lip. "I have tried, but I do not recall everything Father told me the night before he passed. I remember only two things but I know he said more. He said not to marry until I was certain, and then he said, to first keep myself alive."

"He said that?"

Sawney took a deep breath and let it out. "Aye, he must have guessed what was coming and wanted the clan to live on. Now we choose between keeping ourselves alive and going back to fight."

"We are Justin's clan now. We are all together and we are safe. Perhaps he would not want us to go back."

"Aye, but we are smaller now than the Haldane and certain to be set upon by stronger clans. Besides, we left your Mother behind."

"I will go get her as soon as we have a home to bring her to. I had planned to do that even before we left." Keter smiled, reached over, and playfully socked Sawney in the arm. "Your father is right about one thing. A wife may warm your bed at night, but she can make you regret it in the morning."

Sawney lowered his voice to make sure no one could hear. "More than I regret Campbell's barley Ale?"

"Perhaps we will learn to love it. Good night to you, cousin, tomorrow we begin our new home." Keter stood up and was about to leave when Sawney stopped him.

"Then we agree we should tell Laird Campbell the truth?"

"Aye, he might take back his offer to let us stay, but so be it. Ask to speak to him after the morning meal."

AT SUNRISE, MACKINZIE grabbed an apple to nibble on and went outside to sit on the tree stump and watch the castle doors. An hour later, she was still there and as usual, the serving people carried food in and the strangers came and went without noticing her. None of them was Paisley and she was becoming increasingly worried.

The next to come out of the huge double doors was Brin and when Laird Campbell's daughter walked straight for her, Mackinzie wondered if she'd best run and hide. Instead, she stood up, tossed her apple core in the bushes, and wiped her mouth.

"Paisley wishes to see you, although I cannot guess why," said Brin.

Mackinzie almost called Brin a scunner, but just yesterday, she vowed not to do that anymore. She nodded and ran to the castle, burst through the door and started up the stairs. That's when she heard Laird Campbell call her name.

"Mackinzie, what are you up to this time?"

She slowly turned, walked back down the stairs and curtsied to her laird. "Paisley has asked for me."

"Oh, I see, although I cannot guess why she would."

Mackinzie puffed her cheeks, ignored his comment and hurried on up the stairs. Seated at the table, Sawney set his bowl aside and smiled. Now he knew her name and it was a very fitting name for one so enchanting. He liked her, he liked her a lot.

She opened the door to three bedchambers before Mackinzie found the right one. Paisley was wide awake and half sitting up with pillows supporting her head and back. "Are you very ill?" she asked, walking to the side of the bed.

"Nay, not very. I wanted to thank you. You were right, I did need help." Paisley returned Mackinzie's beautiful smile without guessing how privileged she was to receive it. "We did not finish and I have many questions still. Do sit and tell me all about..." A light knock on the door interrupted her. "Come."

Sawney didn't hesitate to walk to the other side of the bed, bend down, and kiss his sister on the forehead. Then he put the back of his hand on her cheek. "No fever this day, I am relieved." Trying not to be obvious, he only glanced at Mackinzie who looked shocked to see him. "I am her brother," he managed to say.

"It was Mackinzie who sent Lenox to get me," said Paisley.

This time he did look at her. "I am very grateful."

She couldn't think of a thing to say so Mackinzie simply nodded.

"Tell me, why did you wish me not to tell Amos and Joel you were..." He could see he had raised her ire and tried to quickly relieve her distress. "Tis only my sister, I'll not tell the Campbells." Again, she did not speak and it was clear he had upset her.

"Mackinzie," Paisley started, "my brother is a good lad. He means no harm to anyone."

"A good lad honors his word."

Sawney narrowed his eyes, "I gave my word not to tell Amos and Joel, nothing more."

He was right, as much as Mackinzie hated to admit it. At length she cast her eyes downward. "I will go now."

"Please stay," Paisley begged. "I have few friends left and I was hoping..."

"Allow me to go instead." Sawney acted annoyed, mockingly bowed to Mackinzie and left the room.

Mackinzie could not help herself and breathed that awful word, "Scunner." Then she caught her breath, realized she had just insulted Paisley's brother and looked to see her reaction.

Paisley giggled, "There are days when I agree with you. Come, sit by me and..."

The door suddenly opened again and Sawney poked his head back in. "Sister, I have decided to tell the Campbells the truth, but please allow me time to do so before you tell Mackinzie. I'd not like all the Campbells to hear it before I've a chance to explain."

No sooner had he closed the door than he opened it again. "And do not say we've had her horse all this time. I see now it was not leading us, it was merely going home and we followed." Again, he closed the door and again opened it. "And..."

"Sawney!" Paisley chastised.

"Very well." This time he closed to door for good.

"'Tis your horse?" Paisley asked.

The last thing Mackinzie wanted to do was lie to her only friend so she changed the subject. "Is he always bothersome?"

"Aye, he has been doing that since he was tall enough to reach the handle. I am older, you see." Paisley expected her to say something and when she didn't, she swore Mackinzie to secrecy and began to tell her what happened.

Sometimes Mackinzie's eyes widened. She nodded occasionally, took on an expression of sympathy at the unbelievably bad things, and smiled at the things Paisley thought were funny. All the while, she marveled at the joy she felt over having a friend. More than that, she could not believe she had a friend who trusted her enough to confide in her.

ONCE HE HEARD THE TRUTH, it was a full three minutes before Laird Campbell spoke. Seated at the long table in the castle's great hall with Sawney, Keter, and Hew across from him, he carefully considered the problem.

First, he wrinkled his brow, brightened his eyes, and then wrinkled his brow again. "I say, 'tis quite a quandary to be sure. 'Twould not be the first time one clan overwhelmed another and threw them out. Most kill all the lads and keep the women and children. There once was a clan by the name of Cammaray, ever heard of them?"

"Nay," said Keter.

"Few have, but they lived on these shores. 'Twas the very same that happened to them. Now they are no more. The Celts sailed these waters years hence and I hear they too have clans. Could be they began ours, but before the Celts, came the Vikings..." Laird Campbell paused in mid-sentence to look at Sawney's large size, then Keter's and Hew's. He scratched the back of his head and changed the subject. "That settles it then."

"Settles what?" asked Sawney.

"You shall live among us and you shall call yourselves Campbells until you return to fight for your land."

Sawney couldn't hide his relief. "We are grateful beyond measure."

"Lads, with little protection for your bonnie lasses and fine children, I'd not sleep nights even after three chalices of ale."

Keter was pleased, but still a little troubled. "Yet we worry we put your people in danger."

"Some of our lads will like a good fight and if they come here, we've the advantage. We will send flocks of sheep against them, force the Davidsons into the ocean and see they all drown.

The mental image made Keter chuckle. "Yet..."

Laird Campbell raised his hand to silence Keter. "My consent is far from unselfish. 'Tis shearing time, we've more sheep than we know what to do with and we could use the help. We take the wool to market, you see, and fill our...the king's coffers with the barter. This year we will hold back more than usual. You will need Campbell kilts for your war and when the sheering is done, you will make more weapons."

It was a good plan and Sawney was pleased. "I have never sheered."

Laid Campbell smiled, "You'll take to it soon enough. First you catch the sheep. The dogs help with that, but 'tis the hardest part. Sharpen your dagger and try to cut the wool and not the sheep."

"Now," he continued, "we've a few empty cottages and the rest of you will stay in the castle with me. I'll be glad of the company. I loathe this place when it is empty and children will rightly liven it up." He paused and directed his next remark to Hew. "You'll be needing protection from our unmarried lasses. Once they've set their minds, I've a devil's time getting them to relent."

Hew was flattered that Laird Campbell thought he would be more sought after than his brother. "How many Campbells are there?"

"Not enough to sheer the sheep. Now, what say you, will you stay?"

Sawney still had a question. "What of your people? Will they tell where we are?"

"To the north, the cliffs cut us off from the next clan. There is a clan on the island to the east of us, but when they sail, they sail south to take their goods to market. England has a great thirst for our wool and fish."

Laird Campbell took a moment to sip water from a goblet. "Were it not for Amos and Joel riding guard over the shores of His Majesty's kingdom, we would hear nothing at all. We have seen few come through the forest as you just did. How you managed it, I do not know. The forest is fraught with any manner of danger such as sudden cliffs and lochs that take days to go around. So you see, the Campbells have few to tell. Nevertheless, I will say the king orders their silence. That should do it." Suddenly, Laird Campbell's eyes widened. "Has the fever passed your way?"

"Aye," Keter answered. "These four months."

"Good, it came to us some time ago and I feared we might pass it to you. We've a laddie not yet recovered."

"Some of our people think Thyme helps," said Hew.

Without another word, Laird Campbell got up, walked to the large wooden doors, opened one, filled his lungs and shouted, "Thyme! Let us all eat our fill of Thyme." Then he walked out the door and let it close behind him.

Alone finally, Keter, Hew and Sawney exchanged worried looks. "'Tis simple, according to him," said Keter.

"If we go to fight first and not let them come here, we are assured the lasses and children are safe," said Hew.

Sawney nodded. "Agreed, but first we sheer the sheep."

"How long do you think that will take?" asked Keter.

Hew slapped his cousin on the back. "I believe we are about to find out."

BRIN CAME IN TO SEE to Paisley's comfort and when it was time for the noon meal, she brought bowls of food for both of the young women. It was such a foreign, thoughtful thing for Brin to do, Mackinzie actually smiled, which took Laird Campbell's daughter completely aback.

As soon as Brin was gone, Paisley continued her story until all was said and she was exhausted. Mackinzie stayed long enough for Paisley to fall asleep and then quietly left the bedchamber.

Sawney was not in the great hall when she went downstairs, but his brother and two other MacGreagor men were still there. After hearing their story, Mackinzie thought enough of the MacGreagors to nod. Then she noticed laird Campbell watching her and quickly went out the door, lest he remembered he was supposed to punish her for tearing a plaid and calling that dreadful woman a scunner.

All that was forgotten as soon as she reached her cottage and went inside. She considered first the way Paisley's brother liked to plague his sister and how Paisley enjoyed it. He did not seem like a laird and indeed did not act like the only one she knew. But then, the only time she talked to Laird Campbell was when she was in trouble.

Next, she thought about Paisley's abduction. Not once had Mackinzie feared such a thing and wondered if it happened often in faraway lands. Perhaps there was more to fear in the world than she knew. She always thought Laird Campbell's warnings were simply to keep her in the village where he could watch her. He often said he cared about her, but how was she to know he truly meant it?

Moreover, she liked Sawney more today than the day before. His open affection for his sister touched Mackinzie's heart. Because she liked Paisley, perhaps it was easier to admire the goodness in her brother. Whatever the reason, she did fancy him.

Mackinzie found her goblet, filled it with water, and went to sit on her tree stump again. She had ample food, which meant she did not need to do any washing this day and perhaps she could see Paisley again.

Joel and Amos came out of the castle dressed in the King's colors, mounted their horses and set out to make their daily ride along the beach. Before the day was finished, Amos and Joel would encounter men from three different clans and make mention of a gray wolf with blue eyes.

However, when Laird Campbell came out and shouted for all the Campbells to gather in the courtyard, Mackinzie decided it was time to go for a walk.

DENA WAS ON HER BEST behavior, catering to her husband's every whim, even though he paid little attention to her except when others were around. She found his actions offensive most of the time, but at least she was now mistress of his clan. She gave instructions to the other women who cleaned and cooked.

Still certain the wealth was in the Keep somewhere, Neasan allowed no one except Dena to enter the top two floors and even she was denied entry to any but her own bedchamber. At times, she gave the reasons for his odd behavior considerable thought. Since he did not say, she was left to suspect it had something to do with Paisley.

William had not yet returned and according to Neasan's less than loyal men, there was no mention of him or the five with him in any of the gossip. Upon that subject, he ranted and raved for at least an hour until a woman came to report her missing chair and table.

The night before, she took them outside, gave them a good scrubbing and left them to dry. That morning, both were simply gone and no one saw a thing.

Neasan's men still had not gotten control of their wives, who began to stick their tongues out at his keep when they walked past. However, his perch in the third-floor windows afforded him a view of nearly everything and he was beginning to spend more and more time there. How else was he to know what was going on?

He had yet to find out who warned the Haldane, who told Carley of his plot to do away with the elders, if indeed he actually said that, and his whalebone had not been put back in the glen where it belonged. Even so, he had a wife now who would behave should any other lairds come to admire him.

On that note, he went back down stairs and turned his attention to his next attack. Which would it be, the Kennedy, the Graham, or the Swintons? Just as he sat down at the head of the table in the great hall, he heard a shout outside.

"Sawney has come back!"

"Neasan raced to the door and yanked it open. "What? Where?"

"A Kennedy saw him," Grant said from across the courtyard. Although none were brave enough to cheer, he noticed several were smiling just before Neasan came out.

"Where was he seen?" Neasan demanded as he walked to Grant.

"In the MacDuff woods."

"Alone or has he raised a full force?"

"The rumors do not say," Grant answered.

Neasan paused to think about that. If Sawney had warriors with him, the rumors surely would say so. If alone, it made perfect sense for Sawney to hide among the MacDuff. They were cowards who would never say no to a man the size of Sawney. "Was he in the MacDuff village?"

Grant cleared his throat. "I do not know, but it is doubtful. The MacDuff would be too frightened to protect him."

"True." Neasan started to pace to the end of the courtyard, stopped and turned. Just as he expected, Bearcha stood with his back against the wall of keep with his arms crossed. "What say you, Bearcha, would the MacDuff willingly hide Sawney?"

Bearcha could not help but smile. "Perhaps. Send word you mean to attack and if they have him they will gladly give him over."

"Indeed they will. Whom should I send to tell them?"

"I will go," said Bearcha, as he stood up straight. He could use the diversion and hoped Neasan would send him.

Neasan rolled his eyes. "You are needed here. Send whomever you will and do it quickly." Satisfied, Neasan went back inside his keep. Sawney was close and he had a lot to consider. As an afterthought, he yelled, "And where is my bone?"

CHAPTER XI

AS SOON AS THE PEOPLE gathered, Laird Campbell introduced the MacGreagors. It did not take long for the unmarried women to figure out only two of the men were married and shrieked their delight, which made Laird Campbell roll his eyes.

He explained the MacGreagor's quandary and made his followers swear not to give their location away...by order of the King. Then he took Keter, Blare and their families to two of the empty cottages so they could settle in. He gave a third, two-room cottage to the three cousins, Lenox, Diocail and Moffet, and left them there, but not until he told them not to bother finding food. He had no doubt the unmarried women would keep them well fed. Again, he rolled his eyes.

That left Paisley, Sawney, Hew, Daniel, and Daniel's three children to live with him in the castle, which suited Laird Campbell just fine. His grandchildren were too old to cuddle, had not yet produced a great-grandchild and he'd taken a shine to little Flora.

NOW THAT PAISLEY WAS out of danger, Sawney and Hew took a walk down several paths to familiarize themselves with their temporary home. Sawney really wanted to see where Mackinzie lived, but she was nowhere in sight and he was disappointed. Then he had a thought. "We left in such a hurry, we should go back to the hill and make certain we did not leave any hint of us behind."

"I agree," said Hew.

Together, they went to the king's massive stable, found their horses, rode out of the village and then along the shore at the edge of the water toward the hill. Just as they were about to round the bend, Sawney spotted her and made his brother stop.

Mackinzie stood on the top of the hill next to the black stallion and never had he seen a more pleasing sight. Though he could not hear what she said, it was plain she talked to the horse and the horse seemed to be listening. Twice, Mackinzie wrapped her arms around the stallion's neck and hugged him. Then she moved away and as she did, the horse came down the hill and began to run along the shore, splashing in the seawater as he went. Too soon, the horse disappeared around the end of the cliffs.

"I thought we came to see if we left something behind," said Hew.

"That we have."

As soon as Mackinzie spotted the brothers, she ran down the other side of the hill and went into the forest. It was perhaps bad manners to run away, but when did she ever care about such things? She did not fear them and was well armed. It was just that she was not in the mood to talk just now, and especially not to two unfamiliar men at the same time.

Mackinzie carefully navigated the rocks over the creek and then hurried back to the castle. If Sawney was on the hill, she could go up to see Paisley without him bothering. She scurried through the castle door, ignored Laird Campbell, and quickly climbed the stairs. When she reached Paisley's door, she softly knocked and waited. A second later, she was invited in and sat in a chair beside her friend's bed.

Paisley smiled and patted Mackinzie's hand. "I told you all about us, now it is your turn and leave nothing out."

Mackinzie hardly knew what to say. It would not do to tell about being orphaned. The last thing she wanted was to be pitied the way she had been each time she was given to a new family. "I saw a wildcat last week."

"Did you? Where?"

"Not far from the hill. It frightened me and I ran home. The lads killed it."

"I have yet to see one and I pray I never do. Tell me, were you born here?"

Mackinzie wrinkled her brow. "I do not think so."

Bewildered, Paisley waited for her to explain, but she didn't. "Have you brothers and sisters?"

"Nay."

It was all Mackinzie was willing to say and Paisley feared it was becoming a one-sided conversation fast. "Dear one, if we are to be good friends, which I hope, you must talk to me."

"It is just that...I do not speak often. I am unaccustomed to it."

"You do not speak to anyone at all?"

"When I must. I wash clothing. That is what I do."

"But they do not speak to you?"

Mackinzie hung her head. "'Tis because I call them a scunner."

Paisley started to laugh and had to hold of her injured side. Sawney abruptly opened the door. He suspected he would find Mackinzie there, so he left Hew to scour the hill and raced back.

"Now that is what I like to hear—laughter." He completely ignored Mackinzie, who looked like she was ready to bolt out the door. "I am back if you need me." He quietly closed the door and went to his bedchamber next door.

"You must rest," Mackinzie said as she stood up.

"Will you come back?"

"I will try."

In his bedchamber, Sawney listened for Mackinzie to leave and then went back to his sister's room.

"You fancy her, do you not?" Paisley asked.

"Sister, she ran from us." He took a seat in the same chair Mackinzie sat in by the bed.

"Why?"

"I do not know. We went to the top of the hill where we first saw the ocean. She was there with her horse, but when she saw us she ran away. Does she fear me?"

"She did not say. Mackinzie is a bit strange, but I like her. Do you know what she said? She said she is unaccustomed to speaking."

Sawney was just as confused as his sister, and then he grinned. "In that case, I shall marry her. I find a wife unaccustomed to speaking delightful, compared to a sister who talks too much."

Paisley glared.

NEASAN IGNORED THE women sticking their tongues out at his keep. He had better things to do and standing just out of sight at the third-floor window, he looked instead toward the trees. Gone were his plans for attacking another clan, gone also was his desire to see the whale bone back in the glen.

Quite possibly Sawney was out there somewhere lurking. It suddenly occurred to him Justin's father might have built a secret passageway into the Keep. The possibility almost caused Neasan to tremble. He could easily be murdered in his bed if it was so.

Who would know if there was a tunnel or where it might be, he wondered. Carley would know, but she was a MacGreagor, and would not likely tell him even under the threat of death. No, there was no one left, no one at all.

He recalled a story about the MacGreagors digging a tunnel, which they used to escape a warring clan. That was long ago and before they came to the glen, but why not dig a tunnel here too, just in case? And why not hide all that wealth in the tunnel? That was it. It had to be. He quickly descended the two flights of stairs and began to look around his great hall for a hidden door.

STILL KEEPING TO HER bed the next day, Paisley was restless when Sawney came in to see how she was. Mackinzie had not come back and Paisley was worried something had happened to her.

Sawney rolled his eyes. "Must I go see about her?"

Paisley pretended to pout. "Must I do everything myself?"

"Oh, if you insist, but you will be forever in my debt."

"As if I am not already." She giggled when he winked before he closed the door. Paisley decided a little more rest would do no harm, yet sleep was not easy to come by. It was hard to admit it, but she missed being in love the way her brother was. She missed it very much. What was life all about without a husband and children?

IF PAISLEY WAS WORRIED, then so was Sawney. He had not seen Mackinzie all day either, and if she were around he would have seen her. He looked for her on the hill and by the waterfall, but she was not there. He looked for her on the shore on the way back to the courtyard, walked the paths between the cottages, and then took the one behind the castle to the river. Still he could not find her. Frustrated, he picked up a stone and tried to skip it across the river.

"I am Tavan," said the man sitting on a rock just a few feet away.

Sawney immediately recognized him. "You are the lad who helped my sister."

"Aye, how does she do?"

"Much better. Of course, you know that or we would have sent for you again."

Tavan smiled. "True. My brother tells me your sister and Mackinzie have become friends. I am pleased to see it, very pleased indeed."

Sawney found a rock to sit on not far away, made himself comfortable and got a good look at the old man's elaborately carved cane. "'Tis true, although she has not come to see Paisley this day. Is she unwell?"

Tavan shook his head, noticed him looking at the cane and handed it to him. "I was once a carver and sold my goods at market. Now I am too old."

He handed the cane back and watched the old man's face. "I fear I have frightened Mackinzie."

"I doubt that. Mackinzie does not frighten easily. It is perhaps you who should fear her."

Sawney chuckled. "I have heard the same is true of many a lass. Do you know where I might find her?"

"Rarely does anyone know where she is."

Surprised to hear that, Sawney wrinkled his brow. "Does no one care for her?"

"Aye, many of us care, but she does not let us."

"Why?"

Tavan had said too much already and decided not to say more. If Mackinzie wanted this MacGreagor to know, she would tell him herself. "She will come back when she is ready."

Sawney didn't find that answer very satisfying, but he did not question Tavan further. "If you see her, say my sister wishes her to come." He stood up, nodded and took the path beside the riverbank.

When he still did not find her, Sawney decided to go to the hill one more time. Finally, there she was, looking just as striking, if not more so. The only thing missing was the horse. This time he walked boldly up the side of the hill and when she saw him and turned to run, he yelled, "Paisley sent me to find you."

That made her stop and turn back. "Is she worse?"

He completed the distance between them before he answered, "Nay."

"Oh."

"May I sit?" It took her a moment, but she finally nodded. Careful not to sit to close to her, he crossed his feet at the ankles and sat down in the tall grass. Sawney took in the sight of the ocean for a moment and then sighed. "I can see why you come here, 'Tis the most peaceful place I have ever seen." He could feel her looking at him, but she did not respond so he had to think of something more to say. "My sister told you of our troubles, but I wonder..." he took a chance and looked up at her."

"What?"

"I thought you might like to hear the rest of it."

She looked perplexed. "There is more?"

"We have many stories to tell. My Father's grandfather was married to a lass who loved an English king." As he hoped, her eyes grew wide with disbelief. She did not say a word but she listened and at least she was not running from him. At length, he finished the story and began another. That one held Mackinzie's complete attention too. It was not until he began the story of his grandfather's wager, that she crossed her feet at the ankles, just as he had, and sat down.

Sawney was surprised she sat as close as she did, although she stayed far enough away so he could not grab her. She seemed completely absorbed in the stories and it was fun to glance at the constantly changing expressions on her face.

Suddenly, she interrupted him, "I am a good hunter."

Her comment had nothing to do with the story, but he ignored that in favor of having a real conversation with her. "I like to think I am a good hunter too."

"You are not a hunter, you are a laird."

"True, but it was not always so. First I was a laddie who learned to hunt." He wasn't certain he should ask any questions, but perhaps if he did not ask anything personal. "Do you fish as well?" He waited for a reply, but she only nodded. "We do not have such large fish as yours. Ours are small and very hard to catch."

"How small?"

He held his hands apart and smiled at her disbelief. "It takes many fish to feed a family in the MacGreagor glen." Sawney waited for a response and decided he might be pushing his luck. "We should go back. Paisley will think we are both lost." He got up and held out his hand to her, but Mackinzie only stared at it.

"I will not harm you. Paisley would have my head if I did." At last, Mackinzie smiled. It took her a moment more, but she finally put her hand in his and let him pull her up. She let go quickly, but it was a start and more than he hoped for.

"Come."

"Come where?" he asked.

Mackinzie did not answer. She wasn't certain why, but she decided to show him the shortcut from the hill to the village. She was pleased he followed without asking more questions and showed him how to find the rocks so he could cross the creek without getting wet.

Just before they reached the village, Sawney asked her to stop. "Mackinzie, if we are attacked will you bring our women and children this way? I will be comforted if I know you are caring for them."

She nodded. "I am a good fighter." With that, she hurried away leaving him standing at the edge of the village.

TRUE TO HIS WORD, LAIRD Campbell furnished new clothing for the MacGreagors. Wearing all new things, the women asked for chores, which pleased him very much and Brin was happy to supply them with plenty of mending, a task she sorely hated.

He kept Logan and Flora with them in the great hall. Laird Campbell had a very fine Slype-Groat board complete with smooth coins and at five, Logan was eager to learn how to play. Flora was more than content to play with balls of spun wool, and feeling better, Paisley came down to join them.

As usual, Amos and Joel went off to take their daily ride, but not before Joel specifically nodded to Senga, the meaning of which did not go unnoticed by anyone in the room. Soon the women began to talk about men and Laird Campbell got an ear full, which he enjoyed immensely.

BEHIND THE KING'S CASTLE, shepherds and their collies began to herd sheep down out of the hills to be sheered. The MacGreagors, together with several Campbells, stood in a row near the back of the castle to try to catch them. It looked so simple Sawney was certain the process wouldn't take long at all.

Nevertheless, try as he might, Sawney could not get the hang of catching the sheep, and the sight of his failure was something the Campbell men found thoroughly amusing. He lay flat on his belly in the mud and watched the third ewe sprint out of his grasp.

All the other MacGreagors were catching them, even Hew and Sawney could not have been more chagrinned. "'Tis hopeless," he muttered. He sat up, tried to brush the mud off his kilt, and only succeeded in smearing it. Just then, a border collie barked and forced the ewe to run back toward Sawney. He quickly hopped to his feet, crouched down and got ready to catch it. First, the ewe veered left and as soon as Sawney lunged that direction, it veered right causing him to slip and fall in the same puddle of mud. As if that were not enough, a woman behind him started laughing.

Frustrated beyond words, Sawney turned over, sat up and glared at Mackinzie. "Have you a better way?"

She held a large basket in her arms and her green eyes sparkled when she spoke. "The lasses wash; the lads sheer."

"Are you always so helpful?"

Mackinzie grinned and nodded.

He started to remove the mud from his arms and sling it away. When he looked, her grin seemed even wider and more mocking. "Have you nothing to do?"

She quickly curtsied, walked to the river and set her basket down.

One of the Campbells shouted. "Take better aim, Sawney. 'Tis a hoof the lads try to grab. Take care it does not kick you."

"A hoof?" he whispered still watching her. "I had forgotten that."

Again the dog chased the ewe his direction, he lunged and at last, managed to grab hold of a hind hoof. Just as he was warned, the ewe tried to kick him but he was able to avoid it. Now what should he do?

"Put your hand under the chin," another Campbell yelled.

Sawney did as he was told and soon had control of the sheep. Two men quickly came, set their large baskets down and helped lay the ewe on its side. With two holding the animal still, the third pulled his dagger, began to shear the wool and put globs of it in the basket.

"The wool is dirty," said Sawney.

"Not as dirty as you." The Campbell smiled and then continued shearing. "We can finish this, best try to catch another."

Mackinzie could not help but watch Sawney's next attempt, which put him right back in the same mud hole. She had not laughed so hard in all her life.

Sawney got up, but instead of getting ready to take another try, he ran to her, grabbed her around the waist, pulled her body against his and smeared mud on the side of her face.

Startled, Mackinzie caught her breath. He did not look angry. In fact, he was smiling and she had no idea how to react. He was, after all, Paisley's brother. She was about to decide on a course of action when the expression on his face changed and he kissed her full on the mouth.

Just as quickly, his smile was back. He picked her up, waded into the shallow river and abruptly dropped her. "You need a bath!"

She landed on her bottom, watched him turn his back and walk away. "I hope you can swim," she heard him say. "Better than you," she muttered.

Sitting on his usual rock, Tavan saw the whole thing and grinned. "Are you hurt, lass?"

"Nay." She touched the side of her hair, discovered mud was in it too, and puffed her cheeks. As long as she was all wet, she might as well wash. Mackinzie began to unbraid her hair, stopped and looked at Tavan. "Why did he do that?"

"'Tis only play, child." He was not surprised she had nothing more to say. Tavan watched her unbraid her hair, wash the mud off her clothes and face, and then lean forward to wash her hair. What he would give to know what was going on in that head of hers.

MACKINZIE DID NOT GO to see Paisley that evening, she was too confused. She ate a good meal and after, set up her weaving loom and tried to concentrate on the soft blanket she was making for the baby she hoped to have one day.

Nevertheless, she could not get Sawney's kiss out of her mind. She realized she messed up the last row of yarn, pulled it back out, started again and it wasn't long before her mind wandered back to his kiss. "Tis my own fault," she muttered. She put her weaving away and sat down on the bed to consider what she must have done wrong.

He was a laird and perhaps she should not have laughed at him. Yet even now, the sight of him sitting in the mud made her smile. How could she not laugh? Her thoughts shifted from why he kissed her to the sound of her own laughter and she tried to remember the last time that happened.

Just as quickly, her attention turned to the way Sawney held her against his body. The truth be told, she had not let anyone touch her since she was nine. Everyone knew if they touched Mackinzie, she would scream until her throat was raw. Nevertheless, when Sawney held her she did not scream; she did not think to and she found that perplexing. She let Paisley touch her too and did not protest.

Mackinzie Campbell's world was changing far too quickly and she was not quite certain if that was a good or a bad thing.

IN HIS BED, SAWNEY thought about it too. Paisley would have giggled and tried to smack him if he rubbed mud on her face, but Mackinzie looked disturbed and even a little frightened. The last thing he wanted to do was make her fear him. He should apologize and resolved to do so the next time he saw her. Tired after chasing sheep all day, he turned on his side and went right to sleep.

The next evening, neither Sawney nor Paisley had seen Mackinzie and he wanted to apologize. He looked for her, again without results and finally decided to ask Tavan. A man on the path pointed the way to Tavan's cottage and when Sawney knocked on the door, he was glad to find Tavan at home. He was so tall, he had to duck down once he was invited in. "I came to see if..."

Tavan grinned. "I am guessing you cannot find Mackinzie again."

"You guess well."

"It was you who kissed her, was it not?"

Sawney slowly nodded. For a moment he feared he stood before MacKinzie's father who might not be pleased. Have I frightened her this time?"

"I assure you she fears nothing but a wildcat. Do you fancy her or do you kiss many a lass?"

"I *do* fancy her."

Tavan smiled and offered Sawney a chair. "Sit, there is much you should know about that one before you have your heart set on her."

Sawney listened intently and the more he heard, the more he understood the reactions of the woman he now greatly admired.

Tavan finished by saying, "She may not let you near her again. She will likely run and hide just as she has since she was a wee one."

"I will find her."

"Perhaps, but for her sake see that you feel more than fancy. See that you truly love her first. Her feelings are tender and I do not wish to see her hurt."

Sawney stood up, walked to the door and turned back. "I give you my pledge, I will not hurt her. I intend to marry her instead."

Tavan was thrilled, "If you can find her. I assure you, we have spent years looking for all her hiding places. On the other hand, she will come to do my wash soon. Perhaps you might wait for her to come to us."

THE NEWS CAME SO SLOWLY; Carley began to fear the MacGreagors were indeed dead. Nearly two weeks had gone by since her sons were banished with no new reports of them. Then rumors came so quickly and so varied it confounded even her. A large clan was seen moving north in numbers of nearly a thousand, maybe more. However, they were not MacGreagors; they were Ferguson, or Forbes or maybe Kerr. Another sighting was near the border with England, but that was rebuffed by rumors they moved east or west.

This day they heard a rumor that the MacGreagors boarded a ship bound for the Norse coast.

At last, Grant brought her the news she longed for—men on the paths heard of a gray wolf with blue eyes. Carley's sons were alive and most likely so were the rest of them.

CHAPTER XII

WITH A LOT TO THINK about, Sawney slowly walked back to the castle. He was not certain what to do next and needed advice. Who better to ask now that Paisley was feeling so much better. He softly knocked on her bedchamber door and waited.

With a wide smile on her face, she let him in and then pointed to her soft cloth belt. "Mackinzie brought it while you were gone. It is very soft and does not hurt at all. Is it not very handsome?"

Sawney studied the design and agreed. "Aye, but will it hold the folds of your plaid in place."

"I do not feel them slipping and I had not noticed before, but she wears one also. If it is good enough for Mackinzie, it is good enough for me. Now, would my brother care to take me for a walk or must you wallow in the mud still more this day."

Sawney smiled. "She told you what I did?"

"Indeed. She is convinced she insulted you by laughing. Mackinzie has an odd way of thinking and I did not know what to say."

He took Paisley's arm and opened the door. "'Tis not odd at all, leastwise not for her. I've a story to tell and 'tis not a pleasant one."

They left the castle, crossed the courtyard, and headed down the beach where no one could hear before Sawney began, "Mackinzie was a wee babe when she was found washed up on shore in a bucket.

No others were found and sometime later they heard a ship had sunk."

"Her parents died at sea?" she asked.

"That is what Tavan thinks. She was but two or three weeks old."

"No wonder she does not know where she was born."

"Laird Campbell named her after his mother's clan. Tavan said Mackinzie did not ask about her parents until she was nearly twelve, and she surely knew all the other children had parents. He thinks it was because she trusted no one else to tell her the truth."

"She does not trust any of the Campbells? These must be dreadful people. I had not guessed that."

Sawney took his sister's hand and wrapped it around his arm. "Do not judge them too harshly, there is more. It was the children who taunted her. First they called her bucket and then claimed she was a sea monster."

Paisley closed her eyes and bowed her head. "Did no one try to stop the children?"

"Tavan said she never once told on them. He only knows because he caught them once, but he fears it was much worse. He fears they were hurting her as well."

The look in Paisley's eyes turned to fury. "Children can be so vicious."

"Aye, but suppose it was not just the children who were hurting her? Tavan could never find out, and Mackinzie would speak to no one."

"Someone threatened her."

"A threat she never forgot."

"Is there more?"

Sawney nodded. "The people who cared for her could find no way to give her comfort—she would not let them so much as touch her. Therefore, she was given to other parents and then others until no family was willing to take her."

"She had no home? No brothers to protect her, no sisters to talk to *and* no home? I can think of nothing worse for a child."

"Nor can I," said Sawney. "When she was old enough, she began to hide and the clan spent long hours trying to find her. Be it rain or cold with wild beasts in the woods, Mackinzie cared not and would not answer when they called. She only came around when she was hungry.

Each evening, Tavan left a bowl of food just inside his window where she could reach it. Sometimes she did not come, but when she did, she always put the empty bowl and spoon back where she got it. Beside himself with worry, Laird Campbell finally gave her a cottage of her own."

Paisley laid her head against her brother's arm. "It makes me want to hold her tight and never let go."

"Me too."

"Aye, but brother pity is not a good reason to marry."

"Too late, I loved her before I knew her troubles. Now I long to give her all the love she can endure and protect her. I will not have her hurt again, not by anyone."

"Do you understand what you are asking? She trusts no one and she runs from even you."

"I know, that is why I need your help."

Paisley giggled, "Nay, Mackinzie needs my help. You must manage on your own."

In silence, they walked back and were almost to the castle when he put his arms around Paisley and hugged her. "Do you want to go back inside or..."

"I believe I feel her watching us."

"So do I."

"Perhaps if you leave, she will come."

"Perhaps she will." He kissed her forehead and walked toward the meadow behind the village. Just before he turned the corner, he glanced back and saw Mackinzie standing next to his sister. Sawney smiled.

WITH AN IRON CROWBAR, Neasan pulled up the last board under the stairs, grabbed a candle, and looked, but he found only hard dirt underneath. Even so, he was not willing to give up just yet. He set the candle aside, stood up and began to eye the nearest wall. If there was a hidden door, he aimed to find it. Neasan glanced up and down the inside wall and then began to pry the first stone out.

The lack of shouting from inside the Keep unnerved the clan and several stood in the courtyard wondering exactly what the screeching of wood meant.

Leaning against the outside wall next to Bearcha, Grant covered his mouth with his hand. "Our next laird, once Neasan has gone completely daft, will have no home to go to if we do not stop him."

"Stop him? We do not want to stop him; we want him to hunt for whatever he thinks to find instead of going to war. Did you say the Swintons have William and the other lads?"

"Aye, they are safely captured."

"I do hope Neasan does not hear that. We will be forced to go to war to get them back and it is just the excuse Neasan is waiting for."

"The Kennedys captured the man you sent to the MacDuff. He'll not be coming back either."

"I see." Bearcha paused to think for a moment. "I wonder how many other Davidsons the clans are willing to capture? Perhaps we might send more out."

Grant chuckled. "I hear the Kennedys spit every time someone says the name of Davidson."

Bearcha couldn't help but smile. "Do they now." He stopped to listen to yet another thud coming from inside the great hall. "Perhaps I could suggest we send lads out to find William."

"What reason will you use?"

Bearcha's grin was wide. "Did you not hear? William was seen just yesterday at the Graham market keeping company with a bonny lass and drinking instead of searching." He paused to enjoy Grant's snicker. "Can you let the Grahams know they are coming?"

"Twill be an honor." Grant didn't hesitate to walk down the path and then slip into the woods where he knew the Graham spies were located.

THIS TIME, NEASAN SENT ten men to bring William and his five traitors back, who were supposed to be searching for the first three traitors and Paisley. His life had become one big annoyance after another. Dena kept asking if the roof would fall once he removed more stones, and he finally had to send her outside before he did something rash. It occurred to him that if he could find Justin's wealth, he would take it, ride away and start a new life somewhere far less annoying—if only he could find Justin's wealth. It was, after all, his wealth now. He earned it and it was unfair for Justin to keep it hidden from him. If the man were not already dead, he would kill him!

IT WAS THE FIRST TIME anyone had been in the cottage Mackinzie lived in and she was not at all certain it was presentable. Nevertheless, Paisley asked to see it, and there was nothing she would not do for her. She held her breath, opened the door, and let Paisley walk in.

The first thing Paisley noticed was the beautiful wall covering made of the same soft wool as the belts. There were more belts too and a pile of clothing fit for a newborn in the seat of a chair against the wall. "May I see them?"

"They are not..."

Paisley picked up a small blanket and held the softness against her cheek. "I desperately wanted children, but it was not to be. Do you make these to barter or are they for the child you hope to have someday?"

"They are for me."

Paisley folded the first back up, laid it aside and unfolded the next. When she turned, Mackinzie's forehead was deeply wrinkled. "What is it?"

"I...I do not know many things."

Paisley thought there might be a question in that statement, but she had no idea what it was. "I do not know many things either."

"Did your husband hurt you? I...I once saw a husband hurt his wife."

"That, my husband did not do and 'tis a good thing. My Father would have killed him for it. My Father once said he did not raise me, fret over me, and keep me safe just so my husband could hurt me." Paisley wondered if she should and decided to add, "Sawney is the same. In our clan it is forbidden for a man to hurt a lass, be he husband or not."

"I have no father."

Apparently, Paisley thought, Mackinzie was not interested in what Sawney would do and her brother had a larger hill to climb than he thought. "I see. There are many in Scotland who have no fathers. Lads die in battle or from fevers, but never do they mean to leave their children." Paisley set aside the baby things to admire a wooden shovel hanging on the wall. It had an intricate carving of a border collie in the handle.

"It is from Tavan."

"It is glorious." She turned away from the wall to look at her friend. "If you desire children, then you must want to marry. In our clan, a lass chooses her husband. He must want her and we prefer he loves her, but in the end a lass does the choosing."

"Will you choose another?"

Paisley shook her head. "Nay, I've had my fill of husbands."

"Lenox loves you."

"Lenox? Why do you say that?"

"I saw it in his eyes when I sent him to help you."

Paisley smiled and took hold of Mackinzie's hand. "I suspect you know far more than you let on."

"I saw your brother hug you...twice."

Paisley let go, walked to the table, and picked up a carved wooden goblet. "Our lads hug us very often. My Father did and his father before him. A lad feels more like a lad when he can comfort a lass."

"Sawney comforts you?"

"He comforts all lasses, as do the other MacGreagor lads when we are in need."

"I do not need comfort."

Paisley thought to argue the point and then decided against it. "Perhaps not, but you may like it someday. I am convinced I would die without the comfort of a lad's arms."

MORE AND MORE, CARLEY was enjoying Neasan's frustration. William and his five were not recovered, the man sent to threaten the MacDuff was never seen again and now, the ten he sent to find William were lost. Neasan finally guessed, and rightly so, his men were being captured. It left him seventeen, very well trained warriors down, and he worried the other clans were in the forest getting ready to attack.

If that were not enough, Neasan loudly voiced his rage at not being able to find Justin's wealth. It made Carley smile each night as

A TIME OF MADNESS

she lay down in her bed not a foot from more wealth than Neasan could ever imagine.

More importantly, the Davidsons were turning against their new laird and asking her if she thought Sawney would indeed come back. Sometimes she answered that she did not truly know, but to those she heard loudly shouting in favor of Neasan, she asked why her nephew would. They rejected Sawney and the deed was done. Carley was happy to let them continue to worry; they deserved it.

Still, she constantly kept Bryce in her thoughts and prayed he and the other two could find Sawney and bring them all home. In the meantime, she continued to advise the women who asked about womanly things, carried on with the old ways of bathing each morning and sweeping the path in front of her cottage. Other women were beginning to join her in the old ways, particularly those weary of once placid husbands who were becoming overly demanding.

Those who shouted in favor of Sawney for their next laird, yet did not go with him, continued to feed Neasan's madness with rumors of clans seeing Sawney here or there, alone or with a full force of men. Sometimes, Bearcha greatly struggled to hide his laughter. Yet even he worried that Sawney would not come back and began to wonder who they might make their next laird if he did not.

IT WAS YET ANOTHER day with yet another herd of sheep needing sheering. Sawney and Hew were getting far better at catching them, once the collies chased the sheep their direction. Just as Tavan predicted, Mackinzie would not let Sawney near her so he concentrated on catching sheep.

The Campbells were still grateful for the help, the MacGreagors were happy to do it and no one believed the village needed protecting. Without daily warrior training, it was a good way for the

MacGreagors to keep their reflexes sharp as well as their minds. They just did not expect to have to face danger quite yet.

As soon as one of the Campbells shouted to warn them of strangers, the MacGreagors raced to their pile of swords, quickly tied the sheath strings around their waists, and gathered to protect their laird. Caught outside, the MacGreagor women and children ran to the castle. Kneeling beside the river attending to her wash, Mackinzie quickly stood up and found a place behind a tree to hide and watch.

It was clear the strangers wore Davidson green. However, there were only three and the MacGreagors relaxed a little. Sawney watched the men dismount in the courtyard, take a moment to stare at the imposing castle, and then begin to look around. It was Bryce who spotted them first, quickly tied his horse to a tree, and began to run in their direction. "Sawney!"

Determined not to let a Davidson get close to him, both Keter and Blare stepped in front of Sawney and drew their swords.

Bryce slowed. It was clear they did not trust him and they had good reason not to. Still, he kept his smile and stopped only a few feet away. "Neasan has gone daft. You must come back Sawney, you are our only hope."

"How do we know you have not come to lay a trap for him," Keter asked, his eyes narrowed and determine.

Bryce paused to catch his breath. "I regret not standing up with Sawney and I am not the only one. Neasan made us attack the Haldane. He commanded us to burn their village, but we three would not obey. They hunt *us* now."

Sawney touched Keter's shoulder and urged him to move aside. "Are the Haldane dead?"

"Nay, someone warned them."

Relieved, Sawney closed his eyes for a moment. "I am very pleased to hear that. What of the Kennedy and the Swinton?"

A TIME OF MADNESS 165

"The Kennedys told us which way to look for you. The Macfarlane said they only saw Fergusons, but they did say some of you wore mac...Davidson colors." Bryce suddenly smiled. "The Kennedys have taken to spitting on the ground each time someone says, 'Davidson.'"

That made Sawney smile too, and then he got serious again. "Still, we are only nine lads and even with the three of you, it is not enough to fight Neasan."

"Aye, we twelve and all the Kennedys. They fear Neasan will try to conquer them next. And do not forget the Haldane will help and..."

"Bryce," Sawney interrupted. "Have you ever sheered sheep?"

"Aye, many a time."

Sawney grinned, stood aside, threw out his hand toward the flock of sheep and the Campbells trying to catch them. "'Tis how we are to earn our keep."

Bryce playfully slapped Sawney on the back, "Come with me, lad, I will show you how a master sheep catcher does it."

Sawney barely had time to glance toward the river before Bryce pulled him away, but Mackinzie was there watching and he was glad to know where she was for a change.

IF MACKINZIE HAD ANY one particular advantage over most other people, it was her exceptional hearing and she had not missed a word of what Sawney and his men talked about. Suddenly, she needed someone to talk to, and Paisley would not do.

"He *is* a laird," she whispered, standing close to Tavan. As usual, he was spending his day watching the river flow to the sea. "I did not truly believe it."

"Aye, but he is laird of a very small clan."

Mackinzie leaned a little closer, "Nay, they talk of many others and these three want him to go back."

Tavan stroked his beard a time or two. "Do you fear he will stay or go?"

"I...I fear he...they will all die."

"I believe he fancies you too."

Mackinzie wrinkled her brow and put a hand on her hip. "Which convinces you, his kiss or his throwing me in the river?"

Tavan tried desperately not to laugh. "Did you like his kiss?"

"I hardly had time to consider it. Perhaps, perhaps I did. Is it sinful?"

He wanted to ask why she was just now worried about sin, but he didn't. "If a lass is married and then kisses another lad, it is sinful. But if she is..."

"Oh, I see." Mackinzie looked once more through the trees to see if Sawney was watching her and when he wasn't, she returned to her wash.

Tavan smiled, picked up his carved cane, and headed for the castle. His brother, Laird Campbell, was going to be very pleased to hear this news. They both feared they would never see Mackinzie happily married.

That started it and once more, she was so consumed with thoughts about Sawney's kiss, she hardly knew what she was doing. She'd fallen behind in her washing and it was nearly evening when she glanced back and gasped. Sawney and his men were standing there watching her. Mackinzie rolled her eyes and went back to her work.

"We wish to bathe," said Sawney.

"There is a fine place upriver for bathing," she said without turning around.

"We wish to bathe here. Perhaps you might finish your wash at that fine place upriver."

Mackinzie slowly stood up and turned around. All twelve men were covered in mud and she almost smiled, but caught herself before she insulted Paisley's brother again. Just then, she noticed Sawney start to untie his belt.

Horrified, Mackinzie threw the last wet plaid in her basket, picked it up and started straight for him. Sawney moved out of her way just in time, but not before she had a chance to glance at him and say, "Scunner."

She did not bother to look back even when she heard all of the men burst out laughing.

FEW EVER KNOCKED ON her door and none this late in the evening. She hoped it was Paisley, but when Mackinzie opened it, Sawney was standing there.

"I have come to ask if you will walk with me."

"Why?"

He was not expecting that question and it took a moment to think of what to say. He decided just to tell her the truth. 'Tis how it is done in my clan."

"Oh."

He expected her to ask what was done, but Mackinzie had her own way of thinking and it appeared it was going to take some getting used to. He held out his hand and she looked at it, but she didn't take it. Instead, she stepped out and closed her door.

Sawney clasped his hands behind his back, nodded toward the path to his left and waited for her to begin to walk. It took a moment, but she finally caught on and started down the path. Before he came, he thought of a thousand things to say, but just now, he couldn't remember a one. They had only walked for a little while when he noticed she held her eyes down and soon he realized why. People on the path were staring at her.

There was only one way to avoid that problem. "I prefer to walk along the ocean, do you agree?" He could see the relief in her eyes when she looked up at him and nodded. He turned them around and as they retraced their steps, he glared at those who so rudely stood staring at her. His message was clear and all of them quickly went about their business.

Again, there was silence between them, but after they walked along the shore for a little while, he said, "Mackinzie, the MacGreagors will leave in the morning."

She knew they must, but she did not want to hear it and looked away. "I see."

He was encouraged by her reaction, but only a little. "Will you see to Paisley while we are gone?"

"You will not take her with you?"

"Nay, 'tis too dangerous." Mackinzie looked relieved. He didn't know what to say, so he just kept walking.

She stopped, picked up a shell, walked to the water's edge, and rinsed the sand off. "You can hear the ocean in it."

"So I have heard. May I listen?"

"Aye." Instead of giving him the shell, she held it up to his ear. He didn't seem to think it was positioned right and covered her hand with his so he could move it. For the first time, she looked into his eyes and did not look away. His hand was warm on hers and she liked his touch more than she thought she would.

"How fascinating," said he, finally letting go of her hand. He meant her, but knew she thought he was talking about the shell. He was so close, all he needed to do was take her in his arms, but he only just got her to be with him. Upsetting her now was not what he wanted. He did notice, however, that Mackinzie kept the shell instead of tossing it away.

"Will you come back?" she asked as they began to walk again.

"If I am able. If not, the lads will come for our families."

"Will you die?"

"Not if I can prevent it." He was encouraged even more now that she cared if he died. Nevertheless, it was not the same as consenting to be his wife. "I was hoping…"

"I lied."

"What?"

Mackinzie drew in a forgotten breath. "The horse is not mine."

He smiled, "I knew you were lying."

"How?"

"You are not very good at it."

At last, she curled her lips into a smile. "I have had little practice."

"I am happy to hear that. For my sake, see that you do not practice." He hadn't meant to, but judging by the look on her face, he thought he had confused her. He was wrong.

"You are not angry?"

"How could I be? I have lied a time or two myself."

"Do you lie well?"

He could not help but chuckle. "Very well, but I give you my pledge, I will never lie to you."

"Why?"

In some ways, Mackinzie was still a little girl. Paisley said she was much wiser in the ways of the world than Mackinzie was willing to let on, but just now, he was not so sure. Still, he just promised not to lie to her and he meant to keep that promise. With so little time left before he had to leave, the truth was his best choice. "Because a husband should never lie to his wife." Just as he feared, she stopped and stared into his eyes. "Does that frighten you?" he asked.

She said nothing and instead let her eyes drift down to the middle of his chest. Part of her wanted to run, but there was a part that wanted to stay. What she really wanted was for him to hold her and let her feel his touch again. Then perhaps she would not be frightened at all.

"Mackinzie, I have been too bold and I did not mean to be."

She ignored his words in favor of deciding if she were brave enough to touch him. So many times, she spent her days touching things, but never once had she intentionally touched a man. At length, she decided he would allow it. Slowly, she raised her hand and put the back her fingers against the middle of his neck.

Mackinzie quickly looked up to see if he was disturbed by it and when he did not seem to be, she turned her hand over and gently touched the side of his face. His beard was soft, his skin was smooth and it was enough. She took her hand away and began to walk again.

For the first time in his life, Sawney felt a depth of love for a woman he did not know he possessed. He desperately wanted to hold her and wash away all her years of sadness. Yet the way she touched him, as if to explore his very being, cautioned him to take more time. Time was something he had little of and although he thought of himself as strong, he wondered if he truly had the strength to leave her. She needed him and he needed her even more.

For a time, Sawney considered taking all the MacGreagors back with him included Mackinzie, but suppose he lost the war. No, they were safer living out their lives with the Campbells.

"Well fancy that?" Sawney said after glancing back.

"What"

"My sister walks with Lenox."

"You are surprised?"

He raised an eyebrow. "You are not?"

Mackinzie's smile was glowing. She knew something he did not know and she was very pleased.

So the truth is out, Sawney thought, she did not know many things, but she knew people and she would make a very good MacGreagor mistress. He saw the end of a tree branch sticking out of the mud, but she did not and he grabbed her arm just in time to keep her from falling. He felt her tense a little, so as soon as she had her balance again, he let go.

"You need new shoes," said he.

"Aye, but I must ask Laird Campbell for them."

"You find that troubling?"

She wasn't certain how she should answer and decided not to.

"Does he deny you shoes?"

"Nay." It occurred to her she finally had someone to ask and just blurted it out, "Why must I always ask him? Why can I not just go to the shoemaker?"

Sawney clasped his hands behind his back and explained, "Would that it were so simple. A laird has many things to do before shoes can be made. First, he must know how many others are in need and if the shoemaker has enough leather. If the shoemaker does not, he must tell the lads to butcher a cow, preferably one of the older ones. But before that, the laird must tell the hunters to stop hunting so the meat will not be wasted."

It all made sense to her finally. In fact, a lot of things were making more sense to her. "Oh."

"Shall I ask Laird Campbell on your behalf?" When she nodded, he smiled. "Perhaps I shall ask for two pair just in case the MacGreagor shoemaker is no more, or is out of leather when…when we get home."

"You wish to take me with you?"

"I do. Are you willing?"

It was a big decision. While she had not been happy with the Campbells, she might not be any happier with the MacGreagors. She loved Paisley, she might even love Sawney, but did she have the courage to face a new life in a part of the world she knew little about?

She didn't answer and he did not ask again. Instead, he changed the subject. "Perhaps we should go back. I've shoes to request." Mackinzie did not say she would not go with him, but she didn't joyfully fly into his arms either. He tried to read the expressions on her face as they turned around and walked back toward the village, but she looked away so he could not see. Lenox and Paisley caught up with them in time to relieve their awkward silence.

Lenox stuck out his lower lip and said, "Laird MacGreagor, Paisley threatened to kill me again."

Sawney chuckled, "I am surprised she let you live this long."

Paisley ignored them both, looped her arm through Mackinzie's and began to walk with her. "I would not truly kill him, 'tis but a game we have played since we were children. He tells me I am too willful and I threaten to kill him. I am not willful, save where he is concerned."

"Why does he say you are willful?" Mackinzie asked.

"My dear, I have much to tell you about MacGreagor lads. They are…"

Sawney and Lenox let the women walk away and in a little while Sawney asked, "You fancy my sister still?"

Lenox leaned down and picked up a seashell, "Why do you think I never married?"

"I have wondered about that. You are a good lad, better than most, but I worry Paisley is not yet ready to choose another husband. Did she tell you about Chisholm?"

"Aye, 'tis a pity he killed himself before I got a hold of him."

"I feel the same. Promise you will give Paisley time to recover, she has cried very little."

Lenox tossed the shell away and watched the waves hit the rocks. "She will not cry. She reviled him in the end and is happy to be shed of him. Nevertheless, I promise to wait for a time. I was a timid lad when she married, but I'll not lose her again."

Sawney only had to see the determined look on his friend's face to believe him. He watched Paisley and Mackinzie part ways in the courtyard and then watched Mackinzie walk around to the back of the castle. He waited outside for her to come back, but she didn't. He finally knocked on her door again, but if she was there, she did not answer.

CHAPTER XIII

WHEN MORNING CAME, Sawney was sick at heart. He was certain leaving Mackinzie was the hardest thing he would ever be forced to do, harder even than fighting to gain back the MacGreagor land. While he helped the men ready the horses, he often looked for her, but she did not come. The MacGreagor women came to say goodbye, as did several Campbells, but not Mackinzie.

Keter and Blare kissed their wives and children, Daniel hugged little Flora for several moments, made Senga promise not to marry until he returned and ruffed five-year-old Logan's hair.

Sawney waited until Lenox said his goodbye and then hugged a tearful Paisley. He mounted his horse, nodded to Laird Campbell, and turned to go. There was still one place Mackinzie might be and he held out hope. As soon as they rounded the bend and he saw her atop the hill, his heart began to race.

He rode his horse up the hill, swung down and quickly took her in his arms. It was a moment he waited too long for and he was not about to let it escape him now. To his surprise, she did not pull away and instead, she laid her head against his chest.

At last, Mackinzie let herself feel the joy and the comfort of being in his warm, strong arms. She felt him stroke the back of her hair and drew in the wonder of something she never guessed would be so pleasing.

With his eyes closed, he kept her in his arms, hoping she could feel how much he loved her. When she tilted her head back to look into his eyes, he softly said, "I *will* come back for you." His kiss was long and passionate, but too soon, he took hold of her shoulders and stood her back before he lost all resolve.

She watched him swing up on his horse, ride down the hill, and join the rest of the MacGreagor warriors in the meadow. He paused for just a moment to look back and then he disappeared into the forest.

He was gone just as suddenly as he came. Mackinzie could not seem to look away, hoping beyond hope that he would come back. He had been a part of her life for such a short time, yet he changed everything about her world and now she had an unfamiliar ache in her heart that she feared would never heal.

Tears began to form in her eyes and she quickly brushed them away. She had not cried in years and she wasn't about to start now. Even so, if ever she felt like crying it was now. How was she ever going to force herself to refuse Sawney? Slowly, she turned around to watch the ocean, half expecting the stallion to come and comfort her. He did not and with a heavy heart, Mackinzie finally went home.

THE NEXT DAY, PAISLEY came to see Mackinzie. They walked and talked, about Lenox mostly. Mackinzie did not say much, but she admitted missing Sawney, which pleased Paisley very much. Gavina and Jennet wanted to get to know Mackinzie too and with three women and two children standing around her, it was too much. Mackinzie soon retreated to the top of her hill.

There was a change in the Campbells as well. Word spread quickly that a laird has asked for her hand and some saw her in a whole new light. That pleased Tavan very much. Sawney seemed to be the kind of man who was willing and able to settle the matter if any dared hurt her again.

WEARING THE BLUE COLORS of the Campbells, Sawney and the MacGreagor men rode hard, rested the horses when they needed to and rode hard again. He considered tempting the Macfarlane to fight with him but decided against it. If what Bryce said was true, he would not need them.

He could not get Mackinzie off his mind and on the second night, Keter asked what troubled him most. He might as well tell them, Sawney decided. It would be hard enough for Mackinzie in his world if the clan did not understand her ways. Once he told the men the worst of it, they agreed something more made her hide from the clan, although none dared guess what it was.

Sawney was relieved after sharing her story and finished with, "Therefore, I ask you to help me see to her."

Blare frowned. "I have heard it is the duty of the third in command to see to the mistress. Seeing to Mackinzie, being that she is most bonny lass I have ever seen...save for my wife, 'Twill be drudgery. Yet I shall manage somehow...if I must."

All the men laughed.

THE WOMAN HER BROTHER loved had become as elusive as a red fox and Paisley did not know what to make of it. Mackinzie was seen doing her usual wash and not seen again the rest of each day, nor would she answer her door at night. At her wits end, Paisley finally when to the river, sat on a rock and asked Tavan what to do.

Tavan chuckled. "Aye, well she is upset to be sure. Your brother asked her to live with the MacGreagors once his war is over."

"Does leaving this place upset her?"

"Perhaps, but my guess is she fears something else far more."

"What? Do tell me. My brother loves her so and so do I."

"She fears he will not truly come back for her."

"Oh, I see." Paisley folded her arms and tried to think what she could do. "I cannot promise he will not die, but if he is alive he will come back for her."

"I believe he will too."

"What can I do to convince her?"

"I do not know. Hope can be miserable to someone like Mackinzie. A thousand hopes cannot be pleased unless the first is fulfilled. I dare not imagine what it will do to her if he does not come back."

"Nor can I."

"For now, all we can do is wait for them both."

It was on the morning of the fourth day that they spotted two Kennedy warriors riding toward them. News was what they needed most and Sawney was happy to see his old friends. He was even happier when Eachann and Thomas shared their wine.

"We hoped we would find you," said Eachann as he took back the flask Sawney handed him. "Laird Davidson has gone completely daft." Eachann turned his head to the side and spit on the ground.

Sawney found his gesture amusing. "So I have heard. You must tell me all of it, but first, will the Kennedy's fight with us?"

"Aye, provided you are willing to take back the bone."

"The bone?"

"The one Neasan brought from the sea." Eachann's grin grew wide. "We stole it and the Davidsons helped. I hear tell Bearcha told Neasan it was his own self who ordered the bone gone. He drinks heavily and believes it."

All laughed, but then Sawney got serious. "Bearcha sides with us? We hoped it was so."

"He is the only lad Neasan trusts of late and Bearcha betrays him more often than any other. We have spies in the woods known only to a few, Bearcha tells Grant and Grant tells us what is happening, so we can tell the other clans."

"Why are you not there now?"

Eachann started to laugh. "The MacDuff sent us to find you."

"The MacDuff? The same MacDuff who would rather surrender than fight?"

"The very same. They have gone into hiding for fear Neasan will attack them next. Someone told Neasan you were seen on MacDuff land and they have lost half a lifetime fretting over it. Neasan only sent one lad to demand the MacDuff turn you over, and when we captured him, he could not thank us enough. He says Neasan screams his rage into the night and none can sleep."

"What have you done with the one you captured?"

"We took him to the Swintons where the others are held."

"What others?"

"At last count, seventeen."

"Will they fight with us?"

"Sawney, all of Scotland will fight with you. All you need do is ask. Neasan is a blight on the land and needs getting rid of."

"Why do the MacGreagors not rid themselves of him?"

"Perhaps they do not yet know who to trust or how many will fight against them," said Lenox. "They are family still."

"Brother," said Hew. "We should take the bone back. We can put both ends in the ground and let the wee ones play on it. The people should be reminded daily of their wrong choice."

Sawney nodded. "And someday we will tell our children the story of the bone?"

"That we will." It was good to be going home. There was a woman Hew longed to see again.

LATE INTO THE NIGHT, Sawney, together with Laird Kennedy, Laird Swinton, Laird Haldane, the new Graham laird, and even Laird MacDuff met in Laird Kennedy's keep to plan their attack. With so many available men, it was doubtful they would lose, but Sawney was not willing that any should die. The Davidsons were honor bound to fight, having given their pledges to Neasan, and there was little the MacGreagors could do about that.

Sawney's hope was to so overwhelm them with numbers, they would lay down their weapons and break their pledges. It was a terrible thing for a man to do and each would carry the shame the rest of his life, but Sawney could see no other choice. They were good men, most of them, and some were his relatives. For two more days they made ready, spreading the word Sawney was truly back, sharpening their swords and making new arrows.

CARLEY WAS SO RELIEVED when Grant brought her the news, she wanted to jump for joy. Her sons were with Sawney, they were well and their families were safe. Now all she had to do was wait.

At the same time, Bearcha told Neasan, who marched from place to place, screamed at the top of his lungs and ordered the men to prepared for war. He was excited, the clan was not.

They were somehow short of swords and the tools necessary to sharpen them. Men were forced to commandeer age-old weapons hung on the walls of cottages for decoration or as souvenirs. With no time to prepare, they scurried around finding what they could while worrying they would not survive. Women cried as did children. Neasan went into the Keep and got very, very quiet, which was more frightening to some than facing a battle.

How many men did Sawney have with him? No one seemed to know. It could be twenty, thirty, or a hundred, and some of the Davidsons were bound to be injured if not killed. Furthermore, they were about to fight Sawney, the son of a man they all loved and admired. How had this happened? How had they come to this end?

GRANT AND BEARCHA SAT on the short stonewall in the courtyard and watched. Bearcha tried to think of one more thing that might push Neasan's madness over the edge, hoping he would not order them to fight. "Perhaps I should say Paisley wed another?"

"That might do it," Grant agreed. "Dena says he will not allow her to go into Paisley's bedchamber and it is the only room he has not destroyed."

"Even to find Justin's gold?"

"She says not."

Bearcha shrugged. "I am surprised he has not killed Dena by now."

"As am I," Grant agreed. "She did lie, did she not?"

"I am convinced of it. Dena has no sickness in the mornings and looks well enough."

"I wonder what Sawney will do with her. What does a laird do with a lass who was once mistress and is no more?"

"He will send her away with Neasan, if he lets Neasan live."

"Unless Neasan wins."

Bearcha closed his eyes for just a moment. "I do not intend to let that happen."

"How will you prevent it?"

"You will see. Just now, I best let Neasan know what we just heard about Paisley."

Grant remained seated on the short wall, watched Bearcha enter the Keep and waited. A moment later, something crashed inside and he knew the deed was done. He smiled.

A TIME OF MADNESS

AT DAWN, MEN FROM FIVE different clans mounted their horses and headed for the Davidson glen. When they neared, they slowed so Neasan would not hear them. Then they dismounted, tied their horses to the trees, and followed Sawney on foot into the glen.

To Sawney's surprise, there were no whistles from the guards signaling his arrival, although he did spot a man running through the forest. He drew his sword and kept going, taking step after step closer to the village until he stopped. Soon, sixteen archers ran to the front, knelt down in front of Sawney, and prepared to shoot their arrows at the Davidsons.

Hew stood next to his brother with his sword also drawn and Keter, Sawney's second in command stood on the other side. The ten faithful MacGreagors, dressed in Campbell blue, stood in the middle of the second line with six Haldane on each side of them eager to seek revenge for their burned homes. The third line consisted of Swintons wearing yellow kilts, the fourth of Kennedys in red and wearing dark blue were the Grahams in the fifth line. The MacDuffs dressed in faded green, those that were not in the trees shivering, brought up the rear.

It was an impressive sight and one Bearcha hoped never to see again. Even as quiet as the opposing forces were trying to be, he heard them and rushed to the courtyard to see what was happening. He wondered if he should wake Neasan or leave him to his wine induced coma for a while longer.

At last, Bearcha gave the whistle that signaled danger and almost instantly, cottage doors flew open, women and children fled to the forest, while reluctant men armed themselves and headed for the courtyard. Not one of them neglected to let his jaw drop once he saw the vast numbers of Sawney's forces. Nor did any run and for a moment, Bearcha was proud of each of them.

The crash of a chair hitting the wall in the third-story bedchamber made them all look up, including Sawney's army. It was clear Neasan was awake and now it was up to Laird Davidson to give the command.

Bearcha expected Neasan to come charging out, but the minutes seemed to slowly tick by and still the Keep door did not open. He suspected Neasan was getting dressed, or forgot where he last left his sword, or perhaps he wanted to kill Dena first. He was about to go inside when Neasan finally leaned out of the top window. "What are you waiting for? Kill them, kill them all!"

The Davidsons could not believe their eyes. Neasan was not coming out to fight with them? He was a coward? After all the bragging, the man intended to hide inside, making them fight for him alone? Slowly, they looked down the glen at the massive opposing force.

With a nod of Sawney's head, the missing Davidsons came out of the forest to stand with Neasan's men, but still they were a pitiful force that would surely lose against so many.

He did not want to, but as Neasan's first in command, William ordered his men to line up facing Sawney. He had to remind them of their pledges, but at length, they complied. What else could they do?

Yet Bearcha remained in the courtyard. His sword still in its sheath, Bearcha climbed up to stand on the wall, cupped his hands, and yelled, "Sawney?"

Sawney took a step forward. He hoped they meant to surrender, but he did not think they would. "Aye, Bearcha."

"If a lad gives his pledge to fight for two different lairds, which must he honor?"

Sawney tried to figure out what Bearcha was getting at but he truly had no idea. "The first," he shouted back.

"Do you remember the day we fought the MacNab?"

He was beginning to see what his old friend was up to and turned to look at Hew. Hew's smile told him all he needed to know.

"We were just laddies fighting with wooden swords, yet we won that battle as I recall," said Sawney.

Hew grinned. "Aye, we did, but you would not let us fight until we gave you our pledge."

"Thank you, Bearcha," Sawney whispered then he drove the tip of his heavy sword into the ground in front of him and cupped both hands. "You are right! Let each lad who gave me his pledge come touch my sword to renew it. I command it!"

A mighty shout for joy came from fully half of Neasan's men who rushed forward to touch Sawney's sword.

Disheartened, Dena's father hung his head and with the others, stayed where he was.

Sawney waited until the Davidsons finished touching his sword to become MacGreagors again and went to stand behind him. Then he considered what to do with the rest and once more turned to his brother for advice.

Hew shrugged. "Tell them to surrender."

"He is right," said Keter. "It is madness to fight now."

Again, Neasan screamed from his window. "Traitors! Fight them! Kill them!"

The remaining Davidsons closed ranks, but they did not draw their swords.

"Hear this," Sawney shouted. "I banish any lad who yet faces us." He paused to let his words sink in. "Nevertheless, for the sake of your families I will give sanctuary to any lad who lays down his sword."

Five Davidsons were so relieved, they instantly sunk to their knees, untied their sheaths, and tossed their weapons away. It was not long before they all did the same. The archers stood up, put their arrows back in their sheaths and Sawney was as relieved as all the warriors were. Yet he still had to fight Neasan.

"Neasan! I call you out, Neasan! Fight me to the death!"

In the doorway of Neasan's bedchamber, Dena watched her husband. His men were deserting and Neasan moaned each time one touched Sawney's sword and moaned longer when the rest laid down their swords. His words were garbled, but she heard him say, "How could this have gone so wrong?" Still she watched, ready to run down the stairs should he turn on her. She need not have worried; Neasan remained where he was and continued to mutter to himself. "Where is the gold? Nowhere, there is no gold."

For a moment, she felt sorry for him, but then he slumped to his knees and said, "Even Paisley has deserted me." Dena put her hand on her dagger and thought to kill him herself. Perhaps they might call her a hero if she did, but Neasan was still a very large, powerful man and a dagger in the back might not be enough to kill him. She removed her hand and waited.

There was nothing left. Slowly, Neasan withdrew his dagger and put the tip of it against his skin just below his breastbone. Then he lifted up, put both hands on his dagger, shouted "Why?" and shoved it into his heart.

Dismayed, Dena watched him fall to the side and then watched the blood begin to collect in a pool under him. It was all over and she was no longer a mistress. Never had she felt such disappointment. She could have gone to the window and shouted the news, but she walked down the two flights of stairs instead and took a last look at the home that was no longer hers. Tears began to roll down her cheeks.

When she opened the door, no one but Carley and Bearcha stood in the courtyard. Dena did not even bother to look at them as she walked past, made her way through the surrendered Davidsons and then between the archers. Every eye was on her and every man probably wanted her, but she wanted only one. She did not stop until she stood in front of Sawney with only his sword between them.

"He is dead."

"Good," said Sawney.

"What will become of me?"

She could not hold back her tears and Sawney felt sorry for her. "You should rest, now."

She lowered her eyes for a moment and then looked up at him. "Aye, I am very tired."

He watched her walk to her father and nearly collapse in his arms. Now that he loved Mackinzie, he could not believe he ever found Dena pleasing, but he quickly dismissed that thought. With as much strength as he used to drive it in the ground, Sawney pulled his sword out and held it high in the air. "Neasan is dead!"

The shout of over three hundred men echoed through the forest. Men from all the clans stowed their weapons and greeted their clansmen with smiles of triumph while the thrilled women and children began to pour out of the woods.

SAWNEY LOCKED ARMS with Hew and then went to find Bearcha, the only man who did not join the Davidsons on the battlefield. "You are brilliant!" he said, putting one arm around Carley and smacking Bearcha's shoulder with the other. "I had forgotten that pledge or I would have said something the day of the choosing."

"I only remembered it yesterday."

Sawney suddenly frowned. "Why did you not come to touch my sword?"

Bearcha winked at Carley and grinned. "I was following you when Neasan asked the men for their pledges and he did not remember to ask for mine. My pledge has always been to you."

"I see." Sawney released Carley so she would greet her sons and smiled. "I have heard much about you from the spies in the forest. I wish to hear everything, but first, has Neasan drunk all the wine?"

Bearcha's smile was beaming. "I think we can manage a drop or two in celebration."

In the middle of the excited men, Hew looked for her, but it wasn't until she tapped him on the back that he finally found Charlotte. He was so happy to see her that he quickly wrapped his arms around her. "I have missed you, lass."

"And I you."

Amid the shouts and the laughter, Keter and Blare made their way through the crowd of men and when he reached her, Keter put his hands on his hips. "Mother, you are far too brave."

"I missed you too."

Instantly, he gathered Carley in his arms and held her for a long moment. "We came back, just as we promised."

"I always knew you would."

It was Blare's turn to hug her. Carley had so much to tell and so many questions, she could hardly wait for him to let her go. "You will see Neasan is buried in the graveyard of shame with my first husband?"

"Aye, Mother, we will see to it," Blare answered.

Sawney hugged each of the women, touched all the children, and drank in their smiles. He noticed that when one of the women saw her husband coming toward her, she glared. "We have the old ways back now, and I am glad of it."

"Aye, the old ways," her husband agreed. He looked sorrowful for a moment, and then he grabbed her and kissed her hard. "I am glad of it too."

All Sawney could think about now was Mackinzie and how he wished she were here to see this day with him. He looked again at all the happy faces around him and then held up his hand.

Once they quieted, he shouted. "I will have twenty lads to go back with me for our families. Who is willing?" Happy to have a leader again who was clearly not daft, every MacGreagor raised his hand, as well as two Swintons and three Kennedys. Sawney laughed.

William quickly made his way to Sawney, "Let me go, I have been captured for days, sitting in an empty cottage, and cannot wait to ride a horse again."

"Sawney slapped him on the back. "Then you shall come."

He glanced around once more and as he expected, all the MacDuff were gone. Next, he sought out his brother, who was engrossed in a conversation with Bearcha and Charlotte.

"Hew, I leave you in charge. Bearcha will help you. See that this place is cleaned up before my bride sees it."

Hew was so pleased, his chest swelled. "Done."

"Bride?" Bearcha asked.

Sawney grinned. "I am certain my brother will tell you all about her. She is wonderful and you will like her. All the MacGreagors will."

Standing not far away, Dena bowed her head. "Sawney had a bride and now all her hopes were truly dashed." She turned and started to walk away when she heard Hew say, "She has not agreed to marry you yet, brother." Perhaps there was hope after all. Pretending to show just the right amount of sorrow, she walked down the path toward the cottage she once again would share with her parents.

IN THE EVENINGS OF the much more pleasant ride back to get his bride, Sawney listened to everything the men had to tell about Neasan and his madness. It was the best entertainment ever and he too told all about their journey, the Campbells, catching sheep and of course about Mackinzie. He knew the women had to be beside themselves with worry and he could not wait to get back to them.

CHAPTER XIV

MACKINZIE WAS RIGHT where he left her, standing on the hill watching the ocean. Sawney signaled for the men to go on without him, dismounted, and walked across the meadow. Her hair was down, a breeze lifted the sides of it, and for a moment, he paused just to look at her.

As soon as she noticed the other MacGreagors on the path, she turned and searched for Sawney among them. When he was not there, she hung her head and nearly crumbled to the ground.

Just in time to keep her from collapsing, he reached for her. She turned in his arms and for a long moment, she stared at his face. "I thought...I feared..."

He put his hand on the back of her head and held her even closer. "I gave you my word I would come back," he whispered. "Are you well?"

"Aye, are you?"

"I am now that I am with you." He passionately kissed her, but he could feel her tension and stopped. Something was wrong. "Do I frighten you?"

She giggled. "Nay." Then she leaned back and looked up at him. "Are you certain you are not hurt?"

"We did not have to fight."

Mackinzie closed her eyes and laid her head back against his chest. "Paisley said I would find comfort in your arms and she is right. It is very pleasing." She didn't let him speak before she continued, "Paisley will be happy you are back." This time she looked deeply concerned when she leaned back to look in his eyes. "Her hair becomes the color of the sun."

He could not help but smile. "I will explain it later, but first, will you marry me and come with us when we go home?" She did not answer and he held his breath. "Mackinzie?"

"I am thinking."

"You will be happy there, I promise."

She moved away and turned to watch the ocean. "I cannot."

"Why not?"

"I do not know what I am. Am I Scot, English, or worse, a Celt? They say I am a Celt, they have always said it."

He knew, but he wanted her to tell him. "Why do they say that?"

"Because I came to them in a bucket and no one knows who put me in it."

"Then they cannot know you are a Celt. I say you are a Scot the same as me, the most becoming Scot I have ever seen." Mackinzie giggled and he believe it was the first time he'd heard that. "The MacGreagors will not call you a Celt, I forbid it."

"By order of the king?"

"My good lass, in the MacGreagor clan, I *am* the king." She smiled slightly and then grew silent again. This time he let her be. No one would care that she was found in a bucket, but she cared.

Finally, she looked at him. "You are certain they will not call me names?"

"Not if they wish to be a MacGreagor. We do not hold with such things, even from our children."

"Aye, but if they did, I would not know where to hide."

Sawney took hold of her shoulders and turned her until she faced him again. Then he pulled her close and wrapped his arms around her. "If ever you have a need, this is where you shall hide. I give you my pledge, no matter where I am or what I am doing, you shall always be my first thought. I will gladly hide you in my arms until the day I die."

LENOX WAS THE FIRST to ride into the Campbell village and Paisley ran out of the castle with open arms to greet him. She looked for her brothers among the MacGreagor warriors as they dismounted, but it was not until she saw Sawney leading his horse and walking hand in hand with Mackinzie that she allowed herself to take a breath.

"Hew?" Paisley asked

Lenox hugged her once more. "He is well, we all are."

She was thrilled and ran to her brother, who had the biggest smile on his face she had ever seen. Paisley greeted all the others, while Daniel, Keter and Blare held their families close. The war was won, Mackinzie would become their new mistress, and they could all go home, at last.

THE MACGREAGORS STAYED long enough for the men to get a good look at the ocean and to celebrate Senga's marriage to Joel.

For the first day in years, Mackinzie did not hide. She had a few choice words to say to one of the Campbell women, but after that, she was content to be by Sawney's side. Tavan was filled with glee, as was Laird Campbell at the sight of her constant smile, a sight they vowed not to forget.

The next day, things had changed. Mackinzie spoke little, sometimes grew tense and it was enough for Paisley to knock on Sawney's door late at night after everyone had gone to bed.

He was surprised to see his sister at his door and stepped aside so she could enter. "Are we at war?"

He always had a way of making her giggle and such was the case this time. "Not yet."

Sawney closed the door and held a chair, but Paisley chose not to sit. "It is too much for Mackinzie," she said.

"I agree. Have you a suggestion?"

"It is only that the Campbells are the smaller clan and if she is not comfortable with them, how can she be with all of us?"

"Aye, but these are the people who hurt her."

Paisley walked to his bed and sat on it instead. "I wonder if she will ever tell us what happened?"

"Perhaps when she becomes more accustomed to us."

"If she does not grow silent again. Brother, you intend to make her the MacGreagor mistress. The people will curtsy to her, do what she says without question and she is ill prepared. Even I had difficulty with the demands on me and I am a laird's daughter. What if she hides? Our woods are far thicker than these and we will never find her."

He slowly ran his fingers through his hair. "I had not considered that." Sawney's eyes suddenly brightened. "Never do you come to me with a quandary and no ready answer. What this time?"

"Caught again, am I? Well, perhaps it might do for us to rest far more often on our journey home."

"So you can prepare her?"

"So we all can."

"Agreed. We've no reason to hurry home now that we are well protected, and from what I have seen of the destruction, the lads need all the time they can get to repair the Keep."

"Good." Paisley closed her eyes for a moment. "Brother, what I say now will not please you. Tell her you will bring her back if she is unhappy with us."

Sawney finally sat beside her on the bed. "Paisley, I cannot lose her. What is life to me without her?"

"Does she say she loves you?"

"Nay, not yet."

"You came back for her as you said and now you have her trust. Can you not see, she will feel trapped by us if you do not give her a solemn pledge? Do not *make* her love you. Let her do so when she is content."

"You are saying I should not marry her right away?"

"Aye. When she is ready, she will ask why you are waiting. Then you will know, even if she does not say she loves you."

MACKINZIE HAD HER BELONGINGS ready even before dawn. There wasn't much; a change of clothing, her baby things, the shovel Tavan made for her and the carved goblet. Waiting was not her best feature and when she had checked everything five more times, she gave up and went out the door. There was one person she wanted to see before she left and she was glad to find Tavan up and about.

"Child, I am happy you have come. I have a gift for you." He handed her a sack and watched her face light up when she saw the balls of soft wool in many different colors.

"It was you, I suspected as much." Suddenly, she put her arms around Tavan and hugged him.

He was so shocked, he hardly knew what to do, but if she was willing, he could think of no greater gift and hugged her back. As soon as she let go, so did he. "I give you also a word to take with you. 'Tis this—stand firm against the world, Mackinzie, for your husband's sake. He is a good lad and he needs a wife of great courage."

NOT MORE THAN A FEW moments after she left Tavan, Sawney came to get her and her belongings, but first he assured her he would bring her back if she grew unhappy. She thought it very odd. If she wanted to come back, she doubted he could stop her. Nevertheless, if it pleased him to say so, then she was pleased to hear it.

By the time they were ready to leave, all the MacGreagors knew what had happened to Mackinzie and were warned not to frighten, provoke, or laugh at her childish ways. Once they said their goodbyes, five MacGreagor warriors led them out of the Campbell courtyard. They walked their horses along the water's edge and then turned up the path beside the hill.

Sawney expected her to do it and warned the men to stop when Mackinzie rode her horse to the top. He thought she needed a moment alone, yet he held his breath. If she were going to change her mind, it would be now.

She sat upon the dapple gray Laird Campbell gave her as a going away gift and she was quite overwhelmed by his kindness. He did care about her, he must. Mackinzie was sad to leave her ocean, but not sad to be going with the man she loved. She took one last look, turned her horse, rode down to the meadow, and as soon as she caught up, fell in behind Sawney.

Home, she decided, had a very nice sound to it and with Paisley there too, she was certain this was the life she was meant to have. Still, she had many questions and spent the first day thinking about them. Most of all, she thought about what Tavan said. He was right, nothing frightened her and it was time to show her courage. Heretofore, she would be as bold as Sawney needed her to be.

ACCORDING TO MOFFET, whom Sawney did not take with him, Dena had just enough time to think of a way to rid herself of the woman Sawney intended to marry. There was always the possibility he would marry her before he brought her home, but just in case, she needed to be ready.

Dena played the grieving widow well, although she did mention she did not find Neasan to be a loving husband. The women were back to bathing each morning and she was happy to go with them and answer all their questions. Because everything she said would soon reach the ears of the entire clan, she embellished a few of the details and never once mentioned his obsession with Paisley.

She was the only one who walked behind his box when the men carried her husband to the graveyard of shame. It was her duty and she held her head up high, bearing the pretend sorrow as best she could.

In the afternoons, she took long walks to pretend to ease her sorrow. Most of the time she considered what to do about this Mackinzie woman. There were several ways to prevent a marriage and she thought she knew them all. Perhaps she could embarrass her in front of the clan, frighten her, or better yet, push her off a cliff. The last option would take some doing, but it was certainly worth considering and she knew exactly where a high cliff was.

Dena liked being mistress while it lasted and she was good at it. She had taken to visiting the sick, ordering the meals for her husband, assigning duties, and seeing that all was well, despite Neasan's constant upheaval. For that reason alone, she was far better suited to the position than any other woman could be. Besides, someone from another clan would not know exactly how Sawney liked things. Indeed, Dena was exactly what Sawney and the restored MacGreagor clan needed. All she had to do was convince Sawney of that.

Not asking Moffet and Diocail to keep quiet about Mackinzie before he brought her home, was an error on Sawney's part, Dena thought. Diocail obviously liked Mackinzie, told about the time she called Sawney a scunner, and made mention of her odd behavior, most likely because of the children's name-calling.

Dena listened to every word of the gossip and little by little, she began to learn Mackinzie's weaknesses. A plan was forming in her mind and just thinking about it excited her. Sawney would choose her to be his wife instead, Dena was sure of it.

SAWNEY WAS NOT SURPRISED Mackinzie spoke little that first day. When he occasionally looked back, she smiled to reassure him and when it was time to rest the horses, he went with her to walk the stiffness out. Even then, she did not speak much and he did not require it.

The Campbells gave them enough provisions to make it home, and already it was a far more relaxing journey for the women and children than the one they took to reach the ocean. They stopped to gaze at the far off mountains, to pick flowers, to let Flora and Logan run and play, and for the twenty men Sawney brought with him to get their fill of the beauty of Scotland.

For Mackinzie, having men constantly guard her took some getting used to. They seemed friendly enough and very helpful, especially Blare, who often asked if she needed to stop. No man touched her save Sawney who only did so when he helped her mount or dismount.

So happy to be with their families again, Keter and Blare often hugged and kissed their wives, but Sawney did not and Mackinzie was glad in the beginning. Touching him when they were alone was something far different than an open display of affection. She was unsure what she should or not do. Each time the husbands took the wives in their arms, she watched to see exactly what was permitted in this new clan.

Sawney watched Mackinzie watch the couples and wondered what she was thinking. He longed to hold her that way and often, but if that was what she wanted, she gave him no hint.

When it was time to prepare the evening meal Mackinzie helped, although she needed instructions. Gavina and Jennet knew all kinds of things about food she did not know and it fascinated her. She laughed both at them and with them, watched them add just the right spices, and could not wait to see how it tasted.

Around the campfire after their evening meal, she began asking questions about her new home and Sawney answered each one. Mackinzie did not find that to her liking at all and began to get annoyed. "Does the laird in your clan answer *all* the questions?"

Sawney quickly glanced at the others. "Nay, only the important ones."

"Such as how small the fish are in your river?"

He raised an eyebrow, "You do not believe me?"

"I might if you let someone else answer occasionally."

He grinned, "Lads, show this lass how long the fish are in our river." Every one of them held their hands as far apart as he had that day on the hill.

That made her giggle. "Now I believe you."

From then on, he let the others answer. However, when Sawney offered her his flask of wine and she took a sip, Mackinzie nearly spit it out. "'Tis bitter."

"Nay, Campbell ale is too sweet," said Sawney.

She was astounded, put her hand on his shoulder, and got up. "You did not bring any ale?"

"I did not think to. Do you drink ale often?"

"Only when I can steal it." She suddenly realized what she said and horrified herself, but when she turned to look at the others, they were smiling.

"Only MacGreagor wine is worth stealing." said Keter.

"Says you." She rolled her eyes and went to sit between Jennet and Gavina. "If I teach you, might you make Campbell ale for me?"

Sawney winked at Paisley. "Now that, I will not allow."

"Toe..." Mackinzie caught her breath and covered her mouth. "I vowed I would not say that anymore."

"You are very wise indeed," said Sawney. "I have vowed to throw you in the loch each time you do."

Mackinzie looked at Gavina and then at Jennet. "Fret not, I can out run him."

Everyone laughed and the ice was finally broken.

EACH DAY MACKINZIE spoke more, laughed more, and kept an eye on Sawney, just in case he looked like he was going to toss her in whatever body of water they happened to be near.

They stopped to fish, walked and talked, and in the evenings, they told Mackinzie all about the people she would meet. Some of the stories were sad, but most were happy.

Hunters and warriors from other clans they met along the way told of a great battle. Each account of the fight grew more incredible with the telling and soon it was a thousand men in a glen somewhere and half died. The MacGreagors only smiled and moved on.

The night before they were to ride into the MacGreagor glen, Paisley took Sawney aside. "I wish a cottage of my own and two beds. Mackinzie will stay with me until you are married."

"I thought to have her live with aunt Carley, but your way is better. Done then."

"Sawney, she tries too hard to please us."

He put his food on a rock and leaned down to adjust the shoes that laced up to his knees. "Does she? I had not thought that."

"We have taken her from all things familiar and the change in her is remarkable. I fear she too easily goes from a lass who hides and does not speak, to what you see now? Who can make such a change? If only she would cry, then I would know how to help her."

"Perhaps once we are home."

"Perhaps we might offer to take her back to see the Campbells each spring."

"I agree. Father made few mistakes, but not sending the people out to see the world was one of them. Let the MacGreagors know what a peaceful life they have and be grateful for it."

Both of them paused to listen to the howl of hungry wolves. "They come closer." Paisley whispered.

"Aye, we will keep the fires going this night and see that the horses are free to run if need be. We should have brought a dog."

She reached up on tip-toe and kissed Sawney on the cheek. "Tomorrow we will be home and able to sleep peacefully in our own beds."

In four days, Sawney had not held her and Mackinzie did not understand why. As soon as Paisley went to make her bed, she went to him and blatantly asked him. "Is it forbidden for you to touch me when others are near?"

He smiled, put his foot down, and opened his arms to her. "Never. Is it forbidden for me to kiss the lass I love?" The moment she lifted her head, he lowered his lips to hers and felt the joy he denied himself for four days. Paisley was wrong. Mackinzie's embrace and her kiss was all the proof he needed to be certain she was not trying too hard—she was just becoming the real Mackinzie.

This night, he put his bed beside hers, turned on his side, took her hand, and watched her fall asleep. Never had he been so happy and he savored the moment. He regretted having to share her with so many in the future, but the clan, his father's beloved clan, needed her too.

CHAPTER XV

IN THE DAYS WHILE THEY waited for their Laird to come home, the MacGreagor glen was a flurry of activity that kept everyone busy. In the third-story bedchamber that would now become Sawney's, the builders pulled up the floorboards where Neasan's blood soaked into them and laid new ones. Wooden pegs were used to secure the old ones Neasan tore up, all the feathers were swept up, the bed was put back together, a new mattress was added, and a new trunk now held the things Justin kept in the old ones. All the rumors of what Justin kept in that room were finally set aside and the myth was no more. Some found that sad, for they spent hours speculating on that very subject.

The second floor bedchambers were easier to repair and once done, the women cleaned and made beds for whomever Sawney wanted to live with him. New mortar was used to put all the stones back in the walls of the great hall. Grandmother Glena's colorful pillows were beyond repair, but the feathers were recovered and stored, to be used again if the new mistress desired more made. Broken chairs were put back together and pitchers and goblets, bartered from the Graham market, replaced all the smashed ones.

At last, they were finished and it was Carley who came to inspect the work. She smiled as she examined each room and often nodded, which greatly pleased the builders. When she was finished, she walked to the door. "My mother always had bowls of fresh flower petals everywhere, but I will see to it."

The paths too were swept. The elders, the men, the women, and the children went back to the old ways that didn't seem so bad after all. Anything was better than Neasan.

AT DAWN, SAWNEY SENT two men to tell the clan they were close to home and would arrive by early afternoon. After two more washes on the way home, Paisley's hair was white again. Everyone was excited and even the horses knew they were close to home. Nevertheless, Sawney called a halt just before they left the path to enter the glen.

He turned in his saddle, smiled at Mackinzie and then looked at Paisley. He put his hand on the sheath of his sword and it took a moment, but when she realized, she smiled and nodded. For three generations, few MacGreagors had ever laid eyes on the golden sword, and most thought it was just a myth. Yet, this was the sword his grandfather's friend, Walrick, held high in the air when Neil first led the people to this very glen.

Sawney slowly pulled it out of its sheath. Even he had not seen the golden blade it in the sunlight and was captured by its magnificence. It was fitting and right for Sawney to hold it up high as he brought the MacGreagor Clan home.

The people with him gawked and he had to say the command twice before they began to move again. At long last, they turned into the glen. The warriors in the front parted, let Sawney ride on ahead and as they drew closer to the village, the people began to cheer.

Lenox moved his horse up next to Paisley's. "Is that not the sword you carried?"

"Aye." She turned to grin at him. "Sawney said Neasan would never find the MacGreagor gold."

"So he did," Lenox mutter, "so he did."

Once he reached the people, Sawney handed the heavy sword to his brother. Then he slid down and went back to claim his bride-to-be. He lightly kissed her lips and then whispered in her ear, "Welcome home."

She hugged him once more and then she saw it. She ignored all the people there to meet her and walked straight to the whalebone. Just as Sawney instructed, both ends were imbedded in the ground with only the curve showing.

Soon, he was standing right beside her. "If it displeases you, I will..."

"'Tis the rib of a whale, a giant whale at that." She smiled at him. "I have seen many whales. The bone brings good fortune."

"It did not bring good fortune to Neasan."

"Aye, but you said he gave it to your father. Do you not see, he gave his good fortune away."

Sawney laughed. "The story of the bone has a new ending."

"I brought shells so the children can hear the ocean."

"They will love you for it and so do I. Come, Hew is eager to see you again and we best not keep him waiting."

Hew was surprised when she hugged him and then he began to introduce Mackinzie to everyone. Sawney talked to the men, but he often glanced at her to make certain it was not too overwhelming. She seemed to be fine and he was amazed at how well she fit in.

DENA DID NOT LIKE HER at all, but then why would she? Everyone could see how smitten Sawney was with Mackinzie. The smug little thing had unsightly freckles across her nose and her hair was not truly red. Yet when she was introduced and Neasan's widow, Dena smiled and welcomed her just as she should. There was one thing that made Dena very happy—Sawney did not say she was already his wife and that was good news, very good news indeed.

The smell of beef set to slowly cook in the pit some two days before filled the air and the women were beginning to set out the food for the welcome feast.

Everyone seemed so happy and it made Dena sick. Each time she looked that way, Mackinzie was smiling as though she was oh so pleased. And why not, Sawney hardly left her side. A couple of times Mackinzie caught Dena watching her and Dena wanted to slap that smile off her face.

Unfortunately, Sawney would not be pleased. Neasan would have liked seeing it, but not Sawney. On the other hand...that was it. It was forbidden for anyone to strike a woman and the punishment would be harsh, even banishment. All Dena needed to do was provoke her so Mackinzie would lash out.

Mackinzie didn't look timid at all, which didn't match the stories she'd heard, and Dena wondered how old she was. Of course, babies born in a bucket never knew how old they were. Just then, Mackinzie started to walk toward her. Dena thought to ignore her and leave, but why should she? She belonged here, not Mackinzie.

"Will you show me where to find the loch?" Mackinzie asked.

Dena wanted to deny her, but Paisley was close enough to hear and she thought better of it. At length, she nodded and led the way. So that was it, Dena thought, the bucket wants to be friends with the previous mistress. Of course she does. Next, she would ask her advice, but that was the last thing Dena was prepared to give.

Half way down the path Mackinzie said, "I am sad for your loss."

Dena stopped and turned around. There were a thousand things she could have said, but Mackinzie might tell on her. "You are the only one." Dena turned back around and when they got to the loch, she threw out her hand. "This is where the lasses bathe in the mornings."

Dena expected Mackinzie to start asking all kinds of questions, but she didn't. She only nodded and seemed satisfied to look out across the water. She didn't know if she should leave Mackinzie alone or not, so Dena stayed. It gave her a chance to look her over well. She was taller than Mackinzie, but Mackinzie looked stronger and she might not be easily pushed off a cliff. Perhaps poison would do, if she could get her hands on some. Of course, her first plan was the best.

When she glanced back, Dena was surprised to find Sawney behind her watching them both. Good, she thought, let him see which of us is more pleasing and which would make a better wife. To her chagrin, Sawney motioned for Dena to leave. She did as she was told, but she wasn't happy about it. Nevertheless, she smiled and walked away.

"Are you unwell?" he asked once Dena was out of sight.

"Nay," Mackinzie answered.

He put his arms around her from behind and was glad when she leaned her head back against him. "You are tired."

"I will be happy to see a bed again."

"So will I. Paisley wants you to stay with her, will that be to your liking?"

She smiled. "Thank you."

"The lasses have left new MacGreagor clothing for you in..."

"I brought clothing of my own."

"It was the first indication she might not stay and it greatly disturbed him. "As you wish. If you want to bathe, I will send Paisley. I am certain she would like a bath as well. Come to think of it, I am surprised she is not already in the water. There is nothing she likes better than to be clean."

"I would prefer that."

"Done then." He wanted to kiss her and hold her even longer, but she did not turn to face him and he tried to understand. Still, he did not let go right away and instead, kissed the side of her neck. A million reasons for this change in behavior ran through his mind, but perhaps she was just exhausted. He glanced around, felt certain she was in no danger and walked back up the path.

As soon as he was gone, Mackinzie turned around. "Why do you watch us, Dena?"

She was caught but she owed that woman nothing, especially the truth. The sooner Mackinzie was out of their lives the better. Dena stood up, walked out of the bushes, and turned to face her. I wanted to talk to you still."

"About what?"

Dena had to think fast. "Did Paisley tell you she was abducted?"

"Aye."

"Would you like to see where it happened?"

All her years of watching people's expressions, the way they moved and the look in their eyes told Mackinzie Dena despised her. Yet there was only one way to see what this woman was up to. "Aye."

Dena was pleased, a little too pleased, and she did not hide it well. First, she had to get Mackinzie away from the loch before Paisley showed up to bathe. "Come with me."

Mackinzie followed her and as they went deeper and deeper into the forest, she put her hand on her dagger.

Dena took the path that led from the loch to the back of the graveyard. From there, it was just a few steps to the glen. However, Dena wasn't taking her to the Glen. "Is it true you were born in a bucket?"

Mackinzie drew in a deep breath. "Aye."

Dena wasn't expecting such a simple answer and decided to ask another question, one which was sure to raise Mackinzie's ire. "I have heard you are a sea monster. Is that also true?"

"Aye."

It wasn't working and Dena was thoroughly frustrated as she led the way up the hill behind the graveyard and down the other side. Then she stopped and turned her hate-filled eyes on Mackinzie. "You do not belong here. We are MacGreagors, you are not."

When they stopped, neither of them saw the gray wolf or had any idea they were between the wolf and the burrow in the rocks where she kept her hungry pups. It was a slender, powerful animal with long limbs, small paws and a heavily muscled neck. Dena was closest to the pups, and it was she the wolf concentrated on.

The growl was so soft, Mackinzie barely heard it, but she would know that sound anywhere and began to search the woods with eyes. Quickly, she drew her dagger. When she finally spotted it, the wolf displayed its large teeth, lifted its tail, and took a slow and deliberate step toward Dena. With a high-pitched whine, the wolf lunged.

Dena screamed and put her arms up to protect her face. A split second later, Mackinzie stepped between Dena and the fierce animal. She plunged her long dagger into the wolf's underbelly, but not before it dug its sharp teeth into her shoulder.

In great pain, the animal twisted, released his jaws, and fell to the ground. Instinctively, Mackinzie knelt down and stabbed it twice more until she was certain it was dead. Then she tossed her dagger away. Blood ran down her arm and her chest into her shirt, yet she did not realize she was injured and looked to see if Dena was hurt.

Dena's scream made Paisley and the other's going to the loch swiftly halt. Instantly, each of them turned and ran back to the Keep. Dena's scream also brought men running and before Mackenzie knew what was happening, Hew had her in his arms. The blood horrified him, he quickly turned and carried her up the hill. "She saved me," he heard Dena cry out behind him. As soon as he could, he hurried through the graveyard, across the glen and headed into the courtyard.

Keter took one look at Mackinzie in Hew's arms and raced on ahead to open the door. "Mackinzie is hurt!" Keter shouted. He rushed to the table and with one swipe of his arm, cleared everything off. "It is bad, Sawney."

Several people moved aside and Sawney started toward the door just as Hew carried her in. At first, he couldn't see where all the blood was coming from. "Bearcha, go get the sewer. Paisley, bring cloths. Hurry!"

He let Hew gently lay her on the table, then took her hand and searched his brother's eyes. "What has happened?

"A gray wolf. It is dead."

From behind Hew, Dena sobbed, "Mackinzie killed it."

Sawney looked into the eyes of the woman he loved and tried to smile. She was bleeding profusely and he was terrified she would die. Her eyes were open, but the color seemed to be draining from her face. He lifted the hand he held up while Hew spread a plaid over her. It was taking far too long for Bearcha to bring Rona, and Sawney anxiously watched the door, while Paisley held several cloths against her shoulder and tried to stop the bleeding. Sawney did not want to alarm Mackinzie, so he forced himself to keep smiling. "You are very brave."

Mackinzie closed her eyes. She could almost see Tavan smiling at her and nodding his approval. She had more courage than she knew and he would be proud of her.

Several more people rushed into the room, including Carley and finally Rona, who was better at sewing flesh than anyone. Rona handed her small sack of needles and sinew threads to Bearcha and quickly went to the other side of the table to examine the wounds. She moved Paisley's hand away and cringed. The wounds were bleeding profusely. Rona pulled her dagger and cut away the measure of plaid Mackinzie wore over her shoulder. She then cut the shirt underneath until Mackinzie's injured flesh was exposed. The wolf's teeth not only punctured her skin, it left gashes as it fell away.

If Mackinzie was in pain, she did not show it and Sawney's next thought was to get her drunk so she wouldn't. He was grateful when Keter brought a flask of wine, but Mackinzie pushed it away with her other hand.

"Put honey in it to sweeten the taste," said Paisley. "Here, I will do it."

Rona finished examining the wounds and then said, "Lads, best hold her down. 'Twill hurt when I do the stitching and she must not move." Just as Rona instructed, Keter got ready to hold her head still while Hew got a firm grip on her injured arm.

Paisley hurried back with the sweetened wine and while Sawney lifted Mackinzie's head, she helped her drink. Mackinzie still did not like the taste, but she drank a good portion anyway.

More blood oozed from the wounds and soon, the room was full of people. Blare stood ready to take hold of her legs if need be while Rona threaded her needle. It was after she moved more of Mackinzie's shirt out of the way that they saw it. Four ugly scars ran from the side of her neck all the way across that side of Mackinzie's chest. "'Tis not her first time," said Rona.

At last, Sawney understood why Mackinzie didn't want to wear his colors. MacGreagor shirts had a round neckline that would expose her scars. "Tavan said she feared nothing but a wildcat and now we see why." He made a mental note to bring that to the attention of the weaver, but for now, it was the last of his concerns. Her grip on his hand was still strong and he found that encouraging, but she kept her eyes closed.

Standing near the wall, Dena watched as Rona told Paisley to wipe away the blood between each stitch and got ready to sew the holes in Mackinzie's shoulder closed. She could see Mackinzie stiffen when Rona pinched the skin together and took the first stitch. It made Dena gasp for air.

With each new stitch, Mackinzie squeezed Sawney's hand tighter and bit her lip to keep from crying out. Tears began to run down the sides of her face into her hair, so Sawney took the cloth out of his belt and gently blotted them away. Then he put his mouth to her ear. "I love you, do not leave me." She opened her eyes for a moment and he knew she heard him.

Covered in Mackinzie's blood, Hew leaned closer to his brother. "Where there is one wolf, there are others."

Sawney looked around until he found Bearcha. "Send the lads to hunt them down and see that the children are kept inside."

With too many tears in her eyes, Paisley gave the chore of wiping away the blood to Grant and moved away. She was grateful to be in the arms of first Gavina, then Jennet and then Carley, each of whom struggled to keep from weeping.

Dena could not bear to watch another moment. She could smell the blood from there, Mackinzie was going to die, and it was her fault. She left her place near the wall, went out the door, and made her way past all the people waiting for word in the courtyard. Several looked to her for news, good or bad, but she ignored them and started down the path in the middle of the glen.

It all happened so fast. She remembered seeing the fire in the wolf's eyes, thought she would surly die and the next thing she knew, Mackinzie was hurt and she wasn't. Why did Mackinzie do that? She should be dead, not Mackinzie. Yet, wasn't that what she wanted? Her own words began to echo in Dena's head—born in a bucket—sea monster...

Shame finally overpowered her and when she could stand it no longer, Dena sunk to her knees and wept. "I am sorry...I am so very sorry!"

ONCE THE STITCHING was done and a wide cloth was wrapped around her shoulder, Sawney carried Mackinzie upstairs to the bedchamber he once shared with Hew. It was next to Paisley's old room, she would want to sleep there this night, and he would be comforted to have his sister close. He left the room so the women could remove her bloody clothing, wash her and help Mackinzie put on a clean shirt. Even now, she did not cry out or moan.

He was pleased to see the people were all gone when he went back downstairs. He added extra honey to the flask of wine, grabbed a goblet and waited. Outside, he heard Hew tell the people the sewing was done and all they could do was pray. It was true, so much could still go wrong, the worst of which was a fever. The MacGreagors had overcome many troubles in the past few months, but no one knew how to keep a wound from killing the woman he loved.

An hour ago, the great hall was full of happy people welcoming him home and now it was an empty room hauntingly quiet. He tried to think how he could go on without Mackinzie and then pushed those thoughts aside. She would not die; he would not let her.

When at last he was allowed back in her bedchamber, he helped her sit up a little and then held the goblet to her mouth. She nodded slightly at the sweeter taste and took several more sips, letting the liquid ease down her throat and warm her body. Sawney set the goblet down on the floor and gently lowered her back down. She tried to say something, but he would not let her. "Rest, my love, just rest."

For the remainder of the night, Sawney left the bedchamber only when the women came to tend to Mackinzie's comfort. The rest of the time, he helped her drink each time she woke and needed it. Several times in the night, Paisley came to see about her best friend and her brother, who looked as tired as she felt. There was nothing to be done, so Paisley went to her bed and lay down, clothes and all. Even as tired as she was, she heard it each time Mackinzie woke.

At last, Sawney fell asleep in the chair and Mackinzie had consumed enough wine to sleep just as soundly.

By morning when there was no fever, all were convinced she would not die.

IN THE DAYS THAT FOLLOWED, and even though Sawney asked, Mackinzie never said a word about what truly happened. It was one more secret she intended to take with her to the grave.

The weavers made new shirts for Mackinzie with higher necklines to hide her scars and everyone was pleased when she was up and about, and began to wear MacGreagor colors. The wedding plans were set, the great hall resumed its normal busy activity, and Sawney personally went to all the surrounding clans. He invited each of the lairds who helped him take back the MacGreagor glen and was pleased when they accepted.

With the help of the Swintons, the Haldane rebuilt their tiny village and were happy to take all the things they'd hidden back out of the forest. They believed, and rightly so, they were the only clan in Scotland to have all new homes. Not long after, the subject of the missing horse came up and once more, the Swintons and the Haldane went their separate ways.

IN THE DARKNESS OF the night, Sawney took the golden sword and the remaining jewels back to Carley's cottage and let her hide them once more in her wall. Perhaps someday they would put the jewels back in the golden chalices.

A TIME OF MADNESS 211

MACKINZIE SOMETIMES looked for the black stallion when she walked in the glen, but it did not follow them. It would, however, be included in the story of the bone that Sawney would tell his children someday. She was able to move her shoulder with much less pain now and she eagerly awaited her wedding day.

Nevertheless, there was one thing unresolved and when she thought it was time, Mackinzie went to find Dena, whom she had not seen since that day. Dena was not in her cottage, nor anywhere in the glen and when Mackinzie finally found her, Dena was sitting on a rock, staring into the water of the river.

Mackinzie waited until Dena noticed her and then sat on a large rock facing her. "In my home...the Campbell village, there is a river like this one." Dena would not look at her and Mackinzie was not sure what to say. Not speaking had always been far more comfortable for her, but she could not become mistress over Dena until they settled things. An idea came to her. "Can you forgive me?"

Dena abruptly turned to her. "You have done nothing wrong."

"Aye, but I have. I knew there were wolves close by and I did not say."

Dena looked away. "I knew it too and I did not say. 'Tis my shame, not yours."

"I wager neither of us will ever do it again, do you agree?"

Tears began to cloud Dena's eyes. "Why did you do it? I mean, you took the pain that should have been mine. I have considered it and I cannot understand. Why?"

"Because someone once took the pain for me. Shall I tell you about him?"

"Please do."

"Well, I was once a lass who knew not the sound of her own laughter. Then one day, the lad did something so funny I could not help myself. I laughed until I nearly cried and was astonished by the sound of it. He did other things too that made me want to be a part of his world. And then one day he put his arms around me and took away all my pain. Dena, before the day Sawney held me, I had not felt the arms of another living soul in nearly ten years."

Dena hung her head and let her tears run down her cheeks. "I did not know."

Mackinzie gently brushed a lock of hair away from Dena's face. "How could you? 'Twas mostly my own fault, for I was the one who hid from the world. Now you are hiding from me."

"I am too ashamed. I wanted to be mistress and I did not care who I hurt."

"I see. Have you told anyone this?"

"Nay."

"Then it is ours alone. You are still young and there are many days ahead. Sawney tells me I am to become a matchmaker." Mackinzie puffed her cheeks. "I assure you I know nothing about that, but I will try."

"You mean to find a husband for me?"

"I think you should have a husband who truly loves you. There are five lairds coming to the wedding and two are unmarried. Perhaps one…or both will fancy you."

Dena wiped her tears with both hands and her mood quickly changed. "Do you think so? They will know I lied to catch a husband."

"Aye, but a bonnie lass is still a bonnie lass."

She was so happy, Dena quickly stood up and offered her hand to help Mackinzie. "If you were not hurt, I would hug you."

"If I were not hurt, I would welcome it. Now, come with me to bathe. The other women will be there and if they see we are friends, they will not think ill of you. If they do, they will wish they faced a gray wolf instead."

AND SO IT WAS, THAT the MacGreagors, having survived the madness that was Neasan, attended the joyful wedding of their rightful laird and his bride. Mackinzie wore a ring of flowers on her head and a scarf around her neck made from the soft lamb's wool Tavan gave her.

When the ceremony was complete, she kissed Sawney, left her guests, and headed for the cottage she shared with Paisley. Mackinzie pulled her sack out from under the bed, opened it, and withdrew the carved goblet Tavan gave her. For a moment, she stared at it. She always loved the carving of the wolf and loved it still. Softly, she ran her fingers over it and when she turned, Sawney was in the doorway watching her.

Mackinzie smiled and handed him the sack. "Come with me."

She took his hand, walked with him to the Keep and when he opened the door, she went in. For a moment, she looked around the great hall for just the right place and then went to the table where the MacGreagor lairds always kept their goblets. Carefully, she set her goblet next to his and then turned to her husband. "Finally, I have a family."

Sawney smiled. "Finally, you are mine." He wrapped his arms around her and the passion in his kiss took her breath away.

~ the end ~

TRIPLETS

Book 10
Marti Talbott's Highlander Series
Sample chapter

THREE TIMES THE HANDSOME young men meant three times the trouble. Off to see the king, Tavan goes missing and the betrothed Patrick might be falling for another woman. Abruptly married to save a woman from harm, Callum has no idea his wife intends to run away. Will she truly leave him and if so, why?

CHAPTER I

THE KING OF SCOTS WAS an elder by the time the much younger King of England decided to count all the inhabitants of Scotland. This, the King of Scots called irritatingly ridiculous. If anyone needed to know, he did, and the count changed so often he found no need to know. All the King of Scots cared about were the number of able-bodied men willing to fight should the English want a war.

The message from the King of England stated the need of the count was for the sake of history, and to know how soon their island would be too small to house them all. The King of Scots suggested that if the English would leave, the Scots would have plenty of room and would be happy to write their own history. Rumor had it the King of England was not amused.

Everyone feared a war with England would soon come, but aside from a few skirmishes along the imaginary border between the two kingdoms, a full-scale war did not materialize—at least not yet.

WINTER WAS EXCEEDINGLY harsh in the MacGreagor glen the year the triplets were born. A thick undergrowth of hair on the animals gave them ample warning and time to prepare. The direct descendent of a Viking, Laird Sawney MacGreagor asked the elders what needed to be done and took every advantage of the advice they gave. The clan set aside their normal duties to gather extra wood and peat moss for their hearths and to dry meat so the hunters could stay inside. Builders took a good look at thatched roofs just in case there came a heavy snow, and advised for or against remaining inside. Weavers made new, while mothers darned old socks, and all made certain to hang thick tapestries over windows lacking coveted English glass. Tree sap was used to seal the edges of the tapestries and everyone agreed it greatly helped hold the heat in, although more candles were needed to light the darkened rooms.

Then, on the third day of February, the clan awoke to a blanket of snow on their long, wide glen with an abundance of fluffy white flakes still falling from the sky. The children were thrilled and even the adults had to admit the covering of white on their village was wondrous and beautiful. Yet the colder northern air was sure to come and when it did, they feared they would all freeze to death.

Laird MacGreagor ordered the guards inside as well, for he was convinced none of the lairds in neighboring clans were witless enough to order an attack in that kind of weather.

After the first week, the families doubled up to conserve fuel. By the end of the second week, there were three families to a cottage with twelve families living in the Keep, including and especially the midwives, Sernoot and Grainee.

The MacGreagor keep consisted of three stories with only one very large hearth near the end of the great hall on the bottom floor. Normally, the rising heat from the hearth generated more than enough warmth for the upper floors. Yet in this kind of weather and with so many people inside, there never seemed to be enough for them all without taking turns sitting beside the hearth on the bottom floor. For this cause, and to ward off the boredom a lack of outside activity brought about, they played old games and invented new ones. A game of changing places near the hearth, to the tune of the flute player, soon became a favorite of the children.

Yet the clan needed water and the livestock still had to be looked after, so the men took turns braving the cold, breaking the ice, filling buckets and trying not to fall on slick paths that meandered between the cottages. Packed snow became solid ice and the large courtyard in front of the Keep was the most dangerous. More than one man returned with a twisted ankle or a bruised hip.

In the great hall, a place where the clan normally tended its daily business, the ageing tapestries had also been moved to cover the windows. Lighter colored stones behind them revealed how much soot had collected on the walls over the years, and a good scrubbing was in order, should the weather ever warm up again. On other walls, weapons of various kinds served as decorations. The table, which normally occupied the center of the room, was moved against the wall at night to make room for sleeping. Although the children did not seem to mind, uncomfortable wooden floors made the adults covet the coming of spring that much more.

They were a sea of green kilts for the unusually large men, sun bleached white shirts for all and long plaids for the women. Each wore a matching length of plaid over their left shoulder, and while the women wore shoes that only covered their ankles, the men had long straps that laced up their bare legs to the knee. For warmth in winter, they wore capes or coats made from the wavy longhaired hides of Highland cattle. Some hides were black, some red, some brown and some garments were sewn using a mixture of the colors, which made the men harder to spot in the forest.

MANY A MOTHER AND FATHER kept wee babes in their laps and shared both coat and body heat, for fear little toes would turn that awful black that meant a horrible and dreaded death. Cooking for so many was an all-day affair with not a drop going to waste. Dogs and cats were kept outside and forced to fend for themselves, although the older children made certain the animals had access to places of protection from the cold northern winds. Therefore, the children fretted over pets, the parents fretted over children, the women fretted over having enough food, the men fretted over the livestock and Laird MacGreagor worried they would run out of fuel for the hearths.

To help while away the empty hours, the men took to placing wagers on nearly everything they could think of. Their favorite, of course, was betting on their laird's every move during the birth of his first child. For generations, the men gathered in the great hall as soon as a wife's labor began. Two wager boards were brought out, one for a girl and one for a boy, upon which the men could put their mark. It was understood the losers were expected to take on the chores of the winners for one full week. Once their bets were placed, they drank heavily, said things a woman was not supposed to hear, jeered at the nervous father and waited for the birth.

A LITTLE MORE THAN a year before, Sawney MacGreagor made Mackinzie Campbell his wife, she was about to give birth, and there was no better entertainment than that of watching a first time expectant father. Already Sawney insisted someone stay with her at all times and swore he could hear it every time she so much as moaned, albeit from two floors below. The clan roared with laughter.

Mackinzie's stomach was unusually large and the midwives were so certain she carried twins, Sawney ordered two new boxes made for his sons...or daughters, as the case may be. Every man wanted sons to carry on the family name. Nevertheless, he assured Mackinzie he would be just as delighted with daughters. She didn't believe a word of it.

By the end of her seventh month, Mackinzie could hardly walk and needed help climbing not one, but two flights of stairs to the bedchamber they shared on the third floor of the Keep. When the snow began to fall, she elected just to stay where she was and rest under a mountain of blankets.

At last, warmer air melted the ice and snow, the families returned to their cottages, those that still had a roof, that is and early in the morning of the very next week, Mackinzie moaned loud enough for nearly half the village to hear. Sawney sat straight up in bed. He had just enough time to tell her he loved her, grab his belt and shirt, and wrap his kilt around his waist before the midwives burst into the room and ordered him out.

They shut the door in his face and for a moment, he stared at it. Never had he been so happy and so terrified at the same time. Much could go wrong and many a good woman had given up the ghost trying to bring a child into the world, including his own mother. He could but wait and waiting was not something he enjoyed, nor did he like hearing his beloved Mackinzie in pain. The guilt was his and his alone, but how else was a man to have sons...or daughters?

Suddenly the door opened and Sernoot nearly ran him over. "Have you nothing to do?"

"Nay, I do not," he answered. "What shall I do?"

She scurried past him and was halfway down the top flight of stairs before she answered, "Drink, MacGreagor, that is what all the men do to calm their nerves."

It sounded like a very fine idea to him, yet he was torn between his own need and being too far away from Mackinzie at a time like this. The wine was in the great hall two flights below and he contemplated just how quickly he could dress, retrieve a flask and return.

"Are you still here?" Standing right behind him carrying a length of forgotten string, Sernoot giggled when the sound of her voice made him jump. "The lads are gathering in the great hall, best you keep them company."

"She might need me."

Exasperated, Sernoot put her hands on her hips. "For what?"

Sawney had no ready answer to that question and puffed his cheeks.

"Stoke the fire, MacGreagor, and heat the place. That's what a husband must do to keep the wee one warm."

"I see."

The stricken look on his face was something Sernoot would enjoy telling everyone about for weeks to come. He held the highest position in the clan and was quite possibly the largest of the men, but first he was an ordinary man, confused, concerned and looking as though a sound thought would never again enter his mind. Save for being the first to hold a new life *that* look on the face of every man about to have his first born, was a midwife's delight.

Reluctantly, Sawney descended the stairs, pausing only long enough to slip into a bedchamber on the second floor and dress. All the men were there when he made it down to the great hall, including Keter, his second in command, Blair, his third, and Sawney's brother, Hew, who had recently married. Already the lot of them were laughing at Sawney and he wondered how he could possibly endure hours and hours of it. He saw nothing funny at all.

The question of twins was bound to come up and it posed a particular problem for the men. Who would win the wagers should there be both a boy and a girl? It stirred a hearty discussion among them that lasted quite a while, for no winners at all was unthinkable. Therefore, they decided, they must have a second set of boards for the second child. Two new boards were fetched and the men lined up to choose the sex of the second child, should there be one.

The wine did not seem to help Sawney at all and while the men watched each time he began to pace the length of the room, he was too worried to pay much attention. A wager, he finally realized, had been placed on the number of times he sat and then returned to his pacing. As the hours dragged on and Sawney renewed his march from one end of the room to the other, one man or another would moan his defeat.

Then there were the number of times he stoked the fire to keep the baby warm, should it appear anytime soon, and the number of goblets of wine he consumed, and lest any man forget, the times he ran his fingers through his hair. Best of all was the wager on how often he glanced up the stairs, although he could not possibly see anything from there.

Each man remarked, at one time or another, on how brave Mackinzie was being. She did not scream her pain the way some wives did. In fact, when she stopped moaning and got quiet, it unnerved them all.

"'Tis a boy!" came a shout from above, at last.

Several men moaned their lost wager and Sawney knocked over a chair trying to get to the stairs—only to hear Grainee yell, "Not yet, Sawney."

Again, it grew silent. The wager then rested on a single or a double birth and all the men held their breaths.

"'Tis another boy!" Sernoot yelled.

A third of the men moaned while the others cheered and just as he started up the stairs again, Grainee shouted, "Not yet, Sawney."

He turned and stared at his brother. "How does she know I am coming up?"

Hew shrugged, "Perhaps you have lost the art of being quiet."

"You must be right."

The silence seemed to last a very long time until a nearly out of breath Grainee shouted. "'Tis three boys."

This time the announcement was met with complete silence. Upon that wager, all the men lost. Not once in the MacGreagor clan had triplets been born and no one was more shocked than Sawney. It occurred to him that women died trying to deliver one, therefore, his wife might be in three times the danger. It was clearly his turn to shout, "Does my wife yet live?"

"She does well, Sawney, very well."

He thought he might collapse and embarrass himself, so he quickly righted the chair he knocked over and sat down. "Three sons...three...three," he muttered.

Hew couldn't resist, walked to the bottom of the stairs, cupped his hands and yelled, "Are there more to come, Grainee?"

"Nay, she is finished." Grainee started to giggle, "She called me a scunner when I said there was a third coming."

The men laughed and Sawney grinned. As a baby, Mackinzie was the sole survivor of a shipwreck, and saved only because someone had the foresight to put her in a bucket and set her adrift. Miraculously, she was yet alive when the bucket washed up on the west coast of Scotland, but she grew up without family. Shunned by her adopted clan, she began to call those she disagreed with "Scunner," which was the worst of all insults. Sawney once threatened to toss Mackinzie in the loch for calling him that. He was large enough to do it easily, too. Yet on this night, he was thrilled to hear she had the strength to say it and all was forgiven.

An hour later, the men were gone, two women with babies of their own came to help with the nursing, and Grainee finally let him come up the stairs to kiss his wife and get a good look at his sons.

They were as wonderful as any newborns could be, yet in all the excitement, the midwives neglected to mark which was born first, second and third. Sawney stared at Grainee in disbelief. "You did not mark them?"

Grainee rolled her eyes. "We were a wee bit busy, MacGreagor."

She was right, of course, so he walked back to the bed, knelt down and kissed his wife once more. "I have chosen two names, Patrick and Callum. What shall we call the third?"

Mackinzie weakly smiled. "Tavan is my favorite name."

"Tavan it is then."

WHICH BABY WAS GIVEN which name that first night would be a favorite discussion in the clan for months to come. After all, the midwives were witness to it and later neither of them could tell which child was which.

The babies were very small, so small; two could easily fit in the same box. However, the triplets seemed restless and upset until Sawney put the third in with the other two. The change in them was remarkable and soon all three were asleep. In the morning, he asked the builders for one very large box instead.

Everyone feared the triplets would not live through the night, the next night, the first week, and then their first month. Yet by the time Mackinzie was allowed out of bed, the boys were well on their way to a normal, healthy life. The triplets were content—the rest of the clan was exhausted.

By then, the babies had been moved so often, the question of which was given which name again plagued them. Therefore, Sawney named them a second time and insisted each baby be put back in the box precisely where he was found, until their parents could manage to tell them apart ...if they ever could.

EACH BABY HAD BLUE eyes and thick, light blond hair that did not begin to turn dark like their father's until the first two years passed. Once they learned to talk, an odd pattern began to emerge. Not only did they answer a question at the same time, they answered using the exact same words. Furthermore, the moment one got in trouble, the other two quickly came to his defense.

The boys soon learned their uniqueness offered grand opportunities to trick the adults, a subject Mackinzie brought up on the night of their sixth birthday. Her favorite thing in all the world was to curl up in Sawney's arms at bedtime after all was quiet. Sometimes, she still could not believe her good fortune. After having such a dreadful childhood, she was now truly loved, safe from those who taunted her, and living in a home where Scottish wildcats and gray wolves could not attack her.

Mackinzie had a smattering of freckles across her nose that matched her reddish-brown hair and, unlike her sons, her eyes were green. "Witless, they are not."

"True." Sawney wrapped both arms around her and laid his head against the top of hers.

"You gave them particular places to sit at the table for our meals and they have changed places quite often."

"I know."

She giggled and playfully smacked his arm. "You do not know. Still you do not know which is which."

"Ah, but I do. Patrick is to sit on my right with Tavan next to him and Callum at the end. This night, Callum sat next to me."

"I am amazed. Why did you not call them out?"

"I intend to encourage it instead. When they are grown, the ability to trick others could save lives."

Mackinzie rolled her eyes, "So long as they do not try to trick their wives. Perhaps you might warn against that."

"I shall, although it may not be necessary. They go nowhere without the other two and I hardly think they will ever marry, unless they build a very large cottage to house them all."

"We happen to have a very large cottage. I say they bring their wives to live with us."

Sawney rolled his eyes. "Do you see what you are saying? Three marriages could keep us in crying babies for years. I doubt I could bear it."

She grinned and pulled back to watch the expression on his face. "Perhaps you are right, but could you bear it just one more time?"

He wrinkled his brow and when she nodded, he was thrilled. "Promise to give me a daughter this time."

"Or two...or..."

"Do not say it." To keep her from finishing her sentence, he kissed her passionately.

There was no question in anyone's mind when Sawney was displeased, for he had a glare that made his annoyance abundantly clear. The only one who was allowed to ignore his glare was Mackinzie, who only shrugged or rolled her eyes, but God help the child who tried it and each of them did. Punishment was bed without the benefit of an evening meal and for boys who outgrew their shoes long before they were worn through, food was in great demand.

The punishment for that infraction, and many others, worked quite well until they were old enough to acquire friends, who were only too willing to tie a bucket of delights to the end of a rope lowered from their second floor bedchamber. Eventually, they got caught, which gained them and their friends, a full week of cleaning up after the horses.

OCCASIONALLY, SAWNEY pondered the question of which was his first-born. Surely, a man's firstborn would be the most ingenious, but the triplets seemed to be equally endowed and by the time they reached the clumsy elevens Sawney still could not guess which was the eldest. Because they did not seem to have any idea where their feet were at any given moment, he considered waiting a year to begin their warrior training with real swords. It was dangerous enough with the wooden ones. Yet the other boys their age would be allowed to begin, so he relented and simply held his breath.

There were some detectable differences in the boys when they entered their teens. By then, they had two younger sisters, Colina and Bardie, each born in different years. It was Callum who saw what his mother needed or wanted first, and it was Callum who had far more patience with his little sisters. On occasion, he used plaids over chairs to build pretend castles in their bedchamber so the girls could play Queen of Scots. He was never too busy for them, never harsh and most of all, constantly on guard for their safety.

It was not as though Tavan and Patrick felt less love for their sisters, they were simply more eager to take on the excitement the outside world had to offer. Nevertheless, if Callum wanted to help, they pitched in as well, although their objective was more to speed up the process than to please their sisters. Tavan and Patrick often mocked Callum for being too softhearted where the fairer sex was concerned, and predicted he would soon fall under the spell of some unsightly woman who offered nothing more than a wink and a smile.

Tavan was more like his father than the other two, carefully considering the options before he made a decision, whereas Patrick and Callum sometimes acted first and thought about it later. The differences between them were minor, but they did exist. When it came to choosing a wife, Tavan was in no hurry.

While the triplets did spend a great deal of time together learning to hunt, fish and fight, it was not nearly as much as their parents believed. Tavan took to practicing his skills with a bow and arrow and had more pride in his accomplishments than the other two. He became quite proficient and often challenged the men to a contest.

Patrick, on the other hand, was far more sociable. If anyone knew all the details of a feud between a husband and a wife, two men or two women, he did. He learned the details by gossiping, and enjoyed hearing it as much as the clan enjoyed telling him. More often than not, Patrick could be found surrounded by the fairer sex, one of which he became partial to early in life.

Her name was Finagal and he first took particular notice of her when he found her sitting in the forest behind the village sobbing. At not yet ten, her big brown eyes seemed too large for her head, and perhaps that is why he noticed them in particular. At any rate, her cat died and no matter how hard he tried, she could not be consoled.

The remedy, of course, was to find a new kitten for her and he knew just where to look. He was gone but a few minutes before he returned, put a calico kitten in her lap and enjoyed the first of her very rare smiles.

When she got older, Finagal was not like the other girls. While she enjoyed hearing the daily gossip, she rarely contributed and while the others swooned at the very sight of the triplets, she often would not look Patrick in the eye. It was as if she carried some dark secret she was not willing to share, and never did her demeanor fail to raise his interest.

Completely smitten with her by the time he reached sixteen, he gathered all his courage and decided to find out what her secret was. Yet Finagal was the eldest of ten and he could never find her alone. That is, until one day just after the noon meal, he noticed her sitting by herself on a log that separated the glen from the graveyard. His approach was perhaps too quick, for she seemed deep in thought and a bit startled when she noticed him.

"Has your cat died?"

"Nay."

He hoped to make her laugh or at least smile, but she remained solemn, so he decided that approach was the wrong one. He sat down beside her, stretched out his long legs and crossed them at the ankle. He waited for her to mention what worried her, but she didn't. "I am Patrick."

"I know." She wore her long blonde hair in one thick braid down the middle of her back.

"You do? Most cannot tell us apart still. How have you managed it?"

"I am not certain, but I have always known which is you. There is something different in your eyes, I think."

"The eyes you refuse to look at?"

"I look at your eyes often, just not when they are looking back at me."

"I see. Why is that?"

Finagal took a deep breath and slowly let it out. "I find them too..."

"Go on; is there something wrong with them?"

"Aye, they are too..."

Never before had anyone found fault with his eyes and he was puzzled. "Too frightening, too insulting, too..."

"Too blue." She hardly got the words out before she looked away and hid her smile.

Patrick thoughtfully scratched the back of his neck. "I have always believed them the same blue as my brothers. What do you suggest I do about it?"

"You could stop looking at me."

"That, I cannot do." Her brow was wrinkled when she finally turned to look at him. "Have you not noticed how pleasing you are? How shall it be if the other lads look and I do not? They would think me daft."

Finagal rolled her beautiful brown eyes. "Most already know you are daft."

"Nay, they think one of us is daft, but they do not know which." She flashed her magnificent smile at him finally, his heart skipped a beat and there was no doubt in his mind she was the one for him. If she had been old enough, Patrick would have asked her to marry him that very moment. But then, he was not yet old enough to choose the right wife either, his father often said.

It was not long before Patrick's brothers noticed his attachment to her and once, when he'd had enough of their relentless teasing, he nearly drew his sword. The expression on his face convinced the other two he was ready to use it and he turned his glare first on Callum.

"Wait," said Tavan. "You cannot kill him."

"Why not?" Patrick asked.

"Because then I would have to kill you, which would leave Father with only one son." Tavan slowly began to grin. "On the other hand, run him through."

Patrick couldn't help but smile. "And leave you alone to inherit? I'll not allow that."

"Nor will I," Callum agreed, turning to face Tavan. "We decided I am the first born and I should be the one remaining."

Tavan rolled his eyes. "We were not yet six when we agreed to that, and only because you grew the width of a thumb taller. Now you are not taller, except when your hair stands up as it does when you awake."

"My hair? You should see yours of a morning..."

Therefore, the argument turned from Patrick's admiration of Finagal to the age-old question of who was born first. It was a way of settling all of their disagreements. After that, the other two understood Patrick's seriousness and had only good things to say about Finagal.

Yet in the two years that followed, Finagal never once told her secret and Patrick took it to mean, she was not quite certain she could trust him. For a time, he wondered if someone was hurting her. The punishment for a man who hurt a woman was death and she was well aware if he knew, Patrick would be honor bound to tell his father.

If someone was hurting her and she would not expose them, the offender had to be someone she loved - a brother, an uncle or perhaps her father. Yet when they were together, Patrick looked for cuts or bruises and never saw anything suspicious. He thought to ask her outright, but decided against it. It would be far better if she volunteered the information once she trusted him more. At least she smiled more often now and even laughed occasionally. Patrick was convinced he was making a good match and they would enjoy a very good life together in the MacGreagor glen.

The King of Scots was about to change all their lives.

End of sample chapter.

Pick up your copy of *Triplets* today!

More Marti Talbott Books

www.martitalbott.com

To discover free Marti Talbott books and more historical novels filled with castles and kings, love and war, triumph and tribulation - click here[1].

Follow Clan MacGreagor through multiple generations beginning with *The Viking*[2] where it all began, *The Highlanders*[3] and their struggle to survive, *Marblestone Mansion*[4] and the duke who simply could not get rid of his scandalous duchess, and still more historical stories in *The Lost MacGreagor Books*[5]. Then check out **Marti's contemporary romance/mysteries**[6] in *Missing Heiress, Greed and a Mistress, The Dead Letters*, and *The Locked Room*. Other books include the **Carson Series**[7], *Leanna, (a short story)*, and **Seattle Quake 9.2**[8].

See what's Marti's working on next and sign up to be notified when it is released.[9]

Marti's Website[10] Talk to Marti on Facebook[11]

---

1. http://www.martitalbott.com

2. http://www.martitalbott.com/viking-series

3. http://www.martitalbott.com/highlander-series

4. http://www.martitalbott.com/marblestone-mansion

5. http://www.martitalbott.com/The-Lost-MacGreagor-Books

6. http://www.martitalbott.com/m-t-romance

7. http://www.martitalbott.com/the-carson-series

8. http://www.martitalbott.com/more-marti-talbott-books

9. http://www.martitalbott.com/Home/notify-me

10. http://www.martitalbott.com

11. https://www.facebook.com/marti.talbot

Don't miss out!

Visit the website below and you can sign up to receive emails whenever Marti Talbott publishes a new book. There's no charge and no obligation.

https://books2read.com/r/B-A-OYD-DAO

BOOKS2READ

Connecting independent readers to independent writers.

Also by Marti Talbott

Marti Talbott's Highlander Series
Marti Talbott's Highlander Series 1
Marti Talbott's Highlander Series 2
Marti Talbott's Highlander Series 3
Marti Talbott's Highlander Series 4
Marti Talbott's Highlander Series 5
Betrothed
The Golden Sword, Book 7
Abducted, Book 8
A Time of Madness
Triplets
Secrets
Choices
Ill-Fated Love
The Other Side of the River
Marti Talbott's Highlander Omnibus, Books 1 - 3
Leanna: A Clean Highlander Short Story

Scandalous Duchess Series
Marblestone Mansion, Book 1
Marblestone Mansion, Book 2
Marblestone Mansion, Book 3

Marblestone Mansion, Book 4
Marblestone Mansion, Book 5
Marblestone Mansion, Book 6
Marblestone Mansion, Book 7
Marblestone Mansion, Book 8
Marblestone Mansion, Book 9
Marblestone Mansion, Book 10
Marblestone Mansion, (Omnibus, Books 1 - 3)

The Lost MacGreagor Books
Beloved Ruins, Book 1
Beloved Lies, Book 2
Beloved Secrets, Book 3
Beloved Vows, Book 4

The Viking Series
The Viking
The Viking's Daughter
The Viking's Son
The Viking's Bride
The Viking's Honor
Viking Blood
The Unwanted Bride
Viking Valor

Standalone
Seattle Quake 9.2
Suspects (The Botham/Miracle Murders)

Watch for more at www.martitalbott.com.

About the Author

Marti Talbott (www.martitalbott.com) is the author of over 40 books, all of which are written without profanity and sex scenes. She lives in Seattle, is retired and has two children, five grandchildren and three great-grandchildren. The MacGreagor family saga begins with The Viking Series and continues in Marti Talbott's Highlander's Series, Marblestone Mansion, the Scandalous Duchess series, and ends with The Lost MacGreagor books. Her mystery books include Seattle Quake 9.2, Missing Heiress, Greed and a Mistress, The Locked Room, and The Dead Letters. Other books include The Promise and Broken Pledge.

Read more at www.martitalbott.com.

Made in the USA
Coppell, TX
01 December 2019